Love Flies

Center Point
Large Print

Also by Julia David and available from
Center Point Large Print:

Love Covers

Love Flies

A Novel By

Julia David

CENTER POINT LARGE PRINT
THORNDIKE, MAINE

The text of this Large Print edition is unabridged.
In other aspects, this book may vary
from the original edition.
Printed in the United States of America on permanent paper. Set in 16-point Times New Roman type.

ISBN: 978-1-64358-465-2

The Library of Congress has cataloged this record under Library of Congress Control Number: 2019950807

I dedicate this novel to my niece Riann.
Her beauty and perseverance never cease to
amaze me and our entire family.
Her Love Flies to the heavens and then back
to her sweet home on Galgate Street.
May His love soar in you, covering you with
His wings all your days.

"But she was given two wings
like those of a great eagle
so she could fly to the place
prepared for her in the wilderness.
There she would be cared for and
protected from the dragon for a time,
times, and half a time."
Revelation 12:14 NTL

A HOT, DRY wind tousled the brown hair of the brothers as they straddled the chestnut mare through the tall, parched grass.

"Robbie, did you hear that?" Young Reed Chapman asked as he twisted on the rump of the sweaty horse.

"If you mean my stomach growling, then yes." Robbie gave the mare a little kick. "Let's get home."

"Wait." Reed tugged on his older brother's shirt. "I heard it again."

Robbie pulled back on the horse's mane. "It sounds like some cat stuck in that barbed wire fence that the Polish land grabbers put up." Before he could catch him, Reed slid off the back of the horse landing with a thud.

"Reed, no—" Robbie whined. "We knew we weren't going to get past that fence for a swim in our lake. Dirty Poles, who cares what is caught in their fence. Reed! Leave it be." He watched his pesky younger brother jog through the field toward the long line of wire and posts.

"I will leave without you. Reed! I swear you have the brain of a jackrabbit!" Robbie shouted to his back.

Reed understood two things clearly, he *was* partly jackrabbit, never able to sit still or focus. Any strange noise, or peculiar new sight pulled instantly on his curiosity. And his brother was right, the Polish family who'd bought this land out from under his family didn't deserve any help. But he just had to see.

A tall, nubby oak branched out over the area providing the only shade. An old knotted rope hung from a branch. He knew the Polish had a bunch of children. Robert wanted to fire rocks at them with their slingshots, but Reed hated the idea of shaming their grandparents' time-worn heritage. Their father had lectured them; just as their people had come over to the colonies, America was open for all people needing refuge. *We are to love our neighbors, not despise them,* his father's words echoed.

Abruptly Reed stopped cold. A little girl, maybe five or six was sitting in the dirt somehow caught in the barbed wire. Her huge, brown eyes shocked to see him, yet pleading for his help.

"What happened?" He carefully pulled the wire apart, crouching down, he stepped through. Trying not to scare her, he stepped closer. Tugging on her long thick braid the color of molasses, she choked out words in some strange language.

"I don't know a word you are saying," he said, noticing the thin lines of blood on her hands and cheek, "but your hair is caught around the barbs and in all this other wire. He began to pull on the long, brown braid and saw why she couldn't get free. A tight ribbon held the braid together, and her hair had wrapped around the barbs. It was a tangled mess. "I have to take your hair apart." He watched her, waiting for permission. Her huge watery eyes waited, trying to understand, finally nodding at him. This appeared to be simple. He had two older sisters that twirled and tied their hair in every invention. He slipped the white ribbon off the end and separated the thick strands, carefully pulling on the pieces that had twisted in and around the wire.

"Reed!"

They both looked up.

"Just my brother." He grinned at her red and white spotty face as he freed the last of her hair. "You're a ways from your home. Do you want me to help you back?"

She stood up wobbling, and he gripped her arms to keep her from tumbling back into the fence. Something strange shuddered up and down his skin, like the first refreshing plunge into the blue lake. Quickly, he let go of her pale gray sleeves. She nodded and spoke some squeaky gibberish he couldn't understand. Her hair fell long around her shoulders and past her waist.

"I—I—" he lifted a lopsided grin, "don't know a word of what you just said. And, well, you

probably didn't even understand my question."
A commotion of strange foreign talking came from the field, and Reed realized her mother and siblings were coming to help.

He handed her the ribbon fluttering in the breeze and took her soft little hand, bowed and kissed it. Separating the wire, he carefully climbed back through. Running back to where his brother waited, he smiled shyly, a bit embarrassed. Why did he just kiss her hand?

CHAPTER 1

Fifteen years later

KING GEORGE, A thoroughbred and full-blooded racehorse charged top speed down the tall yellow grass of Chapman land. Reed's muscular body rode as one with the horse, his heartbeat pounding life into his chest. Spotting what he wanted, no, what he needed—he leaned to the left until his magnificent horse read his mind and flew like a bird over the sagging barbed wire fence. He relaxed his hold and the animal pulled back to canter towards the lovely blue lake. Reed pulled them to a stop and swung off King George as his horse meandered to the edge for a drink of cold, lake water. He stared out taking in the magnificent tall trees surrounding the miles of blue.

Oh, how forever and a day he'd missed this spot. The long, wood dock was rough and cracked, and small waves still lapped up against it just as it did after his grandfather built it. The simple rhythm was mesmerizing taking his keen senses to another lifetime. A brilliant blue sky lined with fluffy, white clouds almost took him back to childhood. What would it feel like if he could just run and leap from the end, he thought anticipating the rush he'd feel as the cold water enveloped him?

One of the boards crackled under his weight as he walked to the edge. A slight breeze came up from the water cooling his body after his heated ride on King George. He searched the water, land, dirt, and grass shores as his prized horse grazed along the shoreline.

"This should be mine!" he shouted to the expanse. King flicked his ears in response, and snorted seemingly in agreement with his beloved master. "Can you see the neglect and waste?" He huffed, bending to separate a loose board splintered off the edge of the dock. He chewed his bottom lip and stared past King George to the trees. Lumber for the mill as far as the eye can see.

An old ash tree spread dappled shade over the place where the house had stood. The Polish family had built their own house on his grand-parents' property and needlessly tore down the simple cabin. More aptly, they built a mansion, as some considered it. He could still see the top of the stately three-story brick fireplace—all that remained of the biggest house in the county.

The Polish family had only been in America a few years, and the house was barely finished. The horror of the entire family being gunned down and the home set on fire, set the locals reeling for years. The servants reported it was other Poles that killed the family, but no one was ever charged with the crime.

Years ticked by, and America had its own problems with the war between North and South. President Lincoln had his hands full. The eldest son fighting was enough for Reed's parents, so they thought it a convenient time to send him to England.

Reed sighed raking his fingers through his thick, brown hair. They gave him an unwanted boat ticket away from the land he loved. Intense green eyes surrounded by dark lashes peered contemplatively left to right over the vast timberland that once belonged to his grandparents. He drank in the impressive view. Three hawks made lazy circles among the back drop of vivid white and blue sky. The tops of the trees rustled gently in the breeze, wafting the scent of evergreen from every direction. Sun sparkling on the gentle ripples in the lake, the rolling green hills packed with trees and wildlife, and he saw the perfect spot for soaking in the warmth of the setting sun. In an instant he could recall those days of freedom where they swam and played for hours. It was all too poignant for words and it wasn't his.

How dense could he be? To think the land and nature that he loved would calm his past, calm his today. He shook his head. Robbie will never place a foot against the fertile earth. Sighing, he leaned his head back and tried to pull his shoulders side to side.

No one in their right mind wanted the vicious crime to befall the Polish family. That little girl with the tangled hair didn't deserve the hate taken out on her and her family. But the land, the lake, the trees were to be his and Robbie's one day, his grandfather had clearly promised it. If his grandmother had never sold it out from under her own family, maybe the Polish people would be alive. Now it just rotted and wasted away like the boards under his feet.

A warm breeze blew over him as he watched King George and considered his restless afternoon. Reed undid the top button of his starched white shirt. He'd begged off work early avoiding a stack of paperwork that tried to bore him to sleep. Why did he think he could be a lawyer, so much sitting and reading? He turned to walk back down the dock. At least here he could dream of—

Suddenly, his foot sunk crookedly into the rotted wood. Quickly, his other foot tried to bring balance as his body rolled forward then backward. Just as he tried to yank his foot free and avoid tumbling into the water, he fell backward. With his arm reaching out to catch his weight, his wrist slammed against the wood, taking the brunt of the fall.

"Bloody stupid, rotten dock!" He winced,

holding his throbbing wrist tightly against his chest. Gripping it with his good hand, he tried to wiggle his fingers as the pain shot up his arm. "Perfect, my *right* wrist. Just perfect." He growled, jerking his foot from its wooden trap.

Slowly standing, he held his arm steady and brushed off his nice, wool trousers with his good hand. He carefully walked back and gripped King George's reins. Instinctively he went to grab the saddle horn with his right hand and stopped. Bringing his wrist closer he didn't see any bones out of place, but there was no way he could use it. He breathed in and let out a slow breath. The ache was horrific.

His fingers throbbed feeling twice their actual size. He had two choices. He could ride to his parents' home just over the ridge, or back into town. "Ahhh." He moaned, dropping his elbow onto the saddle. Jumping up, he gripped the saddle with his good arm pulling his body onto the horse.

Glancing in the direction of his parents' home, he rolled his eyes—they had enough to deal with. He gave King George a little kick. He sat tall in the saddle, muscular legs gripping his horse as he pointed George toward town.

His strong, lanky, older brother had come back home from war a Union cripple. His parents already fed and bathed him like a baby. A broken wrist was nothing. His stomach turned; he should have fought. He should have been next in line. He should have never gone to England, and this land should have never been sold.

King George picked up the pace as they passed where the little caretaker's cottage should be. He squinted, trying to see it through the overgrown trees and ivy and he pulled his arm in tighter to his chest. One more glance back at the mansion, now just a tower of an old brick fireplace and blackened mortar. *Grandmother, I wish you could see this land going to waste. And that poor family, the little girl with the sad, brown eyes, and thick dark hair, she should have never burned to death.*

CHAPTER 2

AT DUSK, THE small town of Hancock was about to call it a day. Reed carefully slid off King George in front of the law offices of Chapman and Beasley. As he approached the tall building that housed his office below and his lodgings above, he stopped. Left-handed, he awkwardly turned the knob. How long till his right hand would work again? His partner in business and Oxford college chum's eyes widened at his entrance.

"Chappy. Did you get your itchy muscles satisfied on a stretch with King George?"

"That and a sore wrist." Reed lifted his stiff arm exposing his injury.

"That blimey bugger give you a toss on your gallivant?" Englishman Fred Beasley closed some papers inside his desk drawer. "Your crumpet, your companion, your Cynthia doll would never do that to you." He grinned pulling flat his thinning, light colored hair.

"No." Reed heaved a sigh. "I wasn't gallivanting exactly. I rode out to the Pole's property. The dock is rotten in places and my foot went right through; fell back on the dock. It hurts like the devil. I may be working on contracts with a sloppy left hand."

"Ahh, Chappy, your covetousness for that land has landed you injured. Once again, I might add. I say, old Chap, since you're not good for much, be so kind as to walk my lovely Janice home from the Doc's office, while I finish this filing." He pointed a long thin finger at Reed. "You know you owe me," Fred smirked.

Reed knew the reference well, from their many days of helping each other survive the years at Oxford. When one was down, the other took up the slack. It was a continual joke of who owed who. He reached again with his left hand, going out the door. Fred's wife worked two afternoons at Doctor Nedows's office. A quick walk down two blocks and up on the left. The doctor that served Hancock for more than thirty years had a white clapboard office and house. Reed entered as the little bell rang over the door. The thin, white-haired doctor peeked out from a room, his thick glasses winking in the lowering sun.

"Welcome, young Reed. Nothing wrong with Robbie, I pray?"

"No sir, Fred was trying to finish up, and I agreed to walk Janice home."

"I just sent her to run some ointment to the widow Van Harden." He came out to the foyer and set some papers on a desk. "You seem to be holding that arm a bit close to your chest." He spied Reed over his little spectacles.

"It's nothing." Reed pulled it away from his protective stance. "Just took a fall thirty minutes or so ago."

"I know you Chapman boys are tough as nails. Excuse my folly. Young *men*. Follow me in here and take a seat on my table." He patted the raised cot.

Reed sat, accepting ministrations from the caring man who'd patiently overseen his brother's invalid care.

"Looks like a clean break." Doctor Nedows gently turned his wrist front to back. "Let me set it in a splint for you." He gathered the items. "That fine horse of yours trip you up?"

"No, no. I almost fell through the old dock at the Polish property."

The doctor blew out a long sigh. "Just as horrific as the war, trying to identify those burnt bodies. Just when you don't think life can get harsher." He glanced at Reed, his gentle eyes misting with emotion. Reed had never seen him so sensitive. Maybe he was getting up in years.

The doctor swallowed, clearing his throat. "I was helping your mother one day, trying to get Robbie past some congestion. She shared how much the land meant to you. I guess your grandmother made a hasty decision after your grandfather died."

"First my grandfather's sudden passing, and

then not even a week later—she had sold it out from the family. Both a shock to me, but I was just a kid." He drew in a shaky breath, watching the doctor wrap the white gauze around his wrist. "The only reason I stayed with law school was to come back here and buy it back. The timber alone could help rebuild half the Union's destruction." I don't even know why I go there." He shook his head. "Where do I think a For Sale sign is going to appear from? I don't know." He huffed. "The land should have gone back to probate, years ago. I've searched county records. Nothing. Why hasn't it gone up for auction?" He assessed his secured wrist. "Thanks, Doc, feels better." He started to move from the table. "I shouldn't have rambled on, what do I owe you?"

"Here, son, let me help you," Doctor Nedows said gently helping him off the table. "I know how you relieve your parents every Sunday to help with Robbie."

"Oh yeah." Reed frowned, lifting up his newly wrapped wrist. "This will take some doing to lift Robbie in and out of the bathtub."

"I can help Sunday, don't fret about that." The doctor pursed his lips, pushed up his glasses and finally spoke. "I want to tell you something about that land. See now, I've come to appreciate how you care for your family. So I want to say something I've never told anyone. I've never trusted anyone enough *to* tell. But it's been so many years, and you don't look like a Polish revolutionist." The doctor flashed a faint smile. "I don't think that property can be sold because I believe there might be an heir left."

"Someone in Poland? Some family member?" Reed's eyes widened. "Do you know how they could be contacted?"

"No, no, right here in Pennsylvania." Doctor Nedows peered around the corner toward his front door, checking to see if anyone had entered. "One of the little girls lived. She had jumped out a top window and then she was brought to me. I can only assume a branch or limb broke her fall. I couldn't find any broken bones, but her back was so terribly burned from the heat of the burning house. When I knew she would live, I made arrangements for her at the Lennhurst Indigent Hospital and School for Disabled Children."

Reed felt his spine arise. "Would she still be there?"

"I really couldn't say. That was what, thirteen, fourteen years ago? They changed her name. I insisted no one keep any local records of where she came from. They agreed to strict confidentiality and to take her as an indigent child. Possibly after she healed, she was adopted. She was only five or six, you know. Lovely child. Only now her back would have those dreadful scars." The doctor lifted a triangle sling toward Reed and Reed shook his head no.

Standing, shocked with this new information, Reed watched as Janice entered. One of the Polish children lived? Unfathomable. Could it be the little girl he helped free from the barbed wire that day so long ago?

"Hi Reed. Looks like the doc had to help you get out of more lawyer work." Janice smiled, pointing to his wrist.

His mind flitted like a hummingbird, almost missing her teasing. "Ahh, yes. Fred asked me to walk you to our office."

"He promised me dinner at Walker's Café tonight," she said, gathering her things off the desk chair. "Next Wednesday, Doc?"

"Can you come in at eleven? I'd like your help with a simple surgery."

"I'll be here." She smiled. "Here, Reed, let me get the door for you. Are you sure I'm not walking you home?" she teased.

Reed smiled and looked back at the wrinkled doctor. "I can handle Robbie on Sunday. My folks still have some workers in the mill bunkhouse. I'll get an extra man from there." He hesitated, still stunned by the doctor's disclosure. "Thank you for listening, what you said helps me make some sense of it."

Doctor Nedows blinked under his thick glasses gazing somewhere far away. "You're a good man." Then he eyed Reed, his tone somber. "And a good brother."

CHAPTER 3

REED AWOKE WITH a start. He'd always struggled sleeping past three in the morning. Four years of getting up to work the early delivery route to the food commons at Oxford had provided change in his pocket but left a groove in his brain. Closing his eyes, he tried to think about something besides his throbbing wrist.

No pain was as bad as the inward kind, though. Like the moment he had found his grandfather slumped over a bale of hay in the barn. Maybe the original Chapman land was cursed.

No, his grandfather was old and had worked sunup to sundown every day of his life. Why had he dreamed about it again? Seeing the lake, smelling the familiar grass and trees, no doubt it was due to Doctor Nedows's revelation.

What a bizarre notion, one of the heirs could be living right here in Pennsylvania. Now his body and mind were wide awake. *I could get it back,* his heart beating faster than usual.

First, harvest the timber on that land. Then mill it at the Chapman mill. That would make his father's business profitable again. Of course!

Men coming home after the war, needed jobs, needed lumber to rebuild their homes and lives. It made perfect sense.

He tried to move his wrapped fingers. They felt tight and swollen. A lawyer with a broken writing hand—this was going to be a long week. He remembered the book in the office on the state of Pennsylvania. Certainly he could find out about the Lennhurst Indigent Hospital. Maybe find out where she had moved. If it were the young girl he had helped so many years ago, she would be twenty, twenty-one? Certainly, she would not still be there, but they might have the information he needed.

He pulled his arm over his pillow and rolled to the side grumbling, *That would never work. The doc had said they were sworn to confidence due to her family being murdered.* He dragged his good fingers back and forth over his forehead. He had a law degree from a prestigious university. Four years for a piece of paper he never wanted, but as Fred would say, it must be *bloody good* for something.

REED SAT AT his desk at dawn, picking through local books and law books that might help him with a compelling notion he couldn't shake. Wiry Fred Beasley came in a few hours later and dropped his leather satchel on his chair.

"Chappy, good to see you working with that

terrible injury. I'm at the courthouse till noon today."

"Mmm." Reed never looked up.

"Your sweet, little cup of pudding dined at Walkers' last night." Fred waited without any response. "Cynthia's hand was tucked inside some handsome bloke's elbow; I dare say he was even more dark and dashing than you."

"What?" Reed finally squinted at him.

"Cynthia Icely, the most wonderful pastry in town. Your cabbage. Your darling." Fred approached Reed's thick wooden desk.

"Do you want your wife hearing you talk that way?" Reed huffed, rolling his eyes at him.

"Since the upstanding, young lawyers that we are want the truth and only the truth, she dined with her uncle. But she did ask me about you, and I told her you'd taken a terrible fall."

Reed groaned as he flipped more pages. "Wonderful."

"Why do you reject such a lovely coquette?" Fred's voice missed its usual mocking tone.

"I don't reject the coquette—whatever that is." Reed flipped his left hand in the air at him. "Cynthia is looking for old money and titles. I'm frankly too second class for her. She's okay that I want to own land, *but* she doesn't want me to work on it or get my suit ruffled." Reed shook his head. "Aren't you supposed to be at the courthouse?" As Fred turned toward the door, guilt pricked Reed's conscience. He tried to take the edge from his voice, "I hate melodrama. And by the way Fred, you married the only smart, pragmatic woman in town. Making you smart and rich."

"Well, blimey, I did. Huh." Fred left with a big smile. Reed went back to scribbling some messy notes with his left hand.

LATER IN THE day he stood to return his law books to the shelf. A little knock on the door and his mother peeked in. "I looked through the window first," she said, smiling. "I didn't see you with anyone."

"Come in." He waved her inside, thankful for the break. "I see you got away for a moment." He went to hug her petite frame, assessing she didn't have bad news. "I'm glad to see you."

"I wondered if you'd eaten, so I packed a few sandwiches." She set the basket down on his desk.

"Mmm," he smelled the roast beef. "No one in England can make a sandwich as good as my mother." He opened the paper and took a large bite of thick bread and succulent beef.

"I still don't like to think how thin you were when you came home." She frowned.

"Thin, but alive. Wasn't that the point?" He wished he could take the snippy words back. His parents knew full well how much he'd resented being removed from the war. The hurt in his mother's eyes stabbed at him.

"How is Robbie today?" he asked.

"Sleeping." She turned to brush some dust off a globe sitting on a side table. "Your father is with him." She glanced back and pulled in a breath. "I passed Doc Nedows, he told me you fell on Grandpa's—I mean the dock at the Polish property. I just stopped by to say we'll stay home this Sunday. You need to care for that wrist."

"No." He chewed and swallowed a large bite. "You need the day off." He touched her arm, noticing the pale blue dress she'd worn for years, her salt and pepper hair pulled back in a simple bun. "I'll be there before breakfast as usual and I'll get him up and have Bernie help me with his bathing. You and father go to church and lunch and the mercantile. Take a Sunday drive. I will be fine." He noticed the dark bags under her eyes.

"You know, Reed, one day you will be a parent, and I hope you can love your children without regrets." Her eyes narrowed sternly just as they'd done countless times before throughout his childhood. Listening was not a strong point for him back then and maybe not even now. He had so often pushed her patience to the limit. He nodded.

"I never regret one minute your grandmother selling that land. She left us with enough to pay for your tuition to Oxford. She wanted that for you. Because of those choices, I can stand here and drop a sandwich off for my son. I can see your office, see you become the man God intended. For that, I will *never* regret your move to England." She gently took his wrapped wrist. "One day in the future, you will have our little mill and land, so tell King George to keep you off that Polish land." She squeezed his elbow. "It does have a beautiful lake." She smiled. "But no good can come of living in the past."

Glancing down, Reed took another bite of sandwich and slid the legal papers he'd worked on all day out of her view.

CHAPTER 4

THE NEXT MORNING, Reed glanced up from his desk as Fred walked in the silent law office.

"Reed Chappy Chapman, did you hit your head on that fall?" Fred flopped his satchel on his desk. "Two mornings in a row you are at work before me." He lifted an eyebrow.

"I'm always in before you, but I need your help." Reed tossed and turned on an idea most the night. He couldn't get the documents ready with his poor penmanship. "Actually, I could use Janice's help. She has a better script than you." He stood and met Fred at his desk.

"I know that crazed look in those dashing, green eyes." Fred pulled some paper from his drawer. "Is it illegal?"

"Yes and no," Reed said, earnestly.

"A nod is as good as a wink. I was going to say yes either way."

"Why?" Reed jeered. "Because you *owe me* . . ." they said simultaneously.

"One day we must make a list of what constitutes payback or has been paid back for nursing me through consumption." Fred's long nose pointed up. "Oh, and writing two of my law finals and taking one of my tests in proxy for me." Fred stilled, giving him a curious frown. "Which I never asked you to do, why did you take such a risk? You could have been flogged and kicked out of Oxford and the country."

"Flogged?" Reed shook his head.

"Well then, banished, to say the least." Fred grabbed a roll from his bag and took a bite.

Reed went back to his desk and shuffled his notes. "I'm an American citizen, Mr. Beasley. My brother is now a cripple for serving his country. I would have fought in a minute rather than go to Oxford. And if your country gave me the heave-ho, I wouldn't have been upset. Thinking about you surviving without me would be more difficult. Anyway. Law is not my love, the land is. But I have an idea to use my stellar law degree for my good."

"Yes, I was right close to those pearly gates during that time. Mum was worried, but I too feeble to make it home. Alas, I survived. Mum relieved and," Fred poured himself some water from a pitcher, "then followed you back to your beloved land. Even found the only intelligent woman, you say."

"Thank God for Janice. Now I don't have to be your nanny," Reed huffed returning to his notes.

"Well chum, before you give up that job, I suppose you should know Janice is pretty sure she's expecting."

"No. Are you joking?" Reed waited, his friend so rarely serious.

Fred put the cup down and stepped over to Reed's desk. "Blast it, man, what a thing to joke about. Yes, it's true. Just another thing you didn't learn from time in my lovely England. If you meet a fair maiden, and you smile nice and brew her a decent cup of tea, there is a fair chance she will let you undress her and . . ."

"Stop." Reed groaned. "I just want to say congratulations. Your wife will make a wonderful mother."

"Exactly, and you will be the godfather offering the American moral compass we Brits don't seem to possess." He smiled quickly. "So your nanny days aren't over. Because. You do. Owe me.

"THESE ARE A bit confusing," Janice said, later in the afternoon. Reed had given her his desk and chair so he could pace and translate his scribble to her.

"Who has to sign for failure to occupy the land?" she said, scratching her nose.

Reed's mouth twisted. "It's not supposed to be clear."

"Oh." She crinkled a frown up at him.

Fred walked in and watched them work. "Darling, did you ask him up front how much he's paying you for translating his work."

She dropped the pen in the inkwell. "I don't

31

think this is work. It reads like instructions for sale of the property next to his parents. I think I'm doing him a favor." She walked over to Fred and pecked him on the cheek.

"Gadzooks, I thought only I got your favors."

"Don't be brash, Freddy. You know they're all for you." She winked.

Reed shook his head wondering why he thought this partnership would rise to any professional level. Noticing the perfectly scripted documents Janice had finished, he chided himself. This desperate attempt to get the land wasn't quite professional or ethical, but it was worth a try.

"Sunday, I care for my brother," Reed said. The couple finally turned to notice he was talking. "Could I borrow your buggy for Monday, possibly Tuesday, too?"

"Does this have anything to do with something legal and illegal?"

"Yes." Reed nodded once.

"And the American soil you covet?"

"Yes, and if I go to jail will you care for King George?"

"Like my own son." Fred kissed his wife gently.

"Or daughter," Janice added.

MONDAY MORNING BEFORE dawn, Reed dressed in his best suit, pacing his small room while he practiced his approach. He double checked his

32

supplies. Without stopping, he should be able to make it to Brown Township in about five hours. His lantern glowed in the corner, and he checked his appearance in the mirror. He used to practice his opening statements in front of the mirror before trials, but now Fred preferred trial court. Actually, Fred enjoyed being up in front of people. Which was fine, leaving him with civil and contract law, and time to help his parents at the mill.

He pulled his stiff white collar away from his neck. Why had Fred brought up his misdeeds from years ago? They were just college mates, trying to make it through. Frankly, it didn't seem so criminal at the time. Fred couldn't get out of bed for weeks. Reed fed him broth and helped him to the privy. Fred passed the bar exam by himself. Would any of their clients really care if Reed did some of Fred's school work? As the sun finally peeked into downtown Hancock, Reed blew out his light and headed down the stairs. He paused at Fred's desk and thought of some sarcastic note he could leave, but something felt different.

Fred, his chum, Fred Beasley was going to be a father. That seemed like asking King George to become a fish. Fred and Janice were growing up, making their own little family. Incredible. He sensed a new and strange distance with them. They had a nice home and security here in

Hancock. Why would he feel anything but happy for them? Without the troubled heritage his generations had, they would make their own way here and be content.

Reed went out back and brought King George around to the buggy. Would repurchasing this land make him happy or content? Had he ever been content? He attached the harness around the horse. This trip was likely a wild goose chase, he could easily be back tonight with no answers, but it didn't matter. He held the reins and climbed in the leather bound black buggy. If he didn't make the trip, he'd go crazy wondering what if. He was on his way to find out. Anything was better than never knowing.

AFTER LUNCH, REED pulled King George to a stop outside a large brick building in Brown Township. He would need directions to the Lennhurst Hospital; there didn't seem to be anything by that name in the quiet humble streets. He stepped down and watched a man walk his way.

"Excuse me, sir. I'm looking for the Lennhurst Hospital. Could you give me directions?"

"The asylum?" the man asked.

"Yes, I believe so."

"If you're sure." The man shook his head. "You know what they say, once you go in you might not ever get out."

Reed felt tension in his back knotting. "I'm just

gathering some information—from the hospital."

"All right then. Take a left at the top of that hill," he pointed. "The road winds around for five or so miles. There's a large tan stone wall. They think the wall will keep them all in, yet I heard last week one escaped and was found in someone's chicken coop eating all the eggs."

Reed knew he often had trouble focusing, but why would a patient healing in a hospital "escape?"

CHAPTER 5

THE TREES GREW denser, and a light cool breeze awakened Reed's composure. Pulling King George back from breaking into a canter, he looked side to side. What did the man mean about people getting out? Did Dr. Nedows call it an asylum? Was he paying attention that day? There had to be something amiss for a hospital to be so far from town.

Reed jerked quickly to the left when he'd heard a strange noise. It wasn't a scream. It was more like a barking howl. Blowing out a breath, he rolled his shoulders back and forth, trying to relieve the tension.

"What could that be?" he said aloud, "Come on now, George, let's keep a steady—"

The bellowing echoed again! Reed saw the massive thick tan wall and pulled King George to a stop.

He could clearly see a thin, bald man rocking back and forth on top of the tall stone wall. Clutching the tail of a tattered gown, the man would rock back while flipping his gown up. How he didn't rock off the top was a miracle. He shrieked, then let out a deep moan and laughter echoed through the trees. Reed allowed the horse a few prancing, nervous steps before he squeezed the reins again.

He glanced around. Surely someone would come along. He spotted a small wagon waiting by an outbuilding of some kind, and Reed carefully led King George down the right lane. Just as the wall rocker yelled out again, Reed noticed the poor invalid was naked under the flipped-up gown. He averted his eyes quickly and wondered why the depraved man wasn't being helped.

"Excuse me, sir." Reed set the brake and jumped down. Two men unloading a wagon stopped and gaped at him, jaws slung open. One appeared like a young boy in an old man's body. He smiled crooked and drool slid from the corner of his grin. The other one walked up to Reed and touched his dark wool suit, "You look nice." He swung back to the other man "Is there a burial today, too?" He turned to Reed. "Are you a preacher?"

"No." Reed stepped back from their oddities trying to rethink the words of the man in town aligning them with what he was seeing. "Can you—"Another piercing yell from the man on the wall halted his words. "I need to speak to someone in charge." He waited as they stared at him.

"I can be in charge," the boyish-faced man said, with a silly child-like tone.

"No, no thank you." Reed noticed a large open double door in the thick wall. Leading King George, he walked around the men's wagon, until he could see inside. "Is this Lennhurst Hospital?" Reed called back to the men by the wagon. They smiled at each other and went back to unloading. Feeling something prickle up his spine, Reed gazed into the large opening, noticing some kind of yard inside the tan wall.

He froze in place and squeezed the reins tight. More invalids, dressed like the wall rocker shuffled on the brown grass inside. He watched one bent over bald man pull up his gown and relieve himself against the wall. Another woman shuffled by jerking and pounding her palm against her head.

"Good Lord," he huffed, wavering back. What had Doc Nedows called this place—a hospital for disabled children? Surely, he was at the wrong place! Two rail-thin, short-haired young women started to slap at each other. A nurse with a black dress and dirty white apron yanked on the bony arm of one woman and pulled her to the ground. "Behave!" she bellowed, sharply. As if the nurse could sense Reed watching her, she turned and made eye contact with him. Jerking the balled-up woman off the ground, she moved her away from the other woman. Reed stepped cautiously up to the large opening. He tried to pull his focus away from another woman down on all fours, wildly flipping her hair back and forth. He cleared his throat. "Excuse the interruption, ma'am. Is this Lennhurst Hospital?"

"Lennhurst Asylum, it is, hospital, too." She jutted her chin out. "What do you want?"

"I'm looking for the administrator in charge." He rubbed his fingers back and forth across his forehead, trying not to look past her to the bizarre people shuffling in the yard.

"This here buildn' is a large H. Like the letter?" Reed nodded as if he understood.

"You're at the back part of the H. You need to go around to the front. Follow this road and stay left. There are two large brick towers with a sign between them. That's the front of the building. There should be a gal at a desk that can help you."

"Thank—" Reed couldn't finish, a short, thin teen in rags ran straight for him.

"Daddy, daddy! You came to get me!" The cross-eyed teen with knotted hair moved around the nurse and tried to grab Reed as he jumped back.

"Woody, stop!" The nurse wrapped her arms around him roughly, almost picking him off the ground. "This ain't yor daddy." She nodded to Reed and manhandled the teen back into the yard and pulled the large doors closed.

Reed stilled, his heartbeat erratic, and a small bead of sweat rolled down his spine. He looked up expecting the yelling wall rocker to chime in, but he was gone. Now that the small wagon had left and the thick gate was closed tight, it was too quiet. Unnervingly silent.

He patted King George on the neck and tried to settle himself. "This place is more than a hospital," he said to his horse. The stallion tossed his head back with the same nervous tension Reed carried. "Let's go find the front."

Back around to the front, Reed could see he'd followed the wrong lane. The front of the building was stately with the two tall square towers. The metal sign across the top of the stone towers said, Lennhurst Hospital. A large plaque on one of the towers read, Asylum for the Relief of Persons Deprived of the Use of Their Reason. The other tower had a plaque, School for Disabled Children. A list of contributors' names fell below.

He thought the Polish girl came here to heal from burns. Did Doctor Nedows understand where he'd sent her?

He tapped the reins as King George walked down the gravel entrance. To the left lay a wandering, walking path nestled by a garden with benches hidden amongst the shrubs and flowers. A stark contrast to the back area he'd just seen. A tranquil fountain with a trickling water tried to bring calm to his edginess. Heavy, green ivy masked the same stone walls he had just come around. A couple of women dressed in normal day dresses sat on a bench on the far left of the garden. No nurses with stiff white aprons and thick scowls hovering anywhere.

He tied George to the hitching post and grabbed his shoulder bag. Climbing the wide stairs, he pulled the heavy glass and wood door open. A woman with a proper white dress and nursing hat sat behind a wooden desk.

"How can I help you, sir?" She stood.

Reed had to get his bearings. The hall to the left was long with many doors. The hall to the right was its equal. The wide hallway behind the woman's desk led to the back. The letter H, the last nurse had said. Now it made sense. He drew in a long breath, still trying to compose himself. "I'm here to see your administrator."

"Yes, sir. If you would like to have a seat." She nodded to a bench and walked two doors down to the right.

Reed sat with a rapidly bouncing leg, tapping his heel against the light wood floor. *It doesn't smell like a hospital. The army hospital they had Robbie in was rancid.* Reed felt a bit of something roll in his stomach. He reached into his bag for his legal papers and looked up as the nurse gestured toward the door. *Once you go in, you may never get out,* echoed through his mind causing his stomach to roll again. Reed took one more look back through the long glass doors.

King George stood where he'd hitched him. Swallowing hard, he walked into the office. A man a bit shorter than Reed reached out to shake his hand.

"Good afternoon, I am Mr. Vial. The administrator of Lennhurst."

Reed nodded his head. Mr. Vial's thick, gray, bushy hair and waxed mustache put him somewhat at ease.

Reed shook the man's hand. "Nice to meet you sir. I am Reed Chapman, a lawyer from Hancock. I have a confidential matter to inquire about." Another man sitting at a desk looked up quickly before dipping his head to return to his work.

"Of course, let's step back into my office." Mr. Vial led the way.

ONLY TWENTY MINUTES later, Reed came out the front doors, completely discouraged. Mr. Vial had listened to his vague explanation of how the sale of the Polish land had come to light in his legal office. With a simple request that this legal paperwork be signed off so the land could be returned to the County for auction. *Even the funds could be donated to the Hospital,* was a thought that came to him at the last moment. Did he forget anything?

He climbed into the buggy and turned George down the gravel path. Mr. Vial had been aloof. He had no expression so Reed could discern his reaction to this news. The man had no questions? Reed wondered if the man played poker or if he was always a cold fish.

Some other women slowly walked the garden path. Maybe the damaged young woman lived in the 'back H'? Certainly, Reed had explained, as the administrator, Mr. Vial had all legal rights to sign for her. Tired, he blew out a sigh. He'd ridden hard all day; he hadn't rehearsed any scenario of Mr. Vial's detachment. At least Mr. Vial had agreed to read over the legal papers and speak with him in the morning. Reed didn't want to look back as he drove under the large Lennhurst Hospital sign. A gentle flapping flew across his vision. A purple and yellow butterfly flitted a circle in front of him and over and down the side. By far, this took the prize for the most outlandish day he'd experienced in a long time.

AFTER A RESTLESS night at the Brown Township Hotel, Reed found himself back on the same bench at Lennhurst Hospital, waiting again. Frankly, there was no reason they shouldn't sign for the release of this land. He stood and looked back to where King George waited. What would be his recourse if they refused? Could he come up with another approach?

A door to the left opened. Two older men in suits stepped out. They briefly looked his way before they walked farther down the long hall of doors. Mr. Vial came out with another well-dressed man and they nodded.

"Mr. Chapman, sir. We are ready to meet with you."

Reed felt his heart lurch, unable to read their expressions. Surely they were going to reject his paperwork. He stepped into another office lined with bookshelves and a table in the center. Six heavy chairs surrounded it.

"Sir, if you would take a seat. I would like to introduce our specialist in theory of reality, mind and matter, Dr. Powell."

The older, white-haired gentleman lifted a small smile and reached to shake his hand. "You are a lawyer from Hancock. Is that correct?"

"Yes, sir." Reed pulled on the chair and sat.

"How long have you lived in that area of our state?" Dr. Powell spoke with a calming voice but Reed didn't want to reveal his strong ties to the land.

"Most of my life. I went to Oxford for law school before returning to Pennsylvania."

Dr. Powell nodded slowly, pulling on his chin. "Our committee held a meeting last night and then again this morning." Dr. Powell cleared his throat. "We have some concerns. How do you feel about answering a few more questions?"

Reed's leg began to bounce under the table as he broke out in a cold sweat.

CHAPTER 6

REED SWIPED HIS thick hair off his forehead and swallowed the tightening in his throat. The legal papers were convoluted, yet simple for these educated men. Could they see his manipulation?

"How would I feel?" he questioned coolly.

Dr. Powell chuckled. "I apologize, that is a term we use here a lot. You look a bit tense, is there anything we can do to help you relax?"

Now Reed considered how fast he could forget it all. Dr. Powell had a grandfatherly face, but Reed had already seen the poor souls in the back H. This place was a frightening paradox.

"I understand that . . . that the young Polish girl's identity was to remain unknown." Reed made eye contact, knowing from experience in court how important it is. "I explained to Mr. Vial, I have no intention of disclosing any information except to the possible sale of the dormant land. It would be a simple business transaction that would never have to involve her."

"What if it *was* to involve her?" Dr. Powell leaned closer and Reed inched back.

"Then, if my assumption that she is unmarried is correct, she is welcome to sign for herself, the funds can be sent here. I assume you gentlemen would oversee that."

"Are you a trustworthy man?" Dr. Powell asked with an intense tone.

Reed tried to breathe in short breaths, his mind racing to what the man was really asking. "I am." He spoke with confidence. "My older brother is mentally and physically handicapped from the war. I help my parents care for him weekly." He thought these men could appreciate his family's situation.

The two men leaned close to one another, whispering something. Reed could only pray they were to approve his request and he could be on his way.

"We would like you to meet her," Dr. Powell said. "Her name here is Patience Stephens."

Reed knew his mouth hung open and for the life of him, he could not find a proper refusal. "If you think it's necessary." he finally choked out.

"Wonderful." Dr. Powell lightly clapped his thick hands together. "I asked her to wait on the green bench."

"I will take my leave," Mr. Vial said. "It was nice meeting you, Mr. Chapman."

Reed nodded at him, then looked down at his paperwork sitting on the table. Had he already signed them? Dr. Powell held a folder and added Reed's documents to his. "Let's go find her in the garden."

Reed followed the doctor out the front stairs, thankful for the cool breeze that soothed his constricted lungs. Surely the committee wanted her protected if they had met last night and this morning. Why would they ask a complete stranger to meet her? His stomach twisted, and he glanced up at the thick stone walls wondering how yesterday's wall-yeller had fared. What if she did something similar? Before he could think of a way out of this place, Dr. Powell stopped and let Reed pass.

"There, under the large oak tree; she's sitting on the bench." Dr. Powell pointed, as though he was to go meet her alone? He carefully glanced over to a striking-featured, young woman sitting as still and erect as one of his sisters' porcelain dolls.

"What am I to say?" He flashed a panicked expression to the doctor.

"She has some questions if you don't mind."

Reed looked again and took a series of hesitant steps. The young woman watched a ladybug jump from the outstretched ivy wall. Could it be the little girl from the barbed wire fence? Same thick, brown hair like molasses in the sun, except her braid, wound up in a large bun at the nape of her neck. Heat rushed to his face. *Oh Lord, she is breathtakingly beautiful.*

Eyeing him, she slowly turned. Deep velvety brown eyes, a perfectly formed woman lifted a small innocent smile. She dropped her thick dark lashes, looking at the ground. Heaven help him, as he approached; he felt locked-up, speechless.

She stood stiffly, without bending at the waist. "Hello," she said with a delicate shyness that kept her eyes from reaching his.

"Miss Stephens." Reed bowed and reached for her hand and kissed it. Startled, he quickly let go. It had to be her, the shivery reaction rattling through him was the same. Thunderstruck, he choked, would she remember?

"You are from Hancock, I understand," she said, squeezing her hands together.

"Yes, Miss."

"You know the area well," she said, softly.

"I do."

"You have been out to the land in question?" This time her round eyes fully met his.

"I have." Reed needed this to be over. Meeting a child survivor of that horrible day was shocking and uncomfortable beyond his imprudent imagination. "I feel I can represent your situation and the need to sell the land and move on if you will allow me."

Watching him, her eyes broke away and surveyed the garden and back to him, a resolve flickering in her eyes. "I will allow you sir, to represent my wishes."

"Wonderful." Reed felt his chest take in air for the first time in days. "Let me ask Dr. Powell for the papers to sign." Turning back, she walked a step behind him as Dr. Powell smiled at them both coming down the path.

"What have you decided?" the doctor asked.

"I'm going to allow Mr. Chapman to help me."

"I'm so proud of you, Patience." The doctor rubbed her arm. "Shall we go back in and sign the papers."

Reed led the way back to the large entrance, holding the large glass and wood door open for them. *Let's sign the papers, echoed in his head. Yes, sign the papers and be gone.* Just before they stepped inside, an older woman his mother's age, ran toward Miss Stephens with her hand held out. Patience reached out to her and they hugged. They shook their heads and hugged again. The other woman pulled away with tears in her eyes. Reed had to brush it off, everything about this place was bizarre. Not a minute too soon, they entered the room with the table. Dr. Powell took out his folder and laid three papers on the table. "Let me quickly go over these, before you sign."

For the hundredth time, Reed stood confused.

"This first form is Article One." Dr. Powell rubbed his finger down the paragraph. "We've met with the managers and staff. I've signed the physician's certificate. The administrator has ordered the release."

Do they have to order the release of her signature? Strangely she didn't seem insane, but he of all people understood about conservatorship. Reed raked his fingers back and forth on his forehead.

"Then this is Article Two. It's Patience's certification by her own person releasing Lennhurst from the obligation of care." Dr. Powell grinned at Miss Stephens and she smiled back. "Go ahead and sign here."

She took the quill and signed her name.

"May I ask?" Reed blinked. "These forms are what's needed for her to sign the land off for sale?"

Dr. Powell stood up, glanced down and pulled out Reed's legal forms. "Doesn't it say here, if the land is to go on unoccupied, it must be sold?"

"Yes," Reed sighed, a bit too relieved.

"Her wishes are to leave Lennhurst and go occupy the land." Dr. Powell looked quizzically at the young woman standing close.

"Yes, I'm leaving with you to go to my land." Her chin dipped slightly. "You said you would represent me."

Reed stopped breathing as his gut fell, slamming into his feet.

CHAPTER 7

"SIR . . . DOCTOR POWELL." Reed barely found an audible voice. "Could I speak with you in the hallway?" He looked past the face of Patience Stephens as he went out the door.

"I'm not sure how the misunderstanding happened. And I will apologize for my part now, but she can't just live on her land. Does she understand her home was burnt to the ground? I've been there; it is just old blackened stone and brick."

"We talked about it at length." Doctor Powell nodded. "Though I don't think she knows how to grieve the loss." He paused. "It's difficult for a child when she never saw the bodies or can visit a grave." He frowned. "But we talk of eternity. We talk about the hope of being united with them one day. Once when she was oh, nine or ten," he scratched his wrinkled cheek, "she said Jesus had told her He enjoys having her family in heaven."

Reed rubbed his fingers across his forehead, pinching the bridge of his nose, forcing himself to focus on what was just said. "She thinks I will be helping her? But I can't. I have a busy law practice and, as I've already said, I have other commitments to help my family." *And she thinks she can have a conversation with Jesus in the sweet by and by. Clearly she is demented.* He tried to keep his expression stoic.

Patience walked out the cracked door. "Would you be willing to give me a ride to Hancock? I could stay in the caretaker's cottage."

"By yourself?" Reed knew he sounded harsh. "That home is practically rubble." *Or would be one day.*

Doctor Powell spoke up. "From your papers, do I understand she is the only living heir to that land?"

Reed stared upward, already exasperated and finally nodded.

"And if she can't abide by the conditions, you will help her sell it?"

Reed huffed, thoroughly disturbed. "I suppose so."

"Well, sir, it is 1866 and times are changing. Since she has no one in Hancock to advise her, we felt confident that you would help her see this through."

Reed glanced out the large hall window to see King George waiting. How could he use this for his advantage? *Once she sees the land, certainly bringing back painful memories, she would be eager to sell.* "All right, I can take her to Hancock and help her locate the land."

"Patience." Doctor Powell smiled. "Will you have Turner gather your things and meet Mr. Chapman out front?"

Bowing her head, she curtsied with a straight back and moved down the hall.

Reed shook his head and began to gather the papers on the table. *This is happening, right now?* He cleared his throat. "Is she . . . you know . . . insane?" He had to know what he was getting into.

"Oh no." The doctor chuckled. "She was never supposed to be here this long. But as you know, a terrible crime happened to her family. In the past years, I've been able to do some research. Her father was part of the Polish government. He fought for the liberation of serfdom leading to a political uprising. Surely he fled to America for asylum, attempting to save himself and his family." The doctor took in a deep breath. "But he was unable to hide. They found him." He blew out his held breath.

"She knows her real name is Patyana Stepavov, her father was Fedor, her mother, Alla. Our professional staff discussed her adoption many times. I even talked to my own sweet wife. Patience would have loved having a family, siblings to play with. But we have nine children ourselves; my wife was already busy enough. Our staff has met, and we feel she is ready to live her own life. She needs other experiences to grow. And we

believe we've done our job in keeping her safe."
He paused, judging if Reed was following him.
"Remember, Patyana Stepavov died that day with
her siblings. Our Patience is smart and speaks
English without flaw, yet, is very innocent and
unworldly. I believe this will give her her own
life. The one God intended for her all along."

Reed tried to focus on the doctor's words as he
watched a man tying a long trunk onto the back
shelf of the Beasley's buggy, then tying his things
on top.

Patience came down the steps as yet another
woman came from the garden to hug her.
Remarkable, he stared at her heavy gray plaid
dress belling out from her tiny waist, this young
woman had grown up in an asylum. He forged a
smile to the doctor and moved toward the front
doors. From his first moments at Lennhurst he
was ready to leave. Never in a thousand years did
he think he would be taking a piece of Lennhurst
Asylum home with him.

PATIENCE COULD FEEL Mr. Chapman's presence
waiting somewhere behind her. She had her list
in her pocket and her trust in a mighty God.
Yes, her God would help her; He'd promised
never to leave her or forsake her. She squeezed
Doctor Powell one more time and turned to
see Mr. Chapman waiting. Without greeting
or expression, he held out his hand to help her

56

inside his horse-drawn buggy. Were all young men so serious? Just as she was to take his hand, the beautiful sleek animal looked her in her eye, and she moved past his extended hand.

"And who is this robust friend?"

"Watch yourself." Mr. Chapman spoke up. "He's been known to toss his head and—"

The stallion bent lower as Patience rubbed its face and neck almost nuzzling her.

Reed shook his head. "This is King George."

"I am delighted to make your acquaintance." Patience did another small stiff curtsy, smiling at the horse. "You are aptly named, carrying your royalty like a true king."

Reed spoke up. "We need to go. If the weather holds, we can make it to Hancock by dark."

She turned to Reed and dropped her head to the side. Smiling, she offered him her hand. "You also have a commanding presence, sir. I can see why the two of you are good friends." Patience held Mr. Chapman's hand and stepped up into her seat. Noticing her dress layers took up most of the area, she tried to pull them back to her side as the buggy rocked with his weight. His eyes narrowed as he made a clicking sound with his tongue and tapped the reins on King George.

"If you have any hesitation about this Miss— you need to speak up now."

Patience squeezed her hands in the folds of her dress. "I will try not to be a burden, Mr.

Chapman. I knew as soon as the little ladybug landed in front of me—this was God's will."

"What was God's will?" he said abruptly, as they passed under the Lennhurst sign.

"I always see a ladybug when God is telling me to pay attention." She gazed out to the forest. "I knew assuredly, this was the day I was to leave here forever."

He seemed to question her with his eyes, even rocking in his seat to move away.

"If you say so," he murmured.

CHAPTER 8

THE STIFF SILENCE back to Brown Township only helped Reed regret his decision more. What was he thinking agreeing to take her to Hancock? Why didn't he mention he was an unmarried man? Traveling alone with an unmarried woman—Dr. Powell should have known to find a better arrangement. Had he seen a train station in Brown Township? He could get her a ticket and—what a terrible idea, who knows where she would wander off to and he'd be back to never being able to close the sale. Turning left off the road from Lennhurst, the town came into view.

"Do you need anything from town?" Reed glanced over at her rigid solemn posture. "Have you ever been here before?"

"Yes." She lifted a quick smile and peered at the stores. "There is one place that upsets me. I will try and look away."

"What place?" Reed wondered.

"That one!" She squealed and dropped her face into her hands. She moaned, rocking side to side.

Shocked by her sudden erratic change of disposition, Reed jumped and wondered if she would fall out of the buggy. He switched the reins to his other hand and grabbed her arm. Wincing, as his grip triggered his broken wrist soreness. "Hold up now." He tried to spot what she'd seen, as she whimpered and dropped her head onto his shoulder. A large glass window showcased a huge skinned cow carcass hanging from a hook. "The butcher? You don't like the butcher?"

"Are we past?" She choked.

"Yes. It's behind us. You can look now." Reed let loose of her arm.

She took a deep breath and glanced up at him. "I'm sorry. I said I wouldn't be a burden. But to treat one of God's creations so—so inhumane." She wiped something from under her eye and Reed froze. She had to be the little girl. The same misty, velvet brown eyes haunting his memories. He scooted closer to the edge of the bench seat as he pushed her dress folds away from touching his leg. He felt something strange sweep over his being. It had to be her. Watching the town thin to a few farms and ranches, he smiled. Somehow humorous now, the start she gave him.

"Tell me about what you'd do in town?" he asked.

"Dr. Powell would bring me." She spoke up. "A few years ago. He called it my independent tutorial. We would go to the store and practice buying things—learn about the bank and how it worked." She pressed the folds flat on the front of her dress. "Things like that. So I'd feel somewhat confident," she paused with brown eyes gazing into the distance, "in my future."

"Except for the butcher." The corner of his mouth tipped up while keeping his eyes on the road.

"Yes, true." They rode on for a few minutes of needed silence.

"Dr. Powell encouraged me to make a dream list. I think he knew this day of independence would come for me."

"Something beyond shopping?" Reed questioned.

"Would you like to hear it?" Patience reached into her pocket and pulled out a crumpled piece of paper.

Reed nodded.

"Number one," she sat up straighter beaming, "is Christmas. I would like to participate in Christmas. I've read about churches having services and people singing together. Maybe if no one invites me to a meal, I could cook one for a widow or elderly couple."

Reed nodded again. He remembered the depression of missing Christmas while at Oxford. His sisters and their new husbands, his parents, often extended family all celebrating without him. The strange, isolated Miss Stephens had never known any family traditions. Did she know how to boil water, cook an egg, or potato?

"Number two is a lot like Christmas, but I want

to attend a church with families. I had a church service every Sunday with the other patients at Lennhurst. There were no babies crying and children running around. Do you attend church with your wife, your family?" She turned to face him.

"No." He looked at her quickly and then away. "I mean, no I am not married, and I help with my brother on Sundays so my parents can attend."

"That is admirable. How do you care for your brother? Is he too young to sit still?"

Reed hesitated, he didn't want to talk about his family. It was a bit inconvenient they lived next door to her property—which would be going up for sale tomorrow, if he could find a way.

"Ahh, no. My brother is a few years older than me. He fought for the Union Army. A bridge exploded around him, and the doctors thought his back might have fractured in more than two places."

"Oh, I'm so sorry." She held her hand over her mouth.

"A miracle to all that he lived, but he is an invalid. He has no control over his limbs or voice, nothing really." Reed gripped the reins tighter, feeling the pain shoot up his broken wrist. "I have two older sisters that are married and live out of state."

"I read the weekly papers, so many tragedies, so many died." She swept a piece of loose hair back behind her ear. "What are your sisters' names?"

"My father is Robert Joseph. My oldest sister is Roberta and Rachel is the other."

"Ahh." Her voice was soft. "I see a pattern of names with the letter R."

"What else is on that list?" Reed didn't want any personal conversations, nodding to the paper with her numbered items.

"Number three is to swim again."

"Swim?" he said, wide-eyed.

"I remember a beautiful lake with a large dock. As children, we would run and jump off the end." Her face glowed.

My lake, my dock. Reed locked his jaw. "Young women don't swim. Something Doctor Powell probably forgot to go over."

"Oh." Her dark eyelashes fluttered up and down. "Doctor Powell encouraged the idea of swimming. He said it would be good for . . ." She looked out over the passing scenery.

Reed allowed the horse a few prancing, nervous steps before he squeezed the reins again. "I will take into account you know more about current standards than I do." She carefully folded her paper and pushed it into her pocket.

Reed felt a prick of consciousness. He had no right to quell her dreams. Christmas, church, a swim—it wasn't like she asked for diamonds and frills. Cynthia Icely flashed to his mind.

That southern belle was fancier than Hancock deserved. Her life was in a constant state of need . . . the need to have Reed on her arm, the need for a new dress or hat, and the need for a ring on her finger.

Reed felt a chill run up his spine. When he finally told her he would never move from Hancock, she'd called him a country bumpkin, a lifeless sluggard, and a few other choice names. Her bright red face illuminated her white blonde hair. Just when he was sure that rant ended her infatuation with him, she sauntered into his office with a basket of pastries. Then she said something about her uncle inviting him to dinner. He feigned an excuse that he was required at home. He didn't connect well with unstable women. But, the pastries were good, he conceded.

He glanced sideways at the woman beside him. Patience Stephens sat perfectly erect in the buggy bumping along staring straight ahead and often chewing on her bottom lip. *Heaven above, she is also a completely unstable young woman.* The very thing he disliked was needed for his plan to succeed. Quickly swallowing another pang of guilt, he pressed himself to focus on the road ahead.

CHAPTER 9

THE LATE AFTERNOON air turned cool, and Patience buried her cold hands inside her pockets. As she squeezed her beloved list for her future, tears began to pool in her eyes. Why had she opened up her most cherished thoughts to this stranger? Hadn't Doctor Powell told her about the callousness of some men's hearts? Though Mr. Chapman held her attention with his strength and confidence, and truly she had never seen a man so handsome in face and smile. Still, he did not seem like a friend. His eyes spoke displeasure when she asked for a ride to Hancock. Maybe men and women of the unmarried group were not to be friends? Doctor Powell was strict about any young men wanting to spend time with her at the asylum.

Her last male friend was Elias, the boy with soft blue eyes and tangled blonde hair. He would bring the coal to her room and talk for a few minutes. She would show him her latest drawing of butterflies and fairies. He was a friend. Then just like Anna, he was gone. When someone told her he'd run away, she cried for a week. Just like her, he had no one. What would become of him?

"You look tired." Mr. Chapman broke into her thoughts. "Have you ever traveled this far from the asylum?"

"Only the day I was brought to Lennhurst from Hancock, but I don't remember anything."

"Let's stop here. George can graze, and I'll see what I have to eat." He pulled the buggy off to the side, and King George pulled farther onto some tall grass. "He does have a mind of his own," Reed said, jumping down and holding his hand out to her. Their eyes met, and something flickered inside his steady gaze. Was it sadness? Stepping down, she let go of his warm hand.

Following him to the back of the buggy, "I have a cape in my trunk," she said. "May I get it?"

"Yes, let me help you." He pulled the rope off his luggage and handed his bag to her. "Inside there is a flour sack with food." He lifted the latch on her trunk and opened the lid. She reached for her cape still holding his bag, and their arms collided.

"Of course, you may get it." He reached for his bag and stepped back from their proximity.

Patience pulled the cape around her shoulders and felt the instant warmth. After she turned to see he was walking away, she quickly slipped her list from her pocket into the bottom of her trunk. Her Bible rested on the top of her daily dress, and she decided to leave it there.

She'd always prayed and wondered how God would move in her life. One day, she did want to leave Lennhurst. Doctor Powell had said, if they trusted God, He would show them the way. This had to be the way. How could she have known her parents' land still sat abandoned? Yes, it would be difficult to see the remains of their home, but what if this was part of God's gift to see her dreams come true?

Mr. Chapman stood holding out a napkin. "It is kind of you to share with me." She walked closer and took a piece of ham from the cloth.

"Tell me what you did at the asylum." The censure in his tone back in place.

"Umm." She swallowed her bite. "When I was young and couldn't speak English, every day was about getting well and learning your American language. Then when I grew older, I had a tutor most days."

"You were tutored in all subjects?" Reed chewed a bite of bread. "Did they teach you a trade of any kind?"

"I don't think so. I can draw. But I don't play an instrument or—"

"No, a useful trade. Women are allowed to be nurses or teachers, governesses and the like."

Patience felt the disapproval in his words. "I'm not sure what you're asking, Mr. Chapman."

"A trade would be something that would earn you money. If Doctor Powell explained it, you have to have money to live. How do you plan to live in Hancock?"

Now she was sure where he stood. Troubled with her. "I plan to live on my land and grow a garden and," her words slowed as his brows creased, "take care of myself and the—little creatures God gives me."

Reed ate a few more bites and shook his head and shoved the flour sack back in his bag. "Unbelievable." He stalked to grab the reins and pull King George back around to face the road. "Just unbelievable. Let's go." He growled.

Patience stilled. This man of pleasing features had a cold soul. What did she do with that truth? She turned and walked into the forest. Time with God would be her only comfort.

"Where are you going?" he snapped.

She could hear his steps coming up behind her.

"I need to be alone for a while." She walked on.

"You can't just go for a stroll in the woods." He stopped and then caught up with her again. "Just like you can't live on your land alone and swim and garden with the ladybugs." She could hear his hands slap against his legs. "Miss Stephens, stop please!" He huffed. "It only takes a few minutes to get lost in the woods."

She stopped walking, staring ahead. Without the silence to hear from the Lord, she felt her own frustration rising.

Mr. Chapman's feet rustled in the leaves behind

her. "Please come back. I'm sorry this isn't going well. If you'd like me to take you back to Lennhurst, I will."

Patience waited, trying the deep breathing exercises she'd learned as a child. Doctor Powell always said a hopeless heart was worse than a scarred back. She had to push on.

Turning to face him, she felt light rain sprinkles fall on her face. "I'd like to go on to Hancock. If you would find the tolerance to take me."

Reed tried to control his erratic breathing. One minute she sounded like an innocent child, the next minute a stubborn mule. This wasn't a simple buggy ride down the lane to him. This woman thought she was going to set up house on his land. His grandfather had put his sweat and blood into those acres, building a thriving saw-mill, employing workers, giving their families a decent living. She was ridiculous! A garden and little creatures. He steamed all the way back to the buggy and waited to help her step up. Ignoring his outstretched hand again, she grabbed the side rail and pulled herself in. They rode in silence for an hour, the rain falling steadily.

"Ohh." Patience turned away from the mud flicking up from King George hooves.

"Slow it down George." Reed pulled back on the reins. He didn't want to cover the Beasley buggy in mud, but this slower pace was only going to make the trip longer. What was her plan for arriving in Hancock? There was a decent boarding house on Second Street that would work. He shrugged away from the rain running off the cover, soaking his left arm, and noticed Patience moved closer to the edge of her seat.

People in Hancock knew him, knew his family. How long until someone told her the connection he had to her land? He shook his head and rolled his tongue along his lower lip. Maybe he could take her to the old mill house and leave her until she agreed to sign the land over. Kidnapping was against the law. Murder would be quicker and easier. He blew out a long breath.

"What's wrong?" Her worried voice broke the long silence.

"Nothing." *Except for an irregular pulse, a crazy woman, being cold and wet and—*

"You just moaned. Like you were hurt."

"I did? I didn't mean to." He cleared his throat. *Murder, good lord, now he was losing his mind.* "Half your cape is getting wet—you need to sit closer to the middle."

Shifting a tad to the middle, she tucked her cape in close. "It's getting dark," she whispered.

Her statement met only with the sound of falling rain and the horse's soft trot. "I noticed your wrist is bandaged. Is it hurting you?"

"No." He huffed, raising it up. "This is not what's hurting me."

70

CHAPTER 10

EVEN IN THE darkness, Reed knew this road into Hancock like the back of his hand. Between the two other stops and the rain, it had put them in much later than he wanted. The last hour she had tried everything in her stiffened body not to touch him. But when her head would wobble just so, she would unknowingly lean into his side and rest her head on his shoulder. He must be tired too because he welcomed the warmth she brought to his body, and it didn't hurt that she smelled good.

He led King George back around the alley-way buildings to his office and apartment. The darkened boarding house they'd passed, residents and staff now long asleep, and he was at a loss for what else to do. The buggy jerked to a stop, and she sat up.

"I'm sorry, I think I fell asleep." Dazed, she stood slowly and stepped down.

Reed secured King George and went around back for their things. "We made it later than I planned. This is my office and home upstairs. I will get you settled, and then I can take care of George, and I'll sleep in my office."

Patience took his bag as he lifted her trunk

with one arm, keeping the weight steady with his wrapped hand. "My key is in the front pocket of my jacket." He stiffened and looked away as she reached around him and in his coat pocket.

"Of course." Finding the key, she unlocked the back door.

Reed entered the back of his office and set the trunk down. "Can I leave this down here for now?"

Patience noticed the small staircase. "Yes, especially because I'm not staying."

He glanced at the staircase quickly, rubbing the stubble on his jaw.

"Am I?" She waited till he looked at her.

"No." He felt his face flush red. "I mean for tonight, yes."

She walked past him and peeked into his office. Only a bit of light streamed in from a street lamp outside. "This is where you work?" Her voice wavered, from nerves or the cold, he couldn't tell.

"Yes. Follow me upstairs, and I can get the fire going before I leave you." He struck a match and lit a lantern hanging by the back door. The wood steps creaked under their weight. Feeling a strange brewing inside his gut, he opened his door and sat the lantern on the table. Raking his fingers through his damp hair, he watched her enter timidly.

"I have a woman who launders every week."

He grabbed some clothes off the floor and threw them in the corner. "The bed is clean—you can sleep there." He turned to the brick fireplace and started a fire. "Do you want to put your wet things over this chair?" He moved the chair closer to the crackling fire.

She carefully stepped toward him and turned. As she undid the clasp at her neck, he realized he was to take her cape from her shoulders. As soon as he moved closer, the brewing started to bubble, and he wondered what was happening to him. Taking the cape, he draped it over the chair. Exhausted and worn not ten minutes ago, now turning to face her, he suddenly felt wide awake.

"I need to get a few things and then tend to George." He grabbed a blanket from the wardrobe.

"What is this called?" She pointed to a blue piece of furniture.

"My mother calls it a settee. I call it a sofa." He headed for the door.

"Can you tend to King George while I get in bed and then come back and keep the fire going and . . . sleep there?" She chewed on her thumbnail, nodding slightly to the sofa. "New places can be frightening."

Reed rubbed his temple. Should he be snide and remind her she was going to live on *her land* alone? Why did the innocent longing in her eyes awaken him? Deep brown pools, surrounded by loose pieces of hair glinting in the firelight. "All right," slipped from his mouth before he could catch the mistake. He took the lantern off the table and walked out, closing the door on his absurd but beautiful late-night houseguest.

REED FLINCHED IN his deep sleep, Patience Stephens was riding away on King George.

"Blimey, Reed! What have you done?"

Sitting up quickly, he realized it was just Fred chattering over him, and sun streaming in the window. Rolling his stiff neck side to side, he blinked at Fred.

"Oh Lord." Remembering why he was on the couch, he looked past Fred to see a mass of lustrous, brown hair over his bed and pillow.

"You better be praying to God, Chappy. When Cynthia Icely finds out you're with another woman, she will break both your knees."

"Shhhh." Reed rose and grabbed Fred by the arms, moving him backward. "You need to leave now. I don't want to explain her to you or you to her." His bed creaked, and the men turned to see her pushing up off the pillow.

"Hello," she said pulling the blanket higher. Her long sleek tresses framing her flawless face.

"Lovely cup of tea, Reed. Is she wearing one of your shirts?"

"I swear on your Queen's crown, Fred, you

have to leave this minute." Reed jerked him by the front of his shirt dragging him away.

"All right, all right." Fred finally quit resisting and went through the door. "It's past ten in the morning, and I wanted to tell you there is some mud on my carriage."

"It will be spotless by the end of the day," Reed said as Fred descended the stairs.

"And I'm so proud of you, Chappy. I worried you were cursed with male dullness." Fred took the last step and turned toward their office. "Bloody well done."

Reed reentered his room and leaned against the door. What spell was he under last night? Had he lost every ounce of logic? Would Fred keep the confidence? Of course not. Miss Stephens sat on the end of his bed wrapped in a blanket. He walked to his sofa and pulled his shirt on. "I apologize for him." Reed attacked the buttons. "We work together, and I didn't realize it was so late."

"I don't know what he meant about tea," she said. "Will he be bringing us a cup?"

"No, no," Reed moaned. "You need to get dressed so I can take you to the boarding house." He spied his cup and the kettle and shook his head. "And they can feed you and make tea or coffee or whatever you want." He reached for his billfold. "I will pay for you to stay there for a week." He opened the leather flap, thankful he

75

had some money. "And you can . . ." He finally looked over at her, the way her hair cascaded down to her waist, a large swath of silky, brown tress hanging over her left eye. She resonated with youth, innocence and more sensuality than should be lawfully allowed. Turning away, he grabbed his jacket and headed for the door. "I need to get out." He grabbed the doorknob, willing his thoughts to stay quiet. "Just come down when you're ready."

"Mr. Chapman."

Reed stilled with his back to her halfway through the doorway.

"If you are so kind to take me anywhere, I want to go to my land. I will be staying there."

Right now he was just thankful she stayed put on his bed. If she came too close in this minute, he didn't trust himself. Unlike Cynthia who did everything with her provocative purposes, Miss Stephens's naivety was entirely too intoxicating.

"If that's what *you* want." He closed the door behind him, releasing a familiar low groan.

CHAPTER 11

"THE SUN IS out." Patience couldn't help but find the optimism in the first day of her new beginning. "I wish I could say I remember Hancock, but I don't." She viewed everything she could, left to right, as they drove out of the small town. "There! Is that a church? Is it the one your parents attend?"

"Yes," Reed murmured, "but there are two others you could try. I think the others have more children." He gave King George a tap, and they sped up.

"Your upstairs home is nice." She didn't want to upset him, as he was almost silent this morning. "But why don't you live at your parents' home?"

"I like my independence. I haven't lived at home in years." He kept his eyes forward.

She nodded, they had that in common. She could feel tingles with each road Reed turned down; leading King George confidently. Independence was frightening, yet exhilarating, too. Another path led them up and around into more trees. She recalled her childhood home was secluded, surrounded by large trees. "There was a family, I remember children. Do they still live close to my land?"

Reed rocked in his seat. "No, no children that I know of."

"I remember from years ago. They would be all grown by now."

"So." Reed pulled hard on the front of his jacket. "How do you plan on living? You are going to live out here alone?"

"I wondered if you would know of a widow lady that might want to stay with me." She chewed her lip as the buggy rolled on. It was too far for her to walk to and from Hancock. "I need to purchase a horse, a gentle one." She touched his jacket sleeve. "Tell King George to please take no offense."

Reed looked away, shaking his head. "I saw you hugging women at Lennhurst, were they your companions?"

"No, just other patients I was close to."

"Do you mind me asking why those women were at Lennhurst?" His brow narrowed.

"There were many women committed due to their monthly moods. Their husbands insisted they stay. I read in a book it was normal for a woman to feel vexed at her monthly cycle. I know during mine, I can feel despairing. It only lasts a few days each month then it goes away." She noticed Reed's jaw shifted to the side, and a little muscle was working along his jaw. "I—I think by the frown on your face that is something I should not . . . have said?"

He slowly nodded his head, eyes rolling.

"Oh, my. Look," she breathed in quickly, "I see the top of the stone fireplace." Reed pulled King George back to a walk. Her eyes locked on the rubble of her once grand home. She didn't know how long she sat before she realized the buggy had stopped, and Mr. Chapman stood on the ground waiting for her.

"Wszystko bylo prostu . . ." she whispered.

"What?" He held his hand to her. "I didn't understand those words."

Taking his hand, she looked past him and stepped down in a silent daze. She wanted to remember, why didn't it come back to her? Where was the entrance, the windows? Where was the room she shared with her older sister, Chartvea? She closed her eyes and breathed in the smell. *Yes.* A bit of familiar pine tree and then a swirl of dirt, and she opened her eyes.

Reed walked closer to the fallen stone. "It was grand. I think it possessed five or six fireplaces." He pointed toward the fallen structure.

"Do you remember?" She came alive in the moment. "Had you seen it before it burned?"

REED WANTED TO bite his tongue off. "I just meant, I could tell, from the stones and how they fell. It is amazing with all these

Pennsylvania winters the large main fireplace is still erect." He exhaled relief from avoiding her question. Patience stood with a motionless pale countenance so bereft he questioned if his was a depraved idea. A young woman so unstable; what if she began to cry? A small swirl of dust picked up from the rubble, and he wondered if she remembered that her family had all burnt inside the house. This was like visiting the family burial grounds. He waited while she walked around the perimeter.

"Do you know, Mr. Chapman, who wants to buy my family's land?"

His head popped up. Could he actually be right? Once she saw the destruction, she would want to sell. "That doesn't matter, just know you would have enough money to see the world, travel, buy another home. Would you like to go back to Poland?"

"Oh, sir." She shook her head. "That is the last place I would be safe."

Reed looked away, chiding himself.

Sedate, she walked up to him. "Can we go to the caretaker's home?"

"Do you remember where it is?" His eyes narrowed.

Pursing her lips, she looked around for a few minutes. "Maybe there? It looks like an over-grown path."

"Let's see." He followed her, knowing she was

right. They stopped in front of the old wood-framed cottage. The large front windows covered in planks. She fingered the ivy growing from a tree to the right side of the house.

"Compared to Lennhurst, it is small." She lifted a sad smile.

Reed went to the brick well and dropped a bucket down. The crank, unfortunately, brought up water. "I wouldn't suggest drinking this. Who knows what could have died down there?" He cringed, saying the wrong thing again.

"Would you try the door?" she asked.

Reed walked past her up the one step to the porch. He jerked on the handle, and nothing happened. "It could be latched from the inside." He side-stepped over and pulled lightly on the boarded-up windows. He turned around to see her heading to the back of the small house.

"Miss Stephens, you can see why I don't suggest this as an option for you." He almost tripped over some overgrown bush. She pulled on the back door and stepped back. Pine needles and debris fell from the roof. Ignoring him, she brushed it off and went inside.

"Miss Stephens, please wait." He jogged to the back door as she was stepping quickly backward bumping into him. He grabbed her arms to steady her.

"Something just scurried across the floor," she squeaked shuddering in his arms. "Mr. Chapman, can you go in first?" Moving behind him in the small entrance, she held onto his suit jacket.

Compressing a snicker, he realized he couldn't have planned this better himself. No woman would abide with mice and rats. He walked forward with her attached to his backside. *Bug lover, Patience Stephens is scared. Perfect.* He pushed a door open on the right. They peeked in unison, noticing some dusty furniture and turned over crates. The door on the left was already open and contained an old bed and bureau, nightstand and basin. She still clutched his jacket and waist, so he took five more steps into the open front room. In the dim light, he could see a kitchen area with a small table and chairs on the left and a large fireplace on the right. Two dust covered green chairs sat abandoned. Just when he felt her release him and move to look closer, a mouse came from nowhere and scampered straight for them. She squealed and hopped up; he jumped as she landed in his arms. A laugh slipped out as he realized his arm was under her legs and he was holding her off the ground. "I wasn't startled by the mouse, but you taking flight surprised me." He grinned, wide-eyed.

She smiled shyly. "I just don't like rodents that can crawl up my skirt—touching my legs and underthings." She bit her lip, watching his smile get wider. "That was wrong to say . . . aloud . . . too." She sighed, pressing her hand over her mouth. "Ahh, I need to overcome that."

Now he had to laugh, this whole morning was going better than he thought. "I will carry you out." He turned, needing the fresh air to bring him away from the warming effect her nearness was having on him.

"Wait." She held her hand against the thin wood of the hallway. "I couldn't really see. Would you mind taking me into the kitchen area, and I can stand on a chair?"

Reed tilted his head to the side. They were only a breath apart. Ignoring the pain from his wrist, he hitched her up in his arms and walked her into the kitchen. Setting her feet carefully on the chair, he felt her arm slide off his shoulders and he let his hand linger on her back. He knew there were supposed scars under the layers of her clothing. *What do those scars look like?* His hand felt suddenly warm and overly protective. He let her go.

"Can you remove the wood planks from the windows? Open the front door?" She smiled sweetly.

Thankfully, Fred wasn't here. He'd harass him for being so obliging. "And then we need to go." Reed unlatched the door, pulling it open. Yanking the old planks off the large windows, he set the boards against the cottage. He'd have to come back tomorrow and nail them back.

She clapped her hands. "Fresh air and light."

Her eyes sparkled from her perch. "Look over there in the corner. A broom and bucket and what is that tall strange thing?"

"A washboard." He paused. "Miss Stephens, have you ever done the wash? Have you cooked your own meals? Do you know how to bank a fire? Without this knowledge you—"

"I—I've read about these things. I'm sure I could figure it out."

"See this spot over here?" He huffed and walked between the fireplace and the two dusty green chairs. "It's water on the floor. The roof leaks."

"Only that one spot. That is better than a roof leak in every room!"

He turned to look up at her still standing on the kitchen chair. "Miss Stephens, I can appreciate you wanting to leave Lennhurst. Besides a few peculiar things that you say, you seem able to manage yourself." He stepped closer and held out his hand, trying to soften his tone. "I'll take you to the boarding house in Hancock. It has clean water and bedding. No mice or rats that I know of." He noticed his hand was still suspended, untouched. "You cannot stay here alone, and I have to get back to work." Something flickered in the velvety depths of her eyes. She did have the thickest lashes—

"Mr. Chapman, I need to do this." Her soft voice pulled him back from distraction. "Please understand." She held her thick skirts, stepping down and looked around the small dusty kitchen and living area. Chewing her bottom lip, they could hear something skitter in the corner. With wide eyes and her mouth gaping open, she stepped back onto the chair. "I—" She looked left to right at the dirty floor.

"I—I'm staying."

CHAPTER 12

REED DROPPED HIS rejected, extended hand and shook his head. In one swift movement, he could grab that straight-laced body and throw it over his shoulder. Strangely, the idea of carrying her again appealed to him. Taking her another ten minutes down the road, he could have her tied up in the old mill house. He stepped back, needing to find a rational way to sway her.

"Have it your way." He stepped back further. "No water, no bedding, except for the mattress in the room that I'm sure the mice have been living in." He shrugged. "No fire, it will get cold, and no food." He turned to leave. "I will get your trunk. It sounds like you are sure you want to live here." He marched out the front door and across the path out to where King George waited. He tapped his fingers on the back of the buggy debating how long before she would come running out.

The morning air was crisp as the sun broke through the large trees. He remembered when Robert had built a tree house in the dead of winter. They were young and thought they were so brave—going to sleep all night in the woods.

In the darkness of night, when he was sure they were going to freeze to death, they climbed down and ran inside their home. He supposed growing up at Lennhurst there weren't many life lessons. He stalked to the back of the buggy and jerked her trunk up. It looked like tonight was going to be one.

Returning to Hancock, Reed was awash with frustration. He unharnessed King George and looked at his back door. Last night she had her hand in his pocket at this very place, coming up to his room, sleeping in his bed. He grabbed the brush and gave his horse a few strokes. "You should have seen her George. I left her standing on a chair. She didn't even get down." Reed checked George's hooves. "Don't nicker at me, George. I'm not going back there tonight. Nope. No way. She won't die in twenty-four hours, but *she will* change her mind."

Reed entered the back door of his office, glad to see Fred was out. He poured himself a cup of cold coffee and sat down at his desk. He needed to finish some paperwork and get it down to the courthouse. Rotating his wrist, he grabbed the pen and winced. His wrist had felt fine until he jerked her trunk out of the back of the buggy.

That woman is crazy, he thought. What was he thinking of bringing her back to Hancock? Why hadn't he just taken his bogus, legal claims and burnt them? He gulped from his coffee mug and tried to concentrate on the documents in front of him. The audacity to ask him to find her a companion, *How ridiculous.* She wasn't staying. He wondered if she was still perched up on that chair watching for mice.

He looked down at the papers and tried reading aloud. He could only pray it was cold and windy tonight. She wouldn't try to walk anywhere, would she? On the road home, when she walked into the woods, she didn't seem to understand the danger. Why had she been angry with him? What had he said then? He moaned and started his work again.

Finally, he dotted the last "i" with his left hand and stood, pulling his jacket on. Stomach growling, he planned to grab some food on the walk to the courthouse. As he reached to open the door, he pulled back, Cynthia Icely was already walking in.

"Reed," she drew his name out sounding a little out-of-place Southern and blinked at him. "Where have you been?" Her need to know his every move wasn't lost under her syrupy tone or her pink wide-brimmed hat.

"I've been working. And I still am. You'll need to excuse me. I have to get to the courthouse."

"Reed." She held her ground. "Are you still pouty about my little fit? If you don't want to ever move to London, we don't have to. Visits will be fine with me."

Reed stepped back, blowing out a gusty breath. "Cynthia, I feel it's necessary to tell you, that as I have enjoyed your company and your uncle's hospitality, we aren't a good match. We want different things."

"Oh, stop that now." Her thick Kentucky accent was slipping through not as soft and much broader. "I was raised that a woman only wants what her man wants. So I am happy with whatever you want."

Reed shook his head and walked out.

Cynthia caught up, slipping her arm through his. "You wouldn't shoo me away like a lost puppy, would you?"

"Of course not." Reed tried to slow his steps and ignore what he'd just done to Patience Stephens. "I just prefer you see us as friends. I know all your invitations have had a purpose."

"Oh, you're a scoundrel. You make it sound like I have done nothing but chase you."

Reed pressed his lips together—that sounded pretty much on the mark to him.

"I did stop in to say that *my uncle* wanted to invite you to supper tonight. Besslynn makes the best pot roast, so you need to come." She shook his arm.

"I can't." He looked both ways before they crossed the street. "I should be saying goodbye." He stepped up onto the wooden sidewalk. "I'll be in the courthouse a couple of hours." His stomach growled again as he unhitched her arm from his.

"Perfect, then we'll see you after that." She smiled.

"No, really Cynthia, I have things to do after that."

She stepped closer popping out her bottom lip for a moment before she gave him a sultry smile. "You know you're the finest looking young man in Hancock." She ran her fingers up and down his lapel. "And we make the most handsome couple. Even Fred said I was a lucky girl to have you look my way."

"Fred?" He shook his head. "Never listen to Fred."

"Please, don't make me sour my uncle. Say you'll come tomorrow then. Supper at five."

"I don't know."

"Say you'll try. Please Reed."

"Okay, I'll try." He stepped back from her touch. "But tell your uncle he's welcome to see me at the office anytime."

"Oh, Reed, you do know how to make a girl swoon." She frowned. "I was going to make my mama's pineapple upside down cake. Maybe my talents in the kitchen will warm your dry affections." She turned on her heel and flipped her parasol open over her shoulder nearly popping it in his face.

It was dusk and chilly when Reed headed back

down Main Street to his office. A block down, the Hancock Mercantile glowed with bright oil lamps. Should he get just a few mouse traps? *No,* he gripped his fingers together, *I am not going to aid the squatter on my land.* What if she'd found matches somewhere in the cottage? The flue was stacked with fifteen years of pine needles and debris. That whole place could go up in minutes. He looked over the top of the town's buildings expecting smoke to be rising from the horizon. A little bell rang as Reed entered the mercantile. He grabbed a basket off the floor and began to toss in some bread, apples, and dried meat. Around the aisle back by the brooms were the mouse traps. Tapping his foot, he looked them over, debating. He could make it seem as if he'd come back to help, but undoubtedly she was cold and ready to spend the night at the boarding house. Throwing four traps in the basket, he walked over to the blankets and bedding. Pausing again, he watched the clerk behind the counter finish with a customer.

Dry affections, Cynthia had chided him. *Cold and dry.* Pulling in a stiff breath, he left the basket on the floor and walked out.

After feeding King George, Reed grabbed the lantern and walked into the cold, empty office. Holding the lamp up to his bookshelf, he searched for something old and boring to read. *Philosophy of Justice,* by Dr. Archibald

Cranbourne would do. He grabbed the thick book and headed upstairs. As soon as he stepped in, he stopped and shook his head. It wasn't the maids' day, yet his bed was neatly made, the pillows standing evenly against the wall, the blanket he used laid across the bottom of the bed covers. Even the clothes he'd thrown in the corner were folded and set on a chair. Setting the lantern and book down, he blew the coals back into flame. He'd grabbed his things this morning and dressed downstairs, while she was up here tidying up his quarters. A long moan escaped his lips. Is she cold right now? He dropped his head back. The scene of the flue catching fire flashed over him again. How valuable would his acres of trees be if they were burnt like matchsticks?

"Lord Almighty." He gritted his teeth and grabbed the book, the fire warming the whole room. Slipping his arms out of his jacket, he then laid it on a chair. Was she still perched on that kitchen chair? He moved away, flipping the book open.

The Morality of Justice, Chapter One. He tried to read the first paragraph but slammed the book shut and dropped it on the table. There would be no diversion, no concentration. He squeezed his brows together, no rest, and no peace until he rode out to check on her.

Chapter 13

A STREAM OF moonlight broke through the heavy branches and lit his steps to the front door. Something besides the cold ran up his spine. It was too dark and too quiet. He moved to the left and peered in the living room window. Stepping back to the right, his shadow feathered across the window and floor as something inside moved. A familiar screech flew out from the large mass. Patience jumped up clutching her chest and finally made sight of him.

The front door swung open. "Mr. Chapman! What. Are. You. *Doing?* She stumbled back clutching her chest, the last word a squeak. "You scared the stuffing out of me." Her warm brown eyes were wide and round, aflame with panic.

"I'm sorry." He sounded defensive. "I was just going to check on you." He stepped in and looked around. An old, brown rug with fringed edges lay in front of the fireplace. The two green chairs' seats were pulled up to each other providing an area to sleep on.

"What is tied around your ankles?" He squinted. Even in the dim light, her skirt layers bunched up unevenly.

She bent over and began to untie the strips of cloth, loosening her skirt back to its full girth. Ignoring him, she went to pick up the clothing laying on the floor around the green chairs. Her long, thick braid swung back and forth on her back. The sight of her swept away all his words.

She turned and brushed the loose hair strands behind her ear. "Well, I'm here, and I'm fine." She panted. "Except for my heart palpitations."

He bit back a smile, now feeling the humor of frightening her. "Were you using your other clothes to keep warm?" He nodded at her pile.

"Yes," she said curtly.

"The strips of cloth have anything to do with keeping the mice off your legs?"

"Yes." Her straight back inched up straighter.

What a cad, he told himself as he chewed his bottom lip. He was going to teach her a lesson. Why didn't he buy the mouse traps and bring some food? "I have an idea if you would be willing." He met her softening eyes. "My parents' home is not far from here. I often spend the night when I'm going to help out. I think they would all be asleep; you could get something to eat and have my old room. I can stay in the spare room.

"Would your parents mind? I would love to meet them?"

Reed's gut dropped. "I would bring you back here in the morning. At dawn."

"Oh," her countenance dropped, "oh that would be fine. I'll get my cape."

They closed the front door and walked to King George.

"Hello, my friend, I have missed you." Patience rubbed the horse's nose. Reed waited, holding the reins.

"The buggy is gone, how does this work?" She turned to him.

"Stand here." Touching her waist suddenly unnerved him. "When I give you a lift, put your left foot in the stirrup and swing your other leg over. Or you could jump like when you see mice." He winked.

Cracking a smile, she shook her head at him and jumped with his assistance, landing in the saddle. Reed swung up behind her turning King George. The cold had to be the only reason it felt so good to have his arms around her. He kept George in a slow walk as a thick cloud moved over the moon.

"Is it far?" she asked.

"No." He'd already planned a back route, now untraceable without the moonlight. "How did it go today? Your life beyond Lennhurst."

Her head tilted back and forth. "That's hard to say, I've only been an independent woman two days." She patted King George's neck. "I used the water from the well for a bit of cleaning. I tried to wash an old blanket I found on the floor.

97

I'm not sure I understand the washboard. I tried to wring it out and found myself wetter than the blanket. I wandered around a bit more. I'm sure there had to have been a vegetable garden at one time. I found the lake and the dock." She quieted.

"And . . ." Reed tried to keep his arms loose, free from holding her closer.

"And, it's just not the same without a family. A dock without children running and swimming. My brother used to fish around the lake, and my mother would plan a picnic for us. I don't know. I wonder what spring will bring."

"Spring?" Reed accidentally said aloud.

"I think I'm just a bit desolate without my winged friends."

"You have friends with wings?" Reed questioned.

"I do." She nodded. "Fairies and butterflies and dragonflies and . . ."

"What about birds? Not friends with the birds?" He interrupted.

"They are of another species."

"So in the spring," he squinted. "You will fare better when the small winged creatures return?"

"Yes, that's it. I belong to them, and they belong to me."

Reed shook his head, wide-eyed. "Did Dr. Powell know about this?"

"That I can see and hear fairies? Yes, he knows."

Reed blinked. Hadn't that same doctor told him she wasn't crazy? That she didn't belong at Lennhurst? He caught sight of his parents' property. Thankfully, all the lights were out in the simple, two-story home. "I feel like I should mention this now. Here in our county, people don't see and hear fairies. I can't speak for Lennhurst or Brown Township . . ." *Goodnight, this is a sure-fire reason for her to go back.* "So my offer stands, if you want to go back, I will take you."

"Thank you, Mr. Chapman. I understand many won't understand. I only mention it to you because you seem to keep, uh, keep caring for me."

Her words turned over in his head until he pulled George to a stop. Jumping down, he held his arms out to her, and their eyes met. "Let's see you fly." He challenged.

She swung her leg around as King George side-stepped quickly away. She fell backward, and Reed caught her in both his arms. He looked down meeting her startled, innocent face. "This must make me a butterfly net." He whispered before he dropped her legs to the ground.

The front door of his parents' home was unlocked, and he motioned to Patience to be quiet. Not one night, but two nights in a row, he was hiding a woman in his room. The clock above the mantel ticked away the time just like it had his whole life. He stepped past the family table and into the kitchen. Lifting the bread tin, he grabbed some biscuits and an apple sitting in a bowl. He turned to give them to her and saw her staring in the shadows at the photo of the Chapman children before the war. She looked up at him and gave him a sad, little smile. The old wood floor creaked, and he grabbed her hand and pulled her next to the staircase. "Wait here," he whispered.

Walking down the center hall, his parents' room was on the right, and his grandparents' room now kept Robert close on the left. He tapped on the door and opened it a crack.

"Mother," he whispered.

Pulling her nightcap back, she rose up on one elbow. "Reed, is that you?"

"Yes, I just wanted you to know, I'm sleeping here tonight. I might have to leave early, but I will return to help at the mill."

"All right dear." She laid back on her side. "Sleep well."

Reed rounded the corner and nodded to Patience. As she followed him up the creaking stairs, he realized she, indeed, had the virtue of patience—something he rarely possessed. He opened the door to his room and swallowed hard. His inability to think this through had got him in another sticky dilemma. "You can sleep here," he said, striking a match to the candle on the nightstand. Two twin beds covered in blue and red patchwork quilts occupied each corner just as they had all his life. She stood holding the napkin of food, trusting eyes watching his.

"I'll be across the hall. Do you need anything?"

"I—I know you've been more than kind." She whispered. "But I would love to meet your family. I could ask about church and Christmas."

Reed felt his throat constrict and rubbed the back of his neck. "Christmas isn't for nine months." One corner of his mouth lifted, perplexed by her endearing fixations and the strange erratic pull she was having on him. For a split second the strongest urge to kiss those perfect lips goodnight swept through his veins. His mouth went dry, shocked by the feeling. "I—I think it best we leave before dawn. My brother is an invalid and my mother . . ."

"I understand." The hurt in her eyes apparent as she stepped back holding the door. "Good night and thank you, sir, for the food and warm bed."

CHAPTER 14

PATIENCE AWOKE TRYING to recall where she was. Hearing the door creak, she gingerly rose up. Blinking, a light from the darkness shone in the crack of the door.

"Is it time to go?" she said groggily.

The light moved to the side, and a woman with a brown robe tied at the waist stared at her wide-eyed. "Who are—is my son in the bed with you?"

"No! Oh, no!" Patience pulled the quilt to her chin. "He's in another room."

The woman walked in letting out her held breath in a soft whoosh. "Oh, I think I frightened you." She raised a small smile, her dark hair, streaked with gray and white peeked from her nightcap. "Reed said he wanted to leave early, so I wanted to at least have coffee with him." She pursed her lips. "But now I think, you and I should have coffee." She nodded to Patience. "Wrap in that quilt, let's see if we can have a few minutes before everyone else wakes."

Patience swallowed lifting a slow, nervous smile.

Tiptoeing down the stairs in her bare feet, she followed Mrs. Chapman and quietly pulled out a chair at the large wooden table. The quilt around her arms served for warmth and protection from this unexpected visit. "I enjoyed a few of your biscuits last night." Patience wondered if she'd said the wrong thing again. Reed's mother finally turned and set a mug in front of her. "Thank you, Mrs. Chapman."

"Some cream?"

Patience smiled, and Mrs. Chapman poured. She'd never really liked coffee, but she would partake to have a few minutes in the kindly female surroundings.

"Have we met before?" Mrs. Chapman asked and pulled out her chair.

"No, Ma'am." She looked back towards the stairs. "I just moved here a few days ago."

"Oh, well, welcome to Hancock." Mrs. Chapman lifted another small smile. "How do you know Reed?"

Patience swallowed a sip of coffee. "Oh, this is hot." Tongue stinging, she blew a few breaths over the steaming cup.

"Forgive me, dear, I should have asked your name," Mrs. Chapman whispered.

"I'm Patience Stephens, from Brown Township."

"Nice to meet you. May I call you Patience?"

"Yes, of course." Patience pulled her loose hair behind her ear, remembering Reed's familiar touch from last night. Why did his strong arms make her feel like butterflies flew in her stomach? She'd wanted to meet his family, yet he probably knew they would never approve of her.

"I'm Arita Chapman. My husband is Robert. Our oldest son is Robbie. Has Reed told you about him?"

"Yes, he called him an invalid."

Arita nodded slowly, sadness flashing in her eyes. "Reed is a wonderful brother. He often stays the night and works all day down at the mill and then on Sunday stays here with Robbie, so Robert and I can go to town."

"I would love to be of help." Patience enjoyed being useful at the asylum, Anna had allowed her to be her nurse's aide.

"That's kind of you, dear. Did you mention how you and Reed know each other?"

REED THOUGHT HE heard something and struggled to get his bearings. Swinging his bare feet to the floor, he rubbed his hands back and forth through his hair. From the window in his sister's room, the sunlight started to peek in. He jumped up, grabbed his shoes, and opened the door to cross the hallway. Before his hand could reach up to knock, he noticed the murmur of women's voices floating up from downstairs. "Oh no," he huffed and pounded down the stairs, dropping his shoes with a loud *thunk*.

His mother eyed him first, and as soon as Patience saw him she jumped up and moved away from the table—and him.

"Miss Stephens, what are you doing?" By the flush on her face and the way she gripped the quilt to her chest, he knew he'd said that a bit too sternly.

"Reed." His mother stood. "Your tone suggests she is doing something wrong." She looked back and forth from Patience to him. "Is there something wrong?"

"Someone pounding down the stairs this early is not—" Reed's father came around the corner. "Oh, there is a young woman in the kitchen, uh, wrapped in Reed's bedding." He pulled his plaid robe closed with a tie. Awkward silence lingered. "I guess we are going to spend the morning all standing here looking at each other." He shook his head and went to pour himself some coffee. "By the way, Miss, I'm Robert Chapman, Reed's father."

Patience nodded her head, still looking wary.

"Yes, you should have mentioned you brought a guest home." Arita went to the cupboard and pulled out a bowl. "This is Miss Patience Stephens. She has just moved here from Brown Township."

Robert nodded. "Welcome to our home. If we seem a bit surprised, forgive us. This isn't like Reed." His father gave him a crooked smirk.

"He's usually very predictable, in a restless way." He stepped closer and slapped Reed on the back. "She's very pretty." He turned to Arita. "Sausage or bacon?"

Rolling his eyes, Reed finally found his voice. "I—can I have a word with you, Miss Stephens, upstairs?"

Patience slightly bowed at his parents and went to the stairs.

"Breakfast will be ready in fifteen minutes." His mother called as they walked up. Reed led her back into his old room and closed the door. He paced back and forth, seeing her dress and things laid on his desk chair.

"I can tell you're unhappy with me, Mr. Chapman." She murmured. "It's not the first time."

He stopped pacing and gripped his hair. "What did you say to my mother? Did you tell her where you are from?" His hands now quickly tucking his shirt in.

"I said I was from Brown Township, didn't you hear her say that?" Her lips tightened, and her eyes flashed. "I'd like you to leave."

"Me leave? This is my room," he said, wide-eyed. Why did he want to kiss her one minute and grab her and shake her the next? *Predictably restless, thanks for that, Father.*

"I'd like to get dressed," her voice softened.

"Oh." Reed snapped back to the moment. "Of course." Stepping to the door, he spun around.

"Did you tell her about the land? The reason you are here."

Her chin quivered a split second. "No. Just like you, I doubt she would understand."

REED PUSHED AROUND his eggs and sausage. The four of them sitting around the table eating breakfast was not what he pictured for this morning. Maybe to his fortune, Patience was silent. Her chin wobbled occasionally, her eyes dewy and on the brink of tears. His mother poured a bit more coffee in her already full cup. Keeping his head bowed in front of his plate, he wished he'd had more faith to have his prayers answered.

"Sooo," Arita cleared her voice, "how do you two know each other?"

"Okay," Reed spoke up, leaning back in his chair. "I went to Brown Township a few days ago to help Miss Stephens procure the sale of some land here in Hancock." He inhaled a deep breath. "I thought she would be signing the papers, but she decided she would like to return to Hancock and live on the land." He dropped his fork on his plate. "I've advised her against it, but she thinks she would like to try."

"Live on your land, by yourself?" Arita frowned.

"I asked Reed about maybe finding a widow that would be a companion." She sat straight-backed and took a small sip of coffee.

"Where is this land, how far from town?" Robert asked.

Reed choked on a cough. His foot and knee involuntarily bounced so hard; he cracked his knee on the underside of the table.

"I haven't got my bearings yet," Patience looked up, "but it has a beautiful lake and a dock, a little cottage that I can clean up."

"A lake," Robert said rubbing his chin, "and dock, you say?"

Reed glared at his parents as Patience took another bite. Slightly shaking his head, they both watched his silent message.

"Where is your family, Patience?"

Reed grabbed his napkin and tried to suppress a groan.

"I am an orphan. My family died in a fire."

"A fire?" Arita and Robert looked long at each other. "We are so sorry for that." The last bit of air left at the table vanished, his parents fighting the shock they were feeling. Robert cleared his throat and said, "And I—we are sorry for what your family has been through." The only sound was a bird chittering and chirping in the morning sunshine outside the kitchen window.

Patience looked at each of them.

Robert tapped his son on his shoulder. "Reed, I see your wrist is still wrapped, but might you be so kind as to help me get Robbie up and then we can get to the mill," said his father.

"Yes, sir." Reed rose and dropped his napkin on the plate. "Would you like him in the wicker chair mother?"

His mother barely nodded. "Yes, that would be fine."

Robert and Reed turned the corner and entered Robbie's room. His staunch blue Union uniform hung outside his wardrobe, the brass buttons and buckle glimmering from the early sun rays through his window. His polished boots stood at attention, a painful reminder of Lieutenant Chapman, the man he once was.

"Reed Chapman," his father whispered. "Does that young woman think she is part of the Polish family? The living heir to their property?"

"Yes, sir." Reed breathed a gusty sigh of relief to come clean. "I found her in an insane asylum. One of the Polish children survived. I went through all this because I was sure she would sell. I want to have our land back," he growled out the words. "You know how important it is to me." He pulled back the guard on his brother's bed and stood it against the uniform.

"Asylum? How do you know she's the real heir? Maybe someone read her the account from the papers, and she made all this up?" Robert pulled Robbie's nightshirt up and over his son's head.

"Dr. Nedows is the only one. He said he treated a Polish child with severe burns on her back.

That's how I found out about her location. The asylum staff said she didn't belong there, but they are wrong, she's as daft as a three-dollar bill—she needs to sign over the land and go back."

"I watched her follow your every move, have you done something to lead her on? Did you sleep with her? Under our roof?" His father threaded Robbie's bent arms into a clean shirt while Reed lifted his brother's stiff torso.

"No, of course not. I slept in the sisters' room." It wasn't worth mentioning to his father that she'd slept in his bed at his apartment, and then he'd been *daft* by sneaking her into his old bedroom last night. He pulled on clean socks over Robbie's feet. His father's comments about them being intimate spiked in his brain. Huffing out loud, he rolled his eyes. Just what he didn't need, more fuel in this unavoidable and absurd Miss Stephens distraction.

CHAPTER 15

PATIENCE TURNED FROM drying the dishes as Reed rolled his brother out in a large chair with wheels. She hadn't seen one quite like this at the asylum. Robert tied strips of cloth under his arms and around the back of the chair to keep him upright. He had dark tasseled hair like Reed and a thick brown beard. His limbs were thin and bent, and his head jerked wildly side to side.

Smiling, she walked up to the chair and bent forward. "Hello, Robbie. I'm Patience." She took his hand and squeezed it. He was a beautiful creation whose eyes flashed something cross. "Oh, I see. You would like to be called Rob. Wonderful, thank you for correcting me. Rob, it is. Does breakfast smell good? Your mother is a wonderful cook." His shoulders jerked back and forth, the cloth restraints holding him upright.

"Miss Stephens," Reed said. "You might want to stand back a bit, sometimes he gets a seizure and can fling his arms quite aggressively."

Patience bent closer. "May I touch your cocoon?"

Reed murmured something about a dollar bill

and made a gesture with three fingers in the air to his father. *What did that mean?* Looking back into Rob's eyes he gave her permission.

"This is just a cocoon." She lightly set her hand upon his thin shoulder. "Your strength is still here Rob. I can sense it." She knelt close and took his hands gently inside hers. "Here I still feel your courage and bravery pulse through your skin. You were a soldier. Yes?" She smiled up at him. "Well done, beloved son and brother. There is no greater love than a man who would lay down his life for a friend. And now God has given you this temporary cocoon."

She gently rubbed and lifted his stiff arms and elbows. His head jerked left to right and she held his arms tight. "Believe me, you think it a curse, but no, it is a gift. One day you will have your own metamorphosis and every muscle and every action will begin to move as you so desire. Have you seen the stunning wings that come from cocoons? I have. A new strength will draw your body out. And not just out." She laughed softly. "But out and upward! Just like the butterfly, you will lift from this place and fly to everything God has planned for you. There will be no war inside or outside." She whispered, shaking her head. "No death or pain. Just freedom to run and fly as much as you want." Seeing the mist in his eyes, she stood and carefully held his chin. "You have fulfilled your assignment, brave one, God is well pleased with you." Waiting till the jerking stopped, a lone tear ran over her thumb and she brushed it away from his beard. "Wait and see," she whispered, leaning close. "God will restore all things to you," she smiled and lightly kissed him on the lips.

Patience straightened up slowly and realized the other three were intently watching her. She smiled shyly, looking at the floor of the silent living room. No one moved and she glanced up to see Arita wiping her wet face with her apron. Robert cleared his throat and Reed had his usual look of dismay and discomfort.

"Yes, it was nice to meet you, Rob." She gave him a quick straight-backed curtsy.

REED STOOD AT a thorough loss. At least his parents could see what he'd been dealing with. This illogical, backward, coy woman speaks to bugs, horses and now had a full conversation with his own brother who doesn't speak. And she kissed him! On the lips, no less. And it looked like his brother enjoyed it! Robbie couldn't stop jerking for his favorite meal, but he'd suddenly become still for Miss Stephens from Lennhurst Asylum? Goodnight, the tenderness was . . . was . . . something . . . almost intimately divine.

"What if Patience stays here this morning with me." His mother's shaky words brought the room back upright. "Would you like that, Patience?"

115

"Yes, thank you. If Mr. Chapman doesn't mind."

"It would be nice female company for Arita, of course, I don't mind," Robert said.

Patience's eyes looked from Robert to Reed.

"I think she meant *that,* Mr. Chapman." Arita pointed to Reed, and they all looked at him.

"Ahh, yes, when we come in for the noon meal, I can take you ho— to the cottage or to town or—" He needed a private word with his mother. They had to be a combined front to her leaving, not making his land a possibility for the demented, fortune-teller Patience Stephens.

Later in the morning, Arita wiped her hands on a towel. "Thank you for your help cutting the vegetables."

Patience lifted the hot lid with a towel. "Now that it's bubbling, how long will you cook it?"

"The potatoes and carrots take the longest. I'd say another hour will do."

"Do you have many workers at the mill to feed?" Patience smiled at Rob as his head flung back and forth. He was happy today.

"We'll feed, usually, around ten but we don't have much work this time of year. Building slows down in the winter. When you were asking about a woman who might want to live with you, I know of someone who might be of help."

"Yes?" Patience searched Arita's face.

"We have an older man, Bernie. He's been with

us since before the boys were born. His sister and nephew moved in with him after the war. They help out as they can."

"The boy? How old is he?" Patience could only guess he would love to swim at the lake.

"Oh, Joel is a man. He took a bullet to the shoulder during the war, so he can do a few things, but most of the work at the mill is heavy lifting. He is a good person and helps Bernie and Robert, but his mother, Sarah, is someone you could ask. Do you know how to cook and clean?"

Patience looked over at the stove and could smell the bread baking. Thinking of her wrestling match with one blanket and a silly washboard, she confessed. "Not really." She gave a half smile. "But I have read about these things, and I have money. I could pay her to be a companion and teacher."

"I can tell you where to find her if you are up for a walk?"

"Yes, Ma'am." Patience stood up feeling hopeful.

A FEW MINUTES later, the cool wind awakened her senses as she turned to look back at the Chapman home. Smiling at the wide porch with two rocking chairs and a butter churn, she walked down the road. Arita was a blessed woman to have such a fine home and loving family. To her right, King George grazed in the fenced pasture.

A large two-story barn pulled her closer. Goats wandered in and out, and a cat peeked out from the hayloft opening in front.

"Good day, Kitty." She waved. A cat! She stopped. The cat helps with the mice. *I need to ask Reed about getting a cat.* Continuing down the road she sighed and shook her head. Notably he was only Mr. Chapman, not Reed. Calling him Reed would suggest they were friends. She pulled her cape closer in the front, she didn't want to judge him. Wasn't that something she'd learned from Lennhurst? Some of the most abnormal looking people had the sweetest hearts. Dr. Powell said that some of the sheep at Lennhurst or Brown Township were really wolves in sheep's clothing. He never said what to do with people who were both. Far off to the right, thick stacks of logs lay outside a large open building. Reed stood on a wagon driving the team of horses in front, while two other men began to load the lumber. With tan, denim pants, a white, short-sleeved, linen undershirt exposing strong, muscular arms, and a bandaged wrist, it was hard for Patience not to stare. She'd seen his office, his nice suits and black buggy, but here he looked more like the untamed, impulsive man she'd come to know.

Enjoying the smell of fresh cut wood, she listened to the sounds of the mill. A buzz of activity, another group of men were using a giant saw, back and forth they moved in rhythm. Glancing back at the wagon, she sucked in a gulp, he was off the wagon and walking straight toward her with steely-wolf in his eyes.

CHAPTER 16

WIPING THE SWEAT from his brow, Reed pursued the quick-stepping Patience Stephens. As soon as she saw him, she'd turned on her heel and headed for the mill house as if she thought he wouldn't notice her. Good night, men with sharp blades and pretty women don't mix. What was his mother thinking allowing her to stroll down to the mill area?

"Pati— Miss Stephens. Wait," running to catch up with a lady in a wide bell skirt who wasn't slowing down, he sucked in a breath. "Hold up." He grabbed her arm. "Are you running away from my home?"

"No." She pulled his hand off her arm, not looking him in the face. "Your mother gave me directions, I'm sorry, I'll let you get back to work." She tried to walk around him.

"Directions to where?" He stepped back in front of her.

Patience let out a long sigh. "I'm speaking to a Sarah, your mother recommended her as a possible companion."

Reed clenched his teeth. He hadn't had a chance to talk to his mother. Of course, she would want to help her. "I think Sarah is busy around here. Laundry and—and other things, she does the cooking on weekends."

Reed watched Patience's eyes scowl and felt a stab of consciousness. "Maybe you should wait and let me help you find someone in town?"

"Maybe not." She quickly swerved to move around him.

His eyes widened, the childlike woman was standing up to him. He vacillated between admiration and anger. Just as she'd pulled away from his touch, she could pull away from his control and make everything a bigger mess for him. "Listen." He tried to lighten his voice as he walked backward in front of her forward steps. "Do you want to stay the day today? My mother wouldn't mind, and you seem to have a way with Robbi—uh, Rob. Stay the night and help me tomorrow?" He could only pray. Patience hadn't asked to go to church with his parents. A wagon load of do-gooders would have the whole town on her side.

Her head bobbled a bit, thinking as she tried to keep walking.

"Reed!" Someone yelled from the mill. "Quit socializin' and get this wagon moved!"

"I've gotta go. Stay the day and help me tomorrow, yes?"

"Very well, Mr. Chapman." A familiar softness returned to her face.

"And I think you should call me Reed." He jogged backward toward the mill. "Can I call you, Patience?" He was halfway back to the mill before he saw that shy smile and her head nod yes. Jumping up on the wagon, he remembered Fred always said being a lawyer was half brilliance and half acting. Blast it, he was good.

"LET'S PRAY," his father said at the evening meal. Patience moved her chair over until she could reach Robbie's hand. His father and mother looked at each other and reluctantly reached to hold hands. Robbie swayed back and forth, but Patience held him steady. Under that straight-laced corset was most likely a backbone of pure iron. Reed smirked. Someone said amen, and he took the hot bowl with Robbie's food and stirred it around.

"Is this beef and—?" Grinding out a groan, he stood. "Pot Roast, good Lord. I was supposed to eat at Cynthia's uncle's home tonight." He set the bowl down and walked to the window, shaking his head at the darkness. "Likely more than an hour ago."

"Oh, Reed." His mother drawled, sighing.

"I just said I would try, I've had a lot on my mind." He noticed Patience already picked up the bowl, carefully taking a sample bite before feeding Robbie. He took his seat and grabbed a roll. He didn't want to go anyway. "I will

123

apologize next time I see her," he said, watching Patience out of the corner of his eye. Robbie barely jerked, he was mesmerized by her as she whispered something in his ear between bites.

"Did you have a chance to speak to Sarah, Patience?" Arita asked.

She turned quickly trying to rebalance the bowl in her hand. "Yes. She was kind and willing to help me. We thought maybe Monday through Thursday. I explained how much work there was and what I could pay, and then she could keep her responsibilities here the other days."

"How are you going to pay her?" Reed questioned, catching another of his mother's frowns. "Is she agreeable to spend those nights? Does she know the cottage is dilapidated?"

"Yes," Patience said, dabbing Robbie's chin with her napkin. "And she knows just the cat to bring." Patience turned, smiling at Arita.

"Wonderful." Arita smiled back.

"Cat. Now besides your winged friends you are going to help the cats?" Reed choked down his bite of food.

"I just need its help keeping the mice outside." She blinked those thick lashes twice.

"Ahh." Reed blew out a breath. It seemed her ridiculous plan was coming together. He needed to speak to his mother. And now Sarah and Bernie.

"You know Cynthia Icely's uncle is only

interested in King George?" Robert's tone was lined with frustration.

And sinking her claws in a husband. Reed swallowed a gulp of coffee. "Yes, he's offered me more than what I think he's worth," Reed shook his head.

"King George is a gift from Robert's father," Arita explained to Patience. "Reed was very close to his grandpa. Reed would never sell him."

"I've told him he's wasting his time." Reed stiffened in his chair.

"He knows good horse flesh, thinks he can reproduce his Kentucky life here in our woods of Pennsylvania. Nasty Southerner running from their ruin to impose on us."

"Robert, please." Arita shook her head glancing at Patience.

"King George would never go." Patience spoke up, and they all looked at her. "He and Reed are akin spirits." She must have noticed they were all staring at her. "You know, they both have a commanding presence, unlimited strength, fortitude and a deep capacity for grace. Surely you all must have noticed."

Robbie rocked back and forth making a strange grunting sound. His father gave Reed a cracked frown. "Now that you say that Miss, they are a lot alike. I'll give you that." He nodded his approval. "George is faster though, that's why Mr. Edwin wants to get his hands on him. To race him and breed him. Maybe *we* should do that, Reed." His father nodded. "It would be a fine breed line. Make some extra money to keep the mill going. Huh, why not?"

Reed sat frozen with a quirked expression. Miss Patience Stephens had done it again. Left his feelings dangling between absurdity and endearment.

Robert patted the last bit of liquid from his bowl with his roll. "Maybe we could find a nice filly for your *akin horse.* What would King George like? Some dainty mare from the South, sweet enough to give ya a toothache? Or maybe a mysterious filly to give him a good chase, maybe from far away, like Poland?"

Reed stood quickly, ignoring his father's cackle and testy wit. Gathering the bowls and plates, he affirmed family mealtime was over. Shocking his mother, he declared. "I'll do the dishes." Any activity to get away from those assessing and knowing eyes of his father. He knew his father would not volunteer to help.

CHAPTER 17

THE NEXT MORNING, Arita dressed in her Sunday, green dress with white trim. Setting her gloves on the table, she grabbed a cloth and pulled hot, oat muffins from the oven and set them on the stove top. "I was going to take a baby gift to the Tylers after church," she said, popping the muffins into a cloth-lined basket.

"Please, mother, take your time. Pa— Miss Stephens and I will be fine." He lifted a small smile to Patience, as she held her cup watching the family get ready. His father came in the front door. "Wagon's ready, Arita, what can I carry?" He grabbed their Bibles. "Got your list for the market?"

"Yes, I think I have everything. Thank you, Reed." She walked over and kissed him on the cheek. "You don't have to tell me. I will enjoy the day." She turned to Patience. "I told Sarah you would be at the house today. She said she would stop by."

"Thank you for everything. You have been an answer to my prayers." Patience smiled.

"Would you watch Robbie for a minute?" Reed

asked Patience, as he stepped outside to help his mother in the waiting wagon.

"Mother, please don't say anything about Patience and the land to anyone. Especially to her, I don't want her knowing it was grandfather's land."

"Your father told me what you're up to, and I know how much you want it back, but we won't trample over anyone to get it." She tucked her skirts inside the wagon. "I know she is different, Reed. And I can't believe you almost left her out at that rundown cottage alone." She pulled her coat on and squeezed the button closed around her middle. "The very place her parents were killed. I don't think you intend to be cruel, but you often miss being tactful." She released a sharp breath, and that corrective look covered her soft features. "Don't you dare hurt her."

Reed entered his parents' home and stilled watching Patience tidy up his mother's kitchen. Nowhere in his heart did he want to hurt her. Well, minus that lapse about murder. But he did want justice for his family, and the land back in Chapman hands *was* just. As an outsider, she held all the cards, but didn't know how to play the game. If he played his cards right, she wouldn't learn either.

He glanced at Robbie's crooked body swaying back and forth. He should have been in America and fought for his country. Robbie should be married, having children, building and prospering the mill, the land. The two of them could have built something his grandfather would be proud of.

Patience reached up, struggling to set a plate on a top shelf. *What was driving her?* He debated back and forth. *It's difficult to find a crack in someone's thinking when all their thinking is cracked.* He came up behind her, pushing the next plate in place, desiring to run his fingers down that stiff neck and rigid back. He didn't fight in the war, but he knew how to keep the enemy in close sight.

Cautiously, she moved away from him and folded a dishcloth.

"I remember you had a list," he said. "On our drive from Lennhurst. I'm trying to remember." He ran his fingers over the table top. "There was swimming and church and . . ."

"Christmas," she said softly.

"That's right, Christmas. My mother puts the tree right here." He walked to the other side of the door. "She has a box of handmade ornaments she puts on the limbs." He waited, hoping to keep her in his good graces. "What else is on your list?"

She lowered her head. "Nothing that you wouldn't think as silly."

"Patience." He enjoyed using her name and worked to control his breathing. "I have been to

Lennhurst. It's a . . . strange place. I realize being away from there is all new and imposing. And I have been easily distracted, which is nothing new," he murmured, "and I don't mean to come across as uncaring." That was for his mother.

"Gardening." She walked over to Robbie and began to massage his hands. "I want a large garden, with paths, an enchanting fairy cottage and wandering ivy, benches for sunlight and shade. Besides the little creatures, a place Rob and people like him would enjoy."

Reed couldn't remember the last time Robbie had left the house.

"And I want to dance with people my age." She smiled pulling Robbie's stiff limbs back and forth, up and down. "He jerks and sways so much because he misses walking and running." She rubbed his shoulders. "Oh, yes, you miss dancing." She smiled at Rob. "We had a man that would play the organ at Lennhurst twice a month. The older ladies from the front H taught me a few dance steps, but soon they would start to cry."

"Why did they cry?" he asked.

"They missed their children and grandchildren. Music engages with the soul. No matter how badly the outside has been damaged, they feel from the inside. People at Lennhurst have no ability to hide behind suitable masks, so they are deemed crazy and unacceptable." She picked up a brush from the shelf and began to brush Robbie's hair. Robbie's eyes drooped with bliss.

"So you want to help people with a garden?" He scratched his neck. Bewildered again at the insight and effect she had on Robbie. "People, I mean, that don't hide behind masks, as you call them."

"Yes. And I still want to meet people my age."

Reed nodded. "And me?" He gripped his chest, his tone lighthearted. "Am I too old for you?"

"Well . . . not in age." She smiled coyly and tapped the hairbrush on her palm.

Reed felt the sting. He'd told himself a hundred times he should try to embrace the carefree side of life. A twinkle of teasing remained on her face, and he reached out and grabbed the brush in her hand. She gripped it tighter, and he used the tension to easily pull her close. Without thought, he wrapped his arm around her waist, pinning her arm and hair brush behind her. Their legs collided, bumping Robbie's chair.

Reed squinted and tilted his chin down a notch. "You kissed my brother." Letting go of the brush, he held her waist firm against him and whispered curtly, inches from her face. "On—the—lips." He waited, she didn't look afraid of him, and he knew with the heat rising in his body what he wanted. Observing and holding her stiff body tightly, he dipped his head and watched as her eyes widened to saucers. She pulled back then

131

came forward so fast they knocked foreheads.

"Ahh." Reed released her, holding his head. "Why did you . . . ow, that hurt."

"I thought you were going to kiss me." She blinked, rubbing her forehead.

"I thought I was, too." Reed felt Robbie rocking hard, tilting his head back farther than usual. "And Robbie finds this amusing."

Someone knocked on the door. "What now." He closed his eyes, sighing. "Do I have a red spot?" Turning to open the door, he pinched his lips closed with his teeth.

Bernie and Sarah walked in. "Hey, Reed." Bernie bowed to Patience. "Hello, Miss, I'm Sarah's older brother, Bernie."

"Nice to meet you, sir." Face still flushed; she looked to the ground. "Please call me Patience."

"Your ma said you got a bum wrist." Bernie pointed to Reed's arm. "I was to come help you get Robbie in and out of the tub."

Reed nodded, feeling flustered in every possible way.

"Sarah and Miss Patience can visit while we give him a soak." Bernie smiled.

"I'll get some tea Sarah, or do you prefer coffee?" Patience stepped around Reed, and back into the Chapman kitchen.

An hour later the water was heated. With rolled up sleeves, Bernie and Reed lowered Robbie down into the tub. "That was nice of your gal to think of my sister," Bernie said, holding Robbie steady as Reed washed his body. "I think Sarah will be a great help."

"She's not my gal." Reed caught Robbie's shoulders as he jerked and splashed the water onto Reed's pants. "She's just never lived on her own. I doubt she knows how to build a fire or work a stove." He tried to shake the water off his pants and hold Robbie still.

"Robbie, please!" he said louder than he meant. "Sorry, Bernie, I've got a bit of a headache." He blew out a tired breath. "I know you knew my grandfather well."

"Yes, he was a great man, and I remember you two weren't often seen apart."

"The thing is, that petite, young woman thinks she can make it on grandpa's land. And I know for a fact she can't. So as much as I appreciate your sister helping her, I want to help her move on, to sell it back to us, so we can keep it in the family again."

"What can Sarah do? She can't *not* help her."

"I know, you all are good people. For now, can we all make a pact not to tell her it was once Chapman land? Think about it, why would she want to be on the land where her entire family was murdered? I'm worried it may not be safe for it to get out that she's even there. What if someone still wanted to do her harm?

I think in time, she will be ready to give up."
Reed winced as a wave of water breached the
tub and soaked his shoe. "Robbie . . . *please*." He
groaned.

"All right, Reed," Bernie said with a wrinkled
scowl. "I can see that. I will talk to Sarah."

CHAPTER 18

THE NEXT MORNING Reed leaned his elbow against his desk then lightly rubbed his bruised forehead. Frankly, all his recent injuries revolved around Patience Stephens. The young woman who was to be on her way spent another comfortable day and night at his parents' home. After many silent Sundays with Robbie for company, he had actually looked forward to having a thought-provoking day with her. Just the two of them. Logical and illogical talking around the hearth, making lunch, or teaching her checkers. But Sarah had stayed and spent the entire time going over plans for the little cottage. Just as Bernie and Sarah were leaving, his parents came home.

Blowing out a breath, he tried to focus on the maps sitting on his desk. Maybe he should have snuck out and burnt the cottage down. Knowing her, she would find a way to build a nest in a tree. Something fairies with long thick braids could fly in and out of.

A flash of colorful movement appeared from the office window. A familiar large parasol popped closed, and Cynthia opened his door.

"Oh no . . ." He sighed.

"Reed Chapman." She snapped with a southern drawl. "Did you forget you were to be at supper at my uncle's lovely home?" The parasol tip cracked against the wood floor while her other hand rested on her hip. "You know I haven't lived in this area long, but where I am from, you can be lynched for an invitation ignored."

Reed looked closer. Nope, no humor found in the white of those narrow eyes.

"I was needed at home. I'm sorry, I—"

"Stop yourself." Her gloved hand flew up. "I already know how you can make it up to me. Besslynn told me Hancock has a little spring dance or fling . . ."

"Spring in Your Step?"

"Yes! That's it." She walked closer and sat on the corner of his desk and papers. "I will forgive you if you will escort me to the dance." She leaned in and tapped on his hand. "Your wrist should be better by then. I'll need a strong partner. I am a superb dancer."

Reed leaned back in his chair, clasping his hands behind his head. "It isn't for a few weeks. Can I let you know then?"

"Of course not. I don't like turning all the single men down without good reason. And you Reed, are my good reason. And you owe me."

Reed wondered if she was imitating Fred or if the big bow at the neck of her dress was making her head swell. "I'll try."

"Hum." She dropped her chin. "Like I haven't heard that before."

Reed glanced out the window. He wondered how Sarah and Patience were doing at the cottage today. His father had even asked Bernie and Joel to go and help her.

"Reed. Yoo-hoo. Where are you?"

"You'll need to excuse me. I have a lot to do." Reed stood and went to open the door as Fred was walking in.

"Always entertaining the ladies, I see." Fred eyed them.

"Ladies? What ladies?" Cynthia held her ground.

Reed ground his jaw at his mouthy friend.

"Dear crumpet, that is the loveliest apricot and blue dress." Fred now had her attention. "The lace is remarkable. It's not from here; I can only guess," Fred fingered a piece a little too close to the curve of the bodice.

Cynthia fanned her fingers at Fred. "No, no, this old frock. Something from my season in Kentucky. But I'm so touched that you would notice." She sent Reed a glare as she curtseyed and walked out.

"I guess I *owe her.*" Reed rolled his eyes. "And now I owe you, *again.* Thank you for distracting her."

"Old Man, to have your problems. So many women and only one Reed. You haven't told me how the dark-haired beauty ended up in your bed." Fred dropped his things on his desk and slid his jacket off. "A souvenir from your trip west?"

Reed looked down releasing a low groan. Fred was a wild pistol and also his best friend. "Maybe you should get a cup of coffee because what I'm about to tell you will take a while."

AN HOUR LATER, Reed regretted his decision to think his closest friend would have compassion for him. "Fred, you can quit laughing now. Really, it's not that funny."

Fred continued to hold his gut and rock back and forth, belly laughing. "You went to kiss her and knocked heads! I—I—think I can see the red mark!" He pointed, snorting and bellowing another laugh. "I'm so disappointed in you." Fred cleared his throat, trying to compose himself. "I wanted to hear how flying fairies kiss, probably light and wispy." Still snickering, he made his hands flap like wings and puckered his lips at Reed.

"I should've never told you." Reed frowned and poked at papers on his desk. "And guess what contracts I'm working on? The Hancock city boundary lines versus the County easement. Such a tangle because deeds go back to—" Reed dropped his pen on his stack of papers. "Really Fred, what am I going to do? She's got help now to play house and build a flower garden. What a waste for that land."

"So you've tried something illegal and failed," Fred said. "The obvious thing is to do something legal. You said your parents practically adopted her."

Reed shook his head. "She's an adult, not a child, what are you talking about?"

Fred stood and walked over, pressing ten thin fingers on Reed's desk. "Chappy, Chappy, focus, watch my lips. I'll say it slowly. Just marry the girl. I saw her, she's not an ogre. Besides, all the wife's assets would belong to the husband. Bee's knees, Reed. That little detail has escaped your notice. Then the land is yours!" He waited, bright-faced.

Reed stood. "Get off my desk, did *you* focus at all? Did you remember she's from an *insane* asylum?"

"Exactly." Fred rolled his head back and forth. "She doesn't know any better. Stay married a year and get an annulment. I'll do the paperwork, give her a nice settlement, you get the land . . . for, let's say, for half my fees. I think I still owe you for saving my life and future at Oxford."

Reed paced around the small office. "I couldn't do that. First, my parents would see right through it and disown me. Second, she is like—like a child that still trusts that life is fair and good." He scowled, turning another circle. "Third, all her outlandish optimism about the future, I told you she is odd." He pinched his eyebrows together and felt the pain in his bruised forehead. "I would never do that."

Fred retreated. "Life out in the big world is bound to teach her the hard lessons. We don't all get everything on our list. Except for me." He sat in his chair and looked for some papers in his stacks on his desk. "Or maybe she'll sprinkle some fairy dust on you like she did on your brother, and you'll fall in love or lust or whatever fairies do to men."

Fred picked up his pen and started to work, and Reed went back to his desk. In his mind's eye, he could see the ill-repaired cottage with a soft crackling fire. Patience curled up in her nightgown, reading a book in the green chair. Him walking across the rug to offer her his hand. That sweet, timid smile, looking up at him, with just the perfect amount of determination in those deep, provocative eyes. As she stood, he could run his hand through her long thick hair. The soft molasses waves, and maybe his hands, lightly resting on her hips. Walking her, no better, carrying her into the bedroom and setting her down with the glow of soft candlelight. She would be a willing wife. Delicate, yet eager for his touch, she—

He cleared his throat and glanced up at Fred working. What was wrong with him? What kind of crazy was he to try to steal a kiss? Absurd Fred. Everything was upside down from the first moment he met her.

Had she put a spell on him?

CHAPTER 19

THE RAIN TAPPED lightly against the cottage bedroom window as the evening deepened the shadows. The ladder back chair needed a cushion if it was to be her private spot to think and pray. Patience sat erect, looking around her room in the clean and tidy cottage. She liked the bed on the left wall. Sarah reminded her it's better not to wake with the sun directly in your face. The horsehair and hay mattress had been stuffed anew and found to be mice free. Mrs. Chapman was so kind, lending new bedding, towels, and quilts. Simple gratitude washed over her. The blue and pink patterned quilt was perfect for her. The wash basin table had been placed and chamber pot cleaned. Sarah brought her a mirror saying at her age she preferred not to use it anymore.

Patience smiled at what a hard worker Sarah was. Not much taller than herself with thick arms and hands, Sarah was graced with a strong body.

They all had worked wonderfully together. Joel was the youngest of Sarah's six grown children. He came most days for lunch after he'd helped at the mill. Joel helped with all the dirty cleaning and lifting, even with a weakened arm, he was so generous to supply their every need. Even though he carried his scars from the war, he seemed to have a smile and eagerness for everything they did together. The story of losing his father to pneumonia was difficult, yet he recounted his appreciation to be able to send his mother his army salary and now help her and Uncle Bernie. Joel was a kind, sweet young man.

Patience drew in a deep breath, watching the drops of water run down the blurry glass window. Tonight would be her first night without Sarah. She had paid her far less than what she deserved for all the help this week. Joel refused any pay, saying the lunch and supper was payment enough. She wondered what Dr. Powell would tell her to do in these situations.

Tonight she would be on her own. Lennhurst was quiet at night, but never really soundless. Knowing there was staff wandering the halls, and other women in rooms behind the doors lining the hallway seemed to bring her comfort. Sarah's snoring had kept her awake this last week, but it still eased her mind.

She smiled and turned the knob on her lantern higher. The last time she'd been able to read her Bible was the first night she had tried to stay at the cottage. Thinking of Reed, she shook her head. Standing, she pulled her Bible from her bureau that held her few things from her trunk. Setting her list to the side, she took the lantern and walked out to the small wooden kitchen table. The quiet cottage transformation was mesmerizing. Everything clean and in its place. The black stove that once seemed intimidating was now workable, the cooking heat still filling the long kitchen-living area. After pouring hot water for a fresh cup of tea, Patience decided to sit in the green chair by the fireplace.

Psalm 91 came back to mind. It was the Psalm she was trying to read last week when she was here alone. No light, no fire, no food. It was one of the most frightening nights of her life. She blew on her steaming tea. As soon as it was too dark to see the words of hope, her resolve crumbled. She'd been reciting what she could remember. *You will not fear the terror by night,* the Psalm said. How could she know the sight of her destroyed home would erupt her grand plans? Somehow as long as Joel and Sarah were about, and there was so much work to do, the past didn't bother her this week. She opened up the familiar words again. *The Lord is my refuge . . . no harm will overtake me.* She must have dozed off that night when she heard someone at the door. Something large and dark is all she could make out.

"Oh, Reed." She sighed aloud, "I didn't know I could be so angry and frightened at the same time." She laughed softly from talking to herself. "Thank you, Lord, for sending Reed as Your shelter." As much as she trusted in God's care—that night she was ready to pack up and take his offer to return to Brown Township. But there he was. That same look of suspicion with a glint of tension. Why did it draw her heart to want to soothe his ruffled feathers?

The need to return to Lennhurst was almost out of her mouth when he offered to take her to his parents' home. Riding King George together, the warmth and safety melted around her down to her bones, oh so gently intimate as his arms circled around her. Then the snack and a warm bed, she smiled at his kindness. Reed Chapman was fascinating, difficult, and attractive. Maybe more attractive because he was difficult? She snickered to herself, she did enjoy reading mysteries. If living at Lennhurst had taught her anything, it was God's people are very complicated beings. She took a sip of tea, was she going to pray or keep thinking about Mr. Chapman?

She slipped off her boots and curled her legs under her. That night at his parents' table, Reed forgot he was supposed to dine with a woman named Cynthia and her uncle. He said he wasn't married but maybe involved in a courtship of some kind? But then why did he try to kiss her? She rubbed her forehead; she didn't mean to ram his head. By the time she had pulled back, something in her said to go forward. She slumped pulling taut the skin on her back. This was the disadvantage of being inexperienced. He seemed shocked by her kissing Rob. So shocked *he wanted* a kiss? "Ahhh." She dropped her head back and pulled her Bible closer. She knew nothing of men.

THE NEXT MORNING, she was thankful for the quiet night's sleep and quickly pulled her clothes on. Separating her hair over her shoulders, she took the brush to her long thick hair. Without any company today, she decided to twirl the front strands back out of her face and leave the rest down loose. After finishing her hot oats and bread, she set more water to warm and cleaned her few breakfast dishes. Sarah was a wonderful teacher, but it sounded like a cow and chickens might need to be purchased next.

Holding her warm mug of tea, she looked out the large front windows. It seemed the rain had stopped. Thinking about the ruins just beyond the path the slow drips from the lush trees sluggishly tapped on her soul.

What if it had rained the day those men came to burn down her family's home? Dr. Powell said the newspapers reported gunshots fired. Did they kill her father first? Did her mother watch and feel the terror? Is that why they never came to the attic? Her heart began to race and she tried to tell herself not to picture their faces that day. Her mind would only allow that it was quick and painless. But what about her sisters, Chartvea and Eella? They had their fairy wings on over their matching yellow dresses that day, the attic was their own private playroom. Memories flooded her vision replacing the raindrops on the window.

They'd all stopped their singing and dancing when they heard the shouting and large popping sound. Then chilling silence was followed by banging noises. Even without knowing, fear filled her body and she grabbed her sisters, and they hid in the attic wall cupboard. Someone was pounding up the stairs.

They would wait until her father or mother told them to come out. Then the terror worsened as the smell of smoke filled the attic. She'd whispered to her sisters that maybe a log had rolled out or something exploded in the stove. She was so young, the dizzying panic and fear, emotions that she had never felt before. Desperate and choking, she'd called out for her father and mother, her brother, but no one came.

With smoke burning her throat, she had tried to pull her sisters from the cupboard, but they would not come out. The smoke closed up her lungs. Running to the little attic window, she pushed the window up, squeezed out the tiny opening, desperate for clear air.

Reaching back, she screamed for her sisters to join her. Heat and smoke were rising so fast. Red hot flames growing higher and higher. *Watch me!*

Watch me! She'd screeched. *Follow me, we must jump!* Just as Eella started to move, her window and landing shook. Spreading her arms with her fairy wings, she flew.

Patience staggered back to the kitchen and dropped her tea mug on the table. Wiping the perspiration from her face, she fought the spinning of the room. Coughing, her lungs struggled to inhale the cottage clear air. Why, oh why, hadn't they followed her? She pulled the front door open, desperate for more air, and ran down the soggy path. Looming in front of her were the ruins and the three-story fireplace.

"Chartvea! Eella! Why didn't you jump?" An icy gray breeze blew through her thick wool dress. "Papa . . . why? You said we would be safe here in America." A low sob escaped from the back of her throat. Dr. Powell had talked to her the night before she left. He warned her this place might upset her.

He would ask her right now to tell her feelings. They were coming so fast. "Anger." She yelled. "And sadness." Her voice wavered and her eyes closed. "Confusion and pity. Pity for my family and now for myself. They are all together, and I am here," she whispered. "Alone, so alone." Falling on her knees, she let the tears fall as the rain-soaked ground saturated through the gray fabric of her skirt. Dr. Powell would tell her to find the goodness after the discharge of emotions.

She reclined on her side on the wet ground and looked up to the gray covered sky and back to the stately brick rising above the devastation.

She would never have survived such a fall. Her wings her salvation and yet her flight brought her to this moment of jaded remorse. Drained and wet, she knew it would help to try. "Goodness. Kindness in Sarah and Joel." She swiped the tears off her face. "Goodness in Robert and Arita. In Rob." Her heart swelled for missing him this week. "King George and his fortitude, his zest." She smiled. "And Reed. I see there is virtue and goodness in him."

And now, my child, what goodness for you? The small voice whispered to her. Wet and cold, her back stung from phantom burning. Something was making her get off the ground, and no one was around to see—this she could do.

CHAPTER 20

REED HAD REFRAINED from distraction all week. Sort of. He convinced himself, without constant contact with Patience Stephens, he could get back to his own life. Throwing the heavy saddle on King George, he debated if he really could ride out to his parents without stopping by her cottage. If he got to the mill, certainly Bernie or Sarah would mention her. Would he want to hear second hand how wonderful her little home was now? His simple breakfast turned over in his stomach.

He needed to see for himself, and maybe she had come to her senses? Or he could point out the obvious reasons her plan would still not work. Dressed in work clothes, he pulled his hat forward and swung up on George. Gray skies, no rain and not bitter cold, a short social call to the squatter on his land shouldn't cause him duress.

The land, trees, and path looked the same as the last time he was here. The small stream of smoke rising from the chimney was the only clue someone now lived tucked inside. Jumping down, he tied King George to a branch and patted his neck. "Wish me luck, last time I was here, didn't go so well." An eerie quiet melded with the sound of his feet squishing against the damp ground. Stepping up on the small porch, Reed tucked his shirt in tighter, pulled off his hat, and ran his fingers through his thick dark hair. This time he would knock before he peeked in the windows and frightened her.

Waiting a few minutes after he knocked, he wondered if she was home. Would his mother have invited her over for the day? He knocked again and peeked inside the front windows. Huffing, he shook his head. The place looked clean and cozy. The same green chairs and rug were moved a bit closer to the hearth. The kitchen looked as if people had been living here for years. A mug sat on the table, a tea strainer next to the basin.

"Patience." This time he knocked on the window. "Are you home?" he said louder. After waiting barely a minute, he turned and walked around the back of the cottage. An old rag mop leaned near the back door. The cottage, the trees, everything was serene and still. He knocked on the back door. "Patience, it's me, Reed. Are you in there?" His hand wavered above the knob; he hated to scare her again.

"Patience, I'm coming in." He walked slowly in the back hall between the two rooms. "Patience!" Only the creak of the old wood floors greeted him back. He peeked in the open door on the right.

Her dress and boots lay scattered on the floor. He noticed the water spots and wet hem. The same Bible from the night he had surprised her, laid on her bed. Backing out, he glanced inside the door on the left and jumped back, startled. A tabby cat curled up on the bed, glaring at him. Seeing a large apron hanging from a hook, he guessed it was where Sarah stayed. Feeling like a trespasser, he took one more look in her room. Usually so tidy, did his mother pick her up in a rush? He'd only seen her in this one pair of boots. Did she have other shoes?

Rubbing his palm across his face, he tried to calm his alarm. She should have someone with her at all times. What if something bad happened, frankly he should be held responsible. Maybe she was just out on a walk? Barefoot? Did she understand, wild animals lived in the forest? He quickened his steps out of the cottage and back to King George. Yanking the reins loose, he swung into the saddle. Did he remember seeing wagon tracks coming up the road? Would his parents break his request, would she notice their land shared an old barbed wire fence with hers?

King George trotted around the mansion remains, and Reed searched to see if he could see her. A cool breeze brushed lightly against his sweaty body. Standing up in the stirrups, he swung back and forth, finally riding ahead till he could see the lake. A mass of white and brown

151

floated in the water! "Good God, what—what had happened?"

He clipped King George in the side and seconds later flipped himself off the moving horse. His feet couldn't keep up with George's speed, and he rolled on the wet ground and jumped to his feet. Running with pumping arms, he hit the dock in four long strides and dove into the water. He came up and sucked in a breath only a hand's length from the mass of dark hair and white fabric. Gripping her arm, he yanked. Her wet face glared back in shock and horror.

"Dear God above, Patience!" Reed realized he could stand and jerked her upward with him, swiping the water off his face with his other arm. "What are you doing?" He knew he gripped and dragged her too roughly, but didn't care. This stupidity was the very reason she shouldn't be alone.

"I—I—" Her soaking wet hair and white gown clung to her body as she rose from the water. He still had her arm and steadied her as she faltered stepping up on the bank. Assaulted by the wet shock of her dark eyes and the obvious silhouette of her body, he quickly let her go and turned.

"You—you could have drowned!" He panted, leaning over gripping his knees, the water running out his ears and nose. He shook his head and rubbed his hair. "What were you thinking?"

He turned and noticed her exposed feminine curves and spun back. Falling back to the ground in a heap he jerked his boots off and poured the water out.

"I was swimming." Her voice clipped with short breaths. "I just wanted to f—float a few minutes, and then I was done. The water is c-c-cold, but it helped with the b-b-burning. I wouldn't have drowned." She sucked a short breath. "I didn't hear you, d-d-did you call my name?" she said, with teeth chattering.

"No." Reed stood puffing. Pulling his wet shirt off, he twisting the water from it. "I just saw . . . I thought . . . you had drowned. I thought you were dead." He turned and wrapped his wet shirt around her shoulders. "What did you say? You burned yourself?" While she tried to pull her long, heavy tresses free, he gripped the front of his wet shirt around her chest. Suddenly, feeling relief and those wide open, velvet eyes on him, he pulled her into his arms. Her body shook and trembled against him. He realized she must be freezing and vigorously rubbed her shoulders and back.

"Ahhh." She winced and recoiled from him. Blinking and shaking, she tensed her shoulders and back.

"I'm sorry." He waited, knowing the list of things he should apologize for were endless. George grazed only a few feet away, and Reed grabbed the reins. "Come here, put your foot up in the stirrup." His heart pulsed hard in his neck as he held her arm and helped her into the saddle. *A simple social call I said.* He swung up behind her, and her bare leg, glaring white and so alluring, demanded his attention. *Nothing— nothing with this young woman was ever simple.*

REED DOUBLED UP the wood in the cottage fireplace. Patience had disappeared into her room and Reed could feel his skin begin to find warmth again. The dive and cold water were nothing to the thought of her dead body floating on top of the serene lake. He replayed the scene in his mind and was sure her eyes were closed. Blowing out a slow breath, did he have to replay holding her as she slipped off King George in nothing but a wet chemise and corset? He pulled away from the wood heat and paced in a circle. Patience walked out in a plain gray dress and added some small sticks to the black stove in the kitchen. Her hair was one long thick braid down her back with a wet spot where the end laid against the gray fabric.

"Are your parents expecting you? Would you like something warm to drink?" Though not looking at him, her voice seemed agreeable.

Now to get his voice and heart to find their normal rhythm. "Coffee." He turned, warming up the back side of his wet clothes. "Patience, you shouldn't be swimming. The water is still too cold."

"I know." She murmured, making the coffee. "I will wait for sunshine next time."

"No." He pressed his lips together—some things just had to be set straight. "There should be no next time. You can't just traipse around alone. You know that some animals are dangerous? They come down to drink from the lake." He debated taking the few steps to her in the little kitchen, wanting to see her face. Is she really this backward or truly demented? He watched her move with ease, just like she'd done in his mother's kitchen. Probably ignoring him.

"I thought maybe you were at my folks' house when I couldn't find you." He tried to lower his tone.

She turned with a timid smile and shook her head.

Something strange hit Reed. "Did someone fix the old dock?" He never looked at his swift steps, but the dock had new wood, he was certain.

"I don't think so. Sarah, Joel, and I did a lot of work around the cottage." She walked toward him with a steaming cup. Her gray stocking feet moving silently across the clean wood floor.

"It's none of my business, but you have money." He questioned taking the hot mug. "Enough to pay Sarah for this week. And how many more weeks?"

Patience chewed on the corner of her bottom lip. "I think so. Dr. Powell said I had a benefactor for anything I needed. Joel wouldn't take any pay."

"Forget Joel." Reed scrutinized. "What benefactor? Where does this money come from?" Her clothes were common, nothing fancy or custom.

"I don't know. Dr. Powell never told me."

"Is it Dr. Powell? Did he give you money for clothes and personal things at Lennhurst?"

"I don't know," she said, watching the fire and moving back from the heat. "The staff came and went throughout the years. Every year at different times a new dress or bigger shoes would come in for me. I never asked who they were from. I wasn't the only child there. There were many children in the back H. They had clothes and shoes, food."

Reed had seen the going on of the back H. There was a large difference between the front appearance and what went on in the back.

"Patience, you know you were there to get well and to be hidden?"

Turning to the window, she gazed out, sighing. "Yes, why else would they change my name?" She turned to Reed. "And *you think* someone wants me away from Lennhurst, not to help me but to do me harm?"

Reed's next sip of hot coffee suddenly trapped in his throat.

CHAPTER 21

"DO YOU KNOW why your family came to America?" Reed asked, poking at the fire.

Patience turned from the large front window. "I remember it was the middle of the night. We were awakened by my mother, and she put us in our coats and shoes. Eella started crying, and my mother told her to be quiet. She held a garment bag and began to shove our little dresses and blankets in. She told us to hold hands and follow her. It was dark, and I didn't understand why there was no light. My father ran up the stairs and picked up Eella, and my mother rushed us all into the carriage. My brother held Chartvea and me in his arms as the carriage left. My parents' faces seemed so dark and cold." Her back began to itch. "I don't have many memories of Poland." Stepping away from the crackling of the fire, she pulled on the sides of her skirt. "I remember being on the rocking ship. All of us children were sick. My mother hovered over us all, trying to get us to eat a bite or two. We were told not to go above, but a few times I snuck out and climbed the stairs to see the ocean."

"I can see you doing that." Reed squinted at her.

"I don't remember how we got to Pennsylvania. My father said he learned English from the boat ride." She blew out a tired breath. "I was so young. I just remember wanting my dolls. I never thought . . ." she grimaced, "that something was so wrong with us, that men would kill parents and children."

"The money it took to buy this land, build your home . . . your father must have brought it from Poland." Reed set his mug on the mantel and ran his fingers through his damp hair "There were many political factions in those days. Maybe he had to run." Didn't Dr. Nedows say something about the unrest? "Trust me. I'm a lawyer educated in England. These things happen in every country."

Patience cupped her hands around her neck and closed her eyes. "But to kill the family?" she whispered.

Reed stepped closer, lightly smoothing a fallen strand of her hair from her face. "The South fighting the North. In this very country, do you know many families fought against their own kin? Some brothers could have killed brothers. I'm sorry Patience. You may never know who did it or the real reason for it."

Patience kept her eyes on the floor, their stocking feet almost touching. Leaning slightly

158

in, she slid her arms around his waist, lightly touching his damp shirt. His breath caught at her unexpected gentle touch. Carefully, he pulled her closer and rested his cheek on her temple.

"I can't think of them suffering," she whispered. "It makes my skin burn." Her body shuddered, and Reed felt a strange peace and deep comfort warming him.

"I had to stop the burning today. God told me to be good to myself."

Reed leaned back, gripping her elbows, his dark eyes narrowing. "God told you to go swimming in a cold lake?"

"Your tone of disbelief has returned." Patience stepped away from his hold. "I thought just now you would be a sympathetic friend? I am mistaken. We are as different as morning and nightfall. When I was dressing, I saw you left bruises on my arm. Here, where you grabbed me." She brushed the top of her arm.

His confident stance waivered, and his momentary peace evaporated. Her words brought a distance that he should have been ready for, but had repeatedly let his guard down. He stepped backward, and something squeezed his chest. "I never meant to—to—hurt you." He murmured.

Reed knew his physical actions were not meant to harm her, but what about this heat, this attraction to a crazy woman? What about his motives to get her off this land? "Patience, I . . ." He had no words to justify his ridiculous behavior of late. Certainly, he was the worst version of a friend. "I think I should be going. Do you need anything? Anything I could have Sarah or Bernie get for you?" He sat in her parlor chair and pulled on his soggy boots.

"Ask your mother if I could visit, maybe Monday. I would like to see Rob. And her of course, if she wouldn't mind." Her voice trailed off.

"That's all?" he said, looking up. "All right." He grabbed his hat and looked for his jacket, remembering he hadn't brought one.

"Thank you for coming and . . ." She opened the door for him and stood looking out to the trees.

He focused on her face as he strode toward the open door. Tired rings glowed under her soft eyes, was she going to cry? *Oh Lord, help me just keep moving.* His strides grew longer.

"Reed." She called after him.

He froze, only a few feet away from King George. If she said the wrong thing, he knew he would fly back into her humble cottage and kiss every bruise and tear from her being.

"I have prayed for my enemies, and I believe I have forgiven them." She paused. "Do you think when pain crushes your heart anew that you haven't really . . . forgiven?"

Reed turned lifting eyes that prickled with

regret. He'd never even thought to forgive his grandmother for selling the land. "I think you've done what is right and acceptable." He grabbed King George's reins and swung up in the saddle. "God does not hold your pain or tears as a lack of faith. Your prayers are valid."

Without looking back, he nudged King George toward the lake, needing a reprieve from the unusual emotions squeezing in his chest. Looking closer, he saw something back a few feet from the trail. Five wooden crosses standing in the ground. He pulled George closer. Two were larger crosses and three smaller. He stopped. He carefully searched, but no imprint. They were simple, new and they had not been here before. Maybe Joel or Sarah helped Patience with them. Crosses, the Christian symbol for the death and life of Christ. These had to be her idea. The woman who heard God tell her to go swim. He shook his head and blew out a breath.

Leading King George on, he came to the dock and jumped down. It *had been* repaired. The rotten wood replaced with clean pine. He stepped on it and felt the firmness beneath his feet. Was the wood from the Chapman mill? It had to be Joel or Bernie. Stepping out further, the board he remembered from the day he fell on his wrist was replaced. He moved his wrist back and forth, only a twinge of pain now and then.

He gazed at the soft rhythmic movement of

the blue water and its return to serenity. His land was being invaded. Did he ever think that would happen? First Patience Stephens, now Sarah, Joel, likely Bernie. Patience would have her way with those soft velvet eyes and innocent disposition. Who could resist her? Frankly, he couldn't.

He looked to where he'd found her floating; a large swath of brown hair, pure skin, and white unmentionables. She looked like some feminine creature from a medieval storybook. Had he jerked her arm out of anger? Desperation more like it. Something putrid hurt his nostrils, he'd left bruises on her arm. What a reprobate he was.

Reed returned to King George and trotted out. A scatter of birds flew out from the quiet trees. Who was he to tell Patience what valid faith was? Since his grandfather's death, he'd taken the reins of his own life ignoring the Divine. "God if you listen to the weak of faith, I do want to forgive," he said to the sky. "Holding on to these offenses has only dug me a deeper hole." It felt unorthodox; he'd never prayed outside of a church.

His parents' faith had been his only guide. "I want to forgive my parents for insisting I go to Oxford while my brother fought." He tried again, the honesty resonating within him. "I want to forgive the man who set the explosive and made my brother a cripple." He lifted his chin again and took a deep breath. "I forgive my grandmother . . . for selling this land." Something in his heart constricted, and King George snorted briskly shaking his mane. "And . . . *I forgive,*" he whispered, feeling drained, "Patience Stephens for belonging to it."

CHAPTER 22

LATER IN THE week, Reed walked down Main Street after dropping off the county land assessments he'd finished. What had his law professor said? Land and pride together will divide the earth until the Day of Judgment. He felt the personal truth of the words and noticed the Chapman mill wagon in front of the mercantile.

After last Sunday, hearing neither Joel nor Bernie admitting to fixing the dock or helping Patience with crosses, he wondered what was really going on. Had one of the other mill workers taken to being Patience's newest helper? He couldn't imagine who. He opened the door to find Sarah back by the fabric wall.

"Good day, Miss Sarah. Is everything going well?"

"Yes, Mr. Reed." She pulled out a bolt of rose colored fabric with spritely yellow flowers. "Our Patience needs something besides those heavy dark woolens. We thought we'd turn our hand toward sewing a new dress."

"That's nice." He looked around the store. "Has there been any more repairs or anything like that of late?"

"Joel will finish the chicken coop today. Then we need a small barn for a cow and possibly a horse for her to do her own shopping."

"Humph." Reed squeezed his brows together. He didn't make himself clear.

"Ruffles or trim?" Sarah smiled at him. "I think the trim would be faster. I hoped she could wear it to the town dance."

"What dance?" His brows furrowed. The one Cynthia had talked about? Wasn't that weeks away?

"Some spring to step . . ."

"Spring in Your Step? At the Founders' Hall?"

"Yes, that's it." She tucked the bolt under her arm and grabbed the thread and trim. "It's this Saturday. Joel said he would take her. It's wonderful for the young folk to have some merriment after all the sorrow." She set her things on the long counter. "Will you be attending?" she asked.

Dancing with people her own age sounded like her strange list she'd brought from Lennhurst. "Umm, what? Yes, yes, I'll be there." Panic started to rise in him. "Enjoy the sewing, I'll say goodbye," he said as Sarah waved goodbye.

Patience and people. Lots of people. He shook his head as he crossed the street to his office. Everyone will want to know about her. Her beauty stands out like a new town-square monument. Then the questions. *Where are you from?*

Where do you live now? What will you do with all that land? Your poor, poor family. Did you know it once belonged to the Chapman family? He groaned a low growl as he entered and sat at his desk.

Joel, the seemingly helpful young man, was trying to win her affections. He said he would take no pay for the work around the cottage. Today a chicken coop, tomorrow they'd be building gardens and fairy playgrounds together. Reed stood, shaking his head and then sat down again. Joel probably loves all her idiosyncrasies, finds her sweet and endearing. *That rake. How dare he dance and flirt with her.* He glanced back at his bookshelf. There must be a law against dancing with a beautiful young woman from . . . from . . . an insane . . . He rolled his eyes, throwing himself back against his chair. Frankly, she would turn many single men's heads, and leave him looking like a manipulating fool.

He waited a day before riding out to his parents' home. They needed to talk to her. She just couldn't go. He walked in and kissed his mother's cheek. She stopped kneading bread and greeted him. Robbie rocked back and forth, and Reed watched him wondering how Patience reached him. Grabbing his brother's cold, stiff hands, he tried to rub in some warmth. Could she see inside of him by touching him? Robbie groaned out of the corner of his mouth. Drool ran onto his shirt.

"I need you to talk to Patience." He turned back to his mother as she loaded the bread in the oven. "Sarah said Patience is going to attend the town dance."

"Yes, Patience mentioned it a few days ago. I understand they are sewing a new dress."

"Mother, you know she can't go. People will ask about her. If they find out she is the Polish heir . . ." Reed went to pour himself some coffee. "It will be a hornet's nest of gossip and speculations."

"How is she to have a life here, Reed? She's asked me about church. Do you suppose she is to be a hermit her whole life?" Arita washed her hands and wiped them on her apron. "I told you I wouldn't be a part of you causing her to leave here."

Reed's jaw dropped and snapped shut. "Trust me. I found out I can't cause or push or reason much with her. That's why I want you to talk to her."

"Have you found out who repaired the dock and staked those crosses?" His mother took a bowl off the table and spooned in the soup for Robbie. Robbie jerked back and forth spilling it down his chin.

"No." Reed gripped Robbie's head trying to hold it still. "Who could it be? She told me at

Lennhurst she had a benefactor. This person still gives her money, but she doesn't know who it is. Is it someone who knows who she really is, maybe old family money? Or just a benevolent do-gooder helping orphans?"

"Here's what I will agree to." Arita set the bowl down and wiped Robbie's face. "She is a family friend, staying with us. I don't want anyone knowing she is alone on weekends in that cottage. Your father and I will bring her and see her home."

Reed exhaled, remembering why he loved his mother so much. She was just thinking of Patience's safety. "Thank you, mother." Flashing her a quick smile, he bit his bottom lip. "How much longer for the hot bread from the oven?"

THE SIMPLE ORCHESTRA music drifted out of the Hancock Founders' Hall. Reed pulled back on the reins bringing Fred's buggy to a stop in front of the Hall's brick-layered façade.

"They're nothing like what we have in Nashville." Cynthia tapped a hankie to the corners of her mouth. Her white blonde hair had been transformed into a hundred little rings above her ears. A little band of pink flowers on top of her head joined the two sides.

Reed wondered what Patience would think about seeing him tonight. Would she dance with him? Remembering the way she carefully touched his shirt and waist at her cottage caused tightness in his throat. Would there be any possible way to keep Cynthia off his arm? He pondered the idea of distracting the lovely Cynthia and sneaking out to hide where the men smoke, but he didn't smoke. They walked inside, and at his first scan of the well-lit room there was no sign of Joel and Patience or his parents. Maybe they'd all decided against it. He could only hope.

After visiting with Fred and Janice, they took their leave to dance, and Cynthia pulled him to the dance floor. "Your mate Fred called me a crumpet." She held her gloved fingers in a delicate pose as Reed fumbled trying to find some way to grip that delicate pose and lead in the dance.

"He's teasing. That's all he knows how to do." Reed struggled to find his steps amid the layers of ruffles and ribbons that swished around his feet.

"All his British snobbery." Cynthia lifted her chin. "I don't know how his wife can stand it." They took another turn around the brightly lit dance floor. "I know as a wife I will possess an unending amount of forbearance but—" The dancers slowed as the music twanged to an awkward halt.

A woman gasped. The crowd of swirling dancers stopped to look toward the door. The chattering of couples and groups stilled.

Reed dropped Cynthia's hand, and like one of the mighty Chapman trees falling on his person, the weight of dread upon doom decked him. His debilitated brother flailed his arms rocking his wheeled chair back and forth. A loud, gargled moan escaped Robbie's lips as Patience stood behind him with her hand on his shoulder. Looking innocent and oblivious, she scanned the room wide-eyed.

"Oh dear God, who is—" Cynthia covered her sour pink lips just in time. "Aren't those your parents?"

Reed saw women shuddering and whispering in their husbands' ears. Others showed their disdain by looking at the ground.

"Reed! Is that *your* brother?" Cynthia's snide tone caused a chill to rise up his spine. "You said he was a cripple *not* a spastic." His body swayed still feeling the crushing.

Two women from the church walked over to his parents and greeted them. The music started up again, and Patience smiled; her bright eyes taking in the musicians and the couples dancing. Joel stood behind her and leaned to say something in her ear. Her chin tilted up and smiling she said something back to him. Reed's mind would not work, but his feet had no problem walking to his family.

"Reed." Patience brightened when she saw him. She wore her new rosy dress with yellow

171

flowers. Every beautiful curve that he'd spent many a night trying to forget was flawlessly accentuated. Her hair was up in a thick knot at the base of her neck, two small curled strands, framed her flushed cheeks. "Isn't this amazing! The music and people all dressed up."

He felt a vice grip crush his elbow.

Without taking his eyes off Patience, he said, "Cynthia, I would like you to meet Miss Patience Stephens. She is a friend of the family. And this is Miss Cynthia Icely, from Kentucky."

"Oh, Reed." She jerked his pinched arm. "I'm just a regular Pennsylvania lady now. I believe I've met your parents at church. Howdy, do." She nodded.

Robert and Arita nodded back.

Robbie began to jerk back and forth, and Cynthia jumped back. "Good Lord! I thought he was going to scratch me." She pouted at Reed. "Can you make him stop? People will stare."

"He's just enjoying the music. It's his way of dancing." Patience pulled his crooked limbs up and swayed them as she'd done at the house. Robbie jerked his head back and forth. Drool slipping down his chin.

"Well, then." Cynthia stepped away, holding her posed gloved fingers in the air for Reed. "Let's finish our dance."

Reed locked eyes on Joel for longer than necessary. "We will, as soon as I've danced with

172

Patience." He reached out and separated her from Robbie and deftly whirled her out to the dance floor. He felt himself falling into her surprised, round, luminous brown eyes.

CHAPTER 23

OVER HIS SHOULDER, Patience stared wide-eyed at the seething red face of Cynthia Icely. "Reed, I—I—don't think . . ." He cupped her bare hand, fingers firm against hers and placed his hand on her back. Her hand touched his jacket sleeve as he turned her in between the dancing couples. The music slowed, and she was able to look into his eyes. "You should have finished dancing with her." He swayed her with the soft melody, watching her intently.

"What I want is what I'm doing. Didn't you want to dance with people your age?" The corner of his mouth lifted. "And I wanted you to have an experience different than the old ladies at Lennhurst."

She smiled nervously at the warmth in his green eyes, feeling the quickened pulse from the handsome Reed Chapman dancing her confidently around the floor.

"And though I can't take my eyes off you, out of the corner of my eye, is Hubert Donavan, in the blue suit." He motioned his head slightly as they turned. "He has not taken his eyes off you either. And Barker Fillmore, turning the derby in his hands, he's a widow, with four children but wanting to remarry, he has not stopped watching you." He squeezed her hand. "As soon as I release you, there will be a dash of men. Are you prepared?"

"No," slipped out before she could determine if his smile was genuine.

"And I like how you are gripping me tighter." He raised his eyebrows quickly.

"Please don't tease me." She tried to match his steps but suddenly felt herself stumble. "I wanted to see Robbie enjoy the music." She glanced back to where his parents visited with friends and Joel looked bored. "I—I—think you should return to Cynthia. How would you say it? Your lady friend or sweetheart."

"She is neither." The orchestra's piece came to a lively ending, and everyone clapped. Reed's face serious. "Cynthia and I will never go forward."

"The way she reached in and held your arm— she is very fine, but I don't understand these things." She shook her head and watched for an opening between the people to return to the Chapmans.

"I saw your cat. When I was looking for you," Reed held her attention. "You'll find they often like to play and bat around the mice before they kill them." Patience flinched back. "I know with-out a doubt women like Cynthia," he said holding her eyes, "just love the hunt, the performance, but I have no intention of being her victim."

"Have you kissed her?" Patience wondered if her question was brash as soon as it left her mouth. "Will you kiss her tonight, even if you don't go forward?" The words didn't make sense, but how was she to ever understand these things? What was going forward, really? Reed held a lightly astonished expression as they both turned as Hubert Donavan approached and bowed.

"Mr. Chapman, Miss." He never looked at Reed. If your dance card is not full, I would like to introduce myself and possibly have this next dance?"

Patience wanted to look to Reed for him to respond, but nothing about the short, pale man holding his hand out seemed intimidating. "Yes, thank you." She curtsied, rising to meet Reed's told-you-so smirk with a sweet smile. Suddenly, it was strange and uncomfortable to be dancing with someone else, but maybe now Reed would return to poor Cynthia, the cat.

REED DID NOT neglect his promise to return to Cynthia, but the challenge for the next hour was to keep his eyes averted from everything Patience Stephens. Cynthia still played the part of the frivolous crumpet; is that what Fred had called her? But Patience barely had one man let go of her hand to find another one in its place. He did enjoy watching his parents take a turn around the dance floor. They so rarely got to have fun together. He watched as Patience would return to Robbie's side, someone was there to visit her. Poor Joel must have felt like the tag-along. Reed excused himself from Cynthia when he saw them taking Robbie to the wagon.

"Reed." His mother gestured for him to come around her side of the wagon. "You were right about the hornet's nest. I was asked by four different gentlemen if they could make a social call on our 'family friend.'" They both turned to see Barker Fillmore helping Patience with her cape. "I can't say she's leaving soon, that's lying. And I won't lie."

Reed scratched his forehead. "Just say she has a previous suitor and won't be taking any callers."

Arita shook her head. "Oh, Reed," she sighed. "She wants to attend church. Am I supposed to lie in church?"

"No, no, of course not. I'll think of something." His father and Joel struggled to load the chair holding the swaying Robbie. "I have an idea, I'll see you tomorrow." He kissed her hand and jumped up on the wagon bed, helping pull Robbie into the back. Jumping over the side, he headed straight for Patience. She nodded goodbye to Mr. Fillmore and walked toward him.

"Would you like to spend Sunday with Robbie tomorrow? And me?" He lifted a quick grin. "I can pick you up on my way?"

"Yes, thank you, Reed." She held his out-stretched hand as she climbed in next to Robbie and Joel. He felt a sense of satisfaction as the wagon rolled forward. Then he heard Cynthia laugh with another woman. Fred and Janice walked out of the hall doors.

"Oh, Chappy, what a night for your little project from the crazy house. If half those men even knew—"

"Fred!" Janice slapped his arm. "She looked perfectly normal."

"She looked like a chocolate truffle from Billington's. Every male wanted a taste."

"Oh Fred, you've had too much red punch, mixed with that liquid in your flask. I need to get him home." Janice rolled her eyes and tugged him around Reed.

Reed headed for Cynthia and her gaggle of friends then looked up to see Dr. Nedows's taut face. He felt the air leave his lungs as the doctor scowled at him. "I thought what I told you was in confidence."

Reed looked around quickly, Cynthia still chatted on with another woman. Feeling his blood clot in his veins and pressure began to build in his chest, he tried to suck in more than an ounce of evening air. "I tried sir. I had no intention of bringing her here." His jaw locked, it sounded like a poor excuse even to his ears. "I had a buyer for the Polish land, and I thought she would want the money and never see it again."

"Would the buyer for the land have the last name of Chapman?"

Reed was dead in the grave. "She insisted on coming here. Yes, I just wanted to see the land have its rightful use. I told her *and* the doctor at Lennhurst, coming here was a bad idea."

"Your dance with her tonight didn't look like such a bad idea." Dr. Nedows squinted behind his round spectacles. Reed pulled a finger from his neck and tight white collar. Dr. Nedows wanted to see him squirm, he deserved it and more.

"I know you shouldn't believe me," Reed said, "but I care about her. She's too . . . too strange and innocent. She talks to bugs and thinks she can fly like a fairy. She was a child playing with toy wings when the fire started. She believes she flew from the house."

"Children that go through severe trauma will often attach to a fantasy." Dr. Nedows's face seemed to relax. "It's the only way the brain can compartmentalize the harshness of the truth. Being a fairy is a beautiful, light, whimsical balance that her mind allowed, in order to ward off what really happened. The fact she is showing bravery and independence is a good sign. How was her experience at Lennhurst?"

Reed sucked in the fresh night air. "I think it was good. She talks about Dr. Powell all the time. She has an abnormal sensitivity to animals and . . ." He couldn't find the words for what she had with Robbie. "Love, I guess you would call it love. She is loving and kind and, well, for the life of me, I still don't understand why Dr. Powell released her." He held his mouth ajar. "To me of all people."

"Maybe he thought he could trust you?" Dr. Nedows dropped his chin. "Was he right or wrong?"

Reed looked up over the top of the Founders' Hall, the stars appearing between some dark clouds. He waited feeling things shift in his gut. "I—"

"Reed!" That syrupy voice came up behind Dr. Nedows. "There you are. Please pardon the interruption, sir." Cynthia batted her eyes at the doctor. "My escort has been shamelessly remiss in his duties this evening." She gripped his arm.

"Of course." Dr. Nedows bowed. "I will leave you young people to the party."

Reed shook his head as Dr. Nedows slowly walked away. Cynthia pinned herself to his left arm and waved at the different folks leaving. Unable to find a proper farewell from anyone, Reed locked his jaw against the constriction of blood flow and use of only one arm. He stared at the ground and rubbed a tight knot along his neck.

CHAPTER 24

AFTER SUCH A restless night, Reed wasn't surprised he was dragging the next day. King George walked in a heavy pace almost mimicking Reed's discontent. Seeing Dr. Nedows last night standing behind Fred and Janice nearly knocked him backward. Had he heard Fred calling her his little project from the crazy house? "Fred." He groaned under his breath. "Unbelievable."

Cynthia Icely gave him the cold shoulder all the way home, to his delight. Until in front of her uncle's home, she threw another fit, stomping her foot and dismembering him verbally with what a rogue and scatterbrain he was. The scatterbrain was the only remark that stung. She was painfully correct on that one.

His parents likely wanted to hang him from a large Chapman tree. They didn't deserve to be dragged into his grand schemes. King George ambled onto the Polish property. He'd wanted to spend the day with Patience but also wanted to distract her from attending church with his parents. How long could he keep that up? How could he make Dr. Nedows understand that he wanted to see Patience safe and cared for, too?

Anywhere she wanted. Except on his land. Her foolish, stubborn streak was the reason everything turned upside down.

Before he could dismount, his mouth went dry seeing her standing on the porch. Her cape covered her simple brown paisley dress, and her long, braid tucked in a circle at the nape of her neck. She smiled and walked to King George. The distraction of her pure beauty made him want to curse.

"Hello, dear friend." She nuzzled King George's neck and looked up to Reed sitting in the saddle. "And hello to you."

He stared down at her. The way those thick lashes framed those trusting, round eyes. He couldn't think past how quickly her voice calmed the shuffled noise in his head.

"Are you all right?" She lightly touched his knee. "I know Rob's care is a lot. Please say if you think I'm in the way."

"Yes, Patience Stephens, from Lennhurst Asylum, if you only knew, how much you are *in the way*." A chuckle mixed with a groan came from the back of his throat.

Removing her hand quickly, she stiffened and stepped back. The trees rustled with a light breeze.

"No, no." He needed to snap out of this deranged mood he was in. "I think I was trying to be funny, but my delivery was very poor."

He reached down for her hand. And for the hundredth time, she left it untended dangling in the air. Her eyes narrowed, unforgiving, weighing him head to toe. "Please, I meant no harm. Take my hand and step up on the chopping round next to the ax." Gripping her hand, he couldn't help but notice Joel had split over two cords of wood for her and Sarah. "Now grab my shoulder." Reed pulled as she swung her leg and wiggled up behind him. She locked her hands around his waist as he led King George out from the path.

"Did you enjoy the dance?" He took in a deep breath, she smelled good, like rosewater.

"Yes, thank you," she said softly. Her extended silence made his stomach twist.

"I should be thanking you," he rolled his lips into a thin line, "for bringing my parents and Robbie. It was unexpected but enjoyable to see them dance and visit with their friends."

"They were worried about bringing him out in the evening cold," she said and Reed felt his gut unwind; relieved she was talking to him. "But we all wrapped up in blankets on the way home." She relaxed her grip around his waist, resting her hands lightly on his sides. "Your father was so kind. He came in my cottage and checked all the doors and windows. Banked the fire. I assured him I would be fine."

Reed smiled, imagining his father being the gallant father figure. Taking the long way to his parents' property, he enjoyed such uncomplicated moments with her. Everyone wanted to help her, did she realize this whole town would want to befriend her? Well, except maybe Cynthia Icely.

"Reed, would you help me get Robbie up?" His father spoke after they exchanged greetings and set their coats down in the warm kitchen.

"Yes, I can," he said, following his father into Robbie's room.

"Something occurred to me last night." His father pulled back Robbie's blankets. "When you were dancing with Patience. And the other gentlemen were asking us how long our family friend would be visiting." Reed sighed as he helped pull Robbie up and removed his night-shirt. "That if your grandfather were alive, you would be the heir to that land. But now Patience is the heir." His father threaded Robbie's arms into a clean shirt. "The thing is, one of the things that keeps your mother at odds is what if something happened to us. Who would care for Robbie? Patience is a natural caregiver. Certainly whoever picked her name, did a wonderful job." Reed looked up from pulling Robbie's socks on, he didn't need a law degree to know where this was going. "What if the two of you were to marry? It would keep the other gentlemen from owning the land and provide Patience with safety and security." His father ran his fingers through Robbie's tousled hair. "She is a lovely girl—I,"

186

he cleared his throat, "I didn't know if you'd already made a declaration toward Miss Icely or—"

"No." Reed recoiled from the sting of her last berating. "We have no understanding." He grabbed Robbie under his legs and back, pulling him out of bed while his father held the wheeled chair steady. "I will admit, I've thought a lot about Miss Stephens's future." He remembered Fred's words dug at him all last week. Only his father's suggestion sounded sensible, the two heirs joining for safety and family security.

As Reed slid his brother into the chair, Robbie flung an arm hitting Reed on the backside. "Oww." Reed jerked up rubbing the sting from the slap. "That almost seemed on purpose." They grabbed the straps and tied Robbie's torso to his chair. "For one thing, I don't know if she would agree. I think I've been a poor example of a friend."

"It was just a thought and of course a big decision." His father pulled the rolling chair out. "Your mother prays for her every day."

PATIENCE PULLED THE lace curtains back in the Chapmans' parlor. Maybe if it wasn't going to rain, they could take Rob outside. Something flitted by the corner of her eye. A red and black ladybug! In the house? She went to offer it her finger when the men rolled Rob out. In the space of her glance back, it disappeared. God, in His infinite providence, was going to show her something today.

After Robert and Arita had left for church, she helped Reed feed Rob and started the dishes. "Do you read the Bible? Could we sit with Rob and hear the scripture?" she asked drying the last dish. Reed looked up from reading the newspaper. She knew God had something special in mind for her and often the scripture brought light and hope into her heart.

Reed nodded and walked over to a brown bookshelf. Bringing a Bible to the table, he opened it and sat. "What would you like?"

She folded the towel and sat at the table. "I just finished Psalm 83, and I think I read 84."

"Psalm 85 then." He thumbed through the feathery pages until he found it. "Lord, thou hast been favorable unto thy land." He paused and rubbed the dark stubble on his chin. "Thou hast brought back the captivity of Jacob. Thou hast forgiven the iniquity of thy people, thou hast covered all their sin." He looked up at Patience. "Did you know this is what it said?"

Shaking her head, she didn't understand his question.

He read on. "Surely His salvation is nigh them that fear Him; that glory may dwell in our land. Mercy and truth are met together; righteousness and peace have kissed each other." He cleared his throat and started again, "Truth shall spring out of the earth, and righteousness shall look down from heaven. Yea, the LORD shall give that which is good; and our land shall yield her increase."

He looked up like he'd never heard God speak before or his breakfast didn't agree with him.

"It's wonderful, yes?" She smiled. "Righteousness and peace have kissed each other." Her face started to flush thinking of Reed's attempt to kiss her. "Did you hear Rob? Truth shall spring out of the earth. That's what I want. I want to build a garden of plants and trees revealing the truth of God at every turn. His goodness, faithfulness and abundant supply," she said, smiling at Rob. "A peaceful place where you can feel the sun on your face or the smell of lilac, hibiscus, white amaranth while lingering in the shade. A pond or fountain where my winged friends will rest. We love yellow lantana, purple verbena . . ." She covered a small laugh. "Sorry, I get excited to think of all the beauty the Lord gives." Reed's brows furrowed as someone knocked on the door.

He rose and opened the door to see Joel standing at the stoop.

"May I speak to Miss Stephens?" He looked past Reed. "Good morning, Patience."

She smiled, stood and curtsied stiffly at him. "Good morning, Joel."

Reed offered no greeting, just his tongue

189

pushing against the inside of his cheek, and his dark brows met over the bridge of his nose.

"Would you join me for a quick walk?" Joel asked ignoring Reed's scowl. "I wanted to show you the boxes I built for your garden. Something to start your early seeds in."

Patience grabbed her cape off the hook and stood next to where Reed held the door. She had the strangest sensation he would put his arm out to stop her. Instead, he stepped back and made an exaggerated sweeping gesture with his hand that she was free to pass. Deciding against looking him in the eye, she reached for Joel's outstretched elbow and walked out.

CHAPTER 25

REED WENT INTO his parents' room and looked into the mirror over his mother's dressing table. He should have shaved, but he was tired this morning. Picking up her brush, he tried to brush his thick, dark hair flat. He exposed his teeth into the mirror, did he have bad breath? Without even a decent excuse, she leaves the table and goes off with Joel? One minute they are reading the Bible about the plenty of the land and the next minute she is gone. Talk about lack of focus.

He rolled his eyes in dismissal. It didn't matter, and he wanted to re-read those verses again without her chattering away about her gardens. He went back to the table and turned his brother's chair into the parlor. Stepping toward the window, he pulled the curtain back an inch. "And now I'm going to keep looking out this front window every five minutes. No!" He turned, pointing at Robbie. "No, I'm not."

An hour later, she still hadn't returned, and he'd filled the last of the warm water for Robbie's bath. Undressing his brother and carefully lowering him into the tub, he grabbed the soap and started to lather his hair and body. Robbie dropped a heavy hand down on the water splashing soap in Reed's eyes. He groaned, trying to keep a grip on Robbie's arm and find a towel to wipe his face. Out of his burning sight, he saw Patience come in the back room. "Could you get me a towel wet with water?" He asked as she already turned to help. While blinking back the sting, a towel flashed in front of his eyes. "Thank you." He scowled. "Could you just hold his arm up, just while I get this soap . . . ?" She gripped the top of Robbie's arm as Reed rested the damp towel against his red eyes. Robbie began to flail and pulled from her grip.

"Robbie, leave some water in the tub!" He tried to steady Robbie as Patience hurried from the room. Rinsing him the best he could, he bent and picked up his brother's bent body. As soon as he set him on the bed and began to towel him dry, he caught his thoughtless mistake. His brother's nakedness was probably not appropriate for a young woman. "First the town dance and now this. If you don't tell mother, I won't." Reed rubbed his brother's wet hair with the towel and pressed it to the side.

Patience moved with few words as she fed Robbie lunch and cleaned his face. He wondered if the bath had scarred her connection with his brother. Maybe just the shock, he swallowed a snicker. Helping Robbie to bed for a rest, he looked forward to lunch with her, perhaps even tolerating the details of the new boxes from Joel. He entered the dining room as she set two plates of chicken and potatoes on the table. It smelled wonderful, and he smiled. A knock at the door made them both freeze. "Did you invite Joel to lunch?" He felt his nostrils flaring.

"No." She shook her head.

Reed opened the door to see the dandy from the post office. His short pants showing his stockings. "Can I help you?"

"Ah, yes. Your mother had said the family friend, Miss Stephens was visiting."

Reed opened the door wider, frowning.

"Oh, oh, Miss Stephens. I was hoping to ask the Chapmans and you, of course, if you wanted to join my family for the Sunday meal tonight."

Patience swallowed and came toward the open door.

"My parents can't attend. They care for my brother in the evenings." Reed reached his arm along the height of the open door, and leaned, flashing a curious look at Patience.

"I think that . . . you should thank your family." She answered, searching for words. "And . . . um may we reschedule for another night?"

"Yes, I understand." He bowed, and his two thin strands of hair fell forward poking him in the eye. "Maybe next week then?" He quickly brushed the hair off his face.

Patience smiled her farewell, looking wide-eyed while Reed closed the door.

"Is this going to go on all day?" Reed tried to keep the annoyance out of his voice. His parents would probably arrive any minute.

She went back to the table and sat. "Would you like me to reheat this?" She started to grab their plates.

"No." He touched her sleeve. "Please eat. I just decided I want to ask you about something important, and I can't ask you and deal with this revolving door." He pulled in a deep breath, something irrational pushing him to at least ask. "Just hear me out before you say no." Her face radiated with skepticism. "Or before you say yes."

She put her napkin in her lap. "Very well."

"I was thinking about your situation. My parents don't want to make up a story about you being the visiting family friend, but they don't want people knowing you have times alone in the cottage." Somehow, he thought his words would help him convince himself, but his own palpitating nerves were taking over. "And after today, I'm not sure any of us can keep up with your social calls." Patience picked up her fork, then set it back down, looking embarrassed.

Reed choked, that's not what he meant to say. He scratched his head and stood up. "Give me a minute. This isn't going right." He checked out the front window for any more needy callers and came back. "Okay, let me try again. Since the first time I met you, it was the strangest thing . . ." *Nope, that wasn't going in the right direction.* How did his father's words make sense and none of his would work?

"Patience, listen." He leaned his palms on the table. "If you truly have your heart set on staying here, would you consider marrying me? I love this land, and if you want to make a garden, I will help you. You want to go to church, go. You want to make friends and dance at Christmas, dance. Our marriage would give you the security to make this land your home."

Frozen in the moment, only the faint rise and fall of her chest moved. He wondered if he'd stunned her. His mind flashed to her seeing a wet, and half soaped, naked, crippled man. "And I think we should take more time to get to know one another. Whatever you know about marriage, there will be no rush. No rush at all." His throat constricted shut. He sucked in air through his nose. "Except to have a ceremony, that's simple, maybe here at the house. Maybe next week?

She blinked, face deepening from pink to pale. "I—" she swallowed and took a deep breath, "can I have some time to think and pray?"

"Yes." He stood, stretching the tension in his

back. "And we could live at the cottage. King George and I can ride back and forth to work. We could even ask Sarah to spend the days with you if you want?"

Silent, her gaze widened and she gasped. Her beautiful mouth made a round O and she blinked several times. She spent a minute or two looking down at her chicken. Her eyes lifted slowly as her words rang with sincerity, "Do you care for me?"

"Yes." He answered her truthfully. "Do you care for me?"

The corner of her soft lips lifted, unmistakable goodness in her eyes. "Yes."

Something thumped hard in his chest. "I wish I could ask your father for permission, but you will have to choose for yourself."

She paused, looking over at the settee, rocking chair, footstool, window, hallway, stairs, the door, and finally back to her plate. "Reed, I have things wrong with me. My back is horribly disfigured. No woman would want anyone to see it." Reed wanted to reach across the table and plates but leaned a careful inch toward her. "I don't care. That will be up to you. I will never demand any-thing from you."

She stood and walked to the front window. "Your parents are coming up the road. We would have to have their blessing to marry." She looked back at him.

· · ·

THIRTY MINUTES LATER, Reed thought he'd explained well enough that Patience was *thinking* about his offer of marriage. His father smiled and hugged them like it had happened today. His mother stood with her mouth ajar. "You've had so many new adjustments, dear girl." Arita fingered the Bible laying out on the table. "Marriage would solve some of our worries. But—"

"Arita and I courted a month and then tied the knot." Robert nodded.

"Robert." She frowned. "We knew of each other before that. Times were different." She smiled weakly at Patience. "Can you stay till supper? We could talk more about some of the questions you would have."

Reed felt his face flush. He didn't want to tell his parents he'd already made it clear that *some things* they didn't need to rush until they knew each other better. "I was thinking, if Patience agrees, we could have the reverend here to the house, maybe next Saturday."

"What's wrong with our church?" His mother scowled.

"Or," he nodded a bit nervously, "the church." Reed looked down and grabbed a piece of chicken. His belly constricted from hunger and the reality that his life might be drastically changing.

CHAPTER 26

THE NEXT MORNING in front of Beasley and Chapman, the familiar rumble of wagon wheels and jangle of horses' tack came from out front as Reed looked up from his desk to see Sarah stop the wagon. Patience stepped down from the footplate and straightened her loose hair back behind her ears. He couldn't read her expression, and his coffee and toast rose immediately to the top of his throat. Patience was here with her answer. Fred watched them approach the door.

"Isn't that your little dippy-headed tart?" Fred smiled.

"Fred, please, go use the outhouse or something. Now!" Reed walked to the door and pulled on the handle. Sarah said something to her and walked down the sidewalk. Patience walked in and nodded to the unmoved Fred.

Fred rose and bowed. "Miss Stephens, you look lovely today."

Shyly she looked at Reed, and then with an intake of air, a pale determination grew across her face. She quickly turned back to Fred. "Oh thank you . . . you look . . . ah . . . nice, too."

Fred sat back down and gawked at them.

She pulled in another deep breath. "I was able to talk to my parents."

Reed cleared his throat and grabbed her hand. "Let's talk in the back."

When they were out of sight of Fred's confused face, he turned to her. "Your parents? You mean my parents?"

"No, mine. I go to the crosses by the ruins. I talk to them there."

"And?" Reed wished he could regain his regular heartbeat. "What have you decided?"

She glanced up the steps to his upstairs apartment. "I saw a ladybug last Sunday."

He shook his head, this felt more like another lapse of judgment turned mistake, just like the night he'd taken her up those stairs. "Forgive me." He sighed, rubbing between his eyebrows. "I don't remember what ladybugs stand for."

"For God's providence. They show me the way."

Just like dead parents. Reed had trouble tracking with his rational thoughts, how could he—

"Yes. This Saturday at the church. I'll be there."

Her words finally broke in. "Are you sure Patience?" For all the days of his life and her limited understanding of what this meant for him and his family, he didn't want to be a wicked husband. He just wanted the land and if it came

200

with a beautiful unorthodox woman, so be it.

"I'm sure." Her eyes shimmered with something unsaid.

His hands gently held her forearms remembering in his haste he'd left bruises on her. "What, what are you afraid of?"

Swallowing hard, she turned away and shook her head. "I never allowed myself to believe a man would want me. Would want to marry me. You can't imagine, how many times I wrote it on my list and then I would erase it." A sad laugh escaped. "I couldn't allow myself to dream so extravagantly. It would crush my heart in some strange way. But you, you came one day and took me away from Lennhurst." Her tender, silky eyes met his. "I don't think I have told you, but thank you for taking me away that day. I know you didn't want to." Her cheek rose with a smile and she blinked. A single tear flowed over. He let go of her arm and brushed it away. "Thank you for introducing me to your family. I know you weren't sure about that either." She touched the button on his shirt. "I'm not sure what love and marriage is between a man and a woman. Except in books." She waited. "Your parents, I'm sure they love each other."

Reed nodded slowly, finding her words strangely touching. "Can we just figure it out as we go?" He leaned back to see Sarah coming in his office. "You be patient with me, I'll be patient with you." He smiled. "Is there anything you need for Saturday?"

She shrugged, walking with him into his front office. "I don't think so. I've never been to a wedding. This will be my first."

Reed caught Sarah's sober expression. "Thank you for all your help, Sarah." He opened the door, hoping she wasn't going to give him a piece of her mind. "I will see everyone on Saturday." He waited till the wagon pulled away and glared at Fred.

"Thank you for all the *privacy*." Reed went back to his desk.

Fred stood, and Reed could feel his eyes on him. "So you are seriously joining yourself to that tumble-headed dove? Since you never do anything I suggest, I suddenly feel responsible for a life of carrots in your coffee and birds flying around your house." Fred lifted his palms in the air. "Have you prepared your independent, stubborn soul for the dizzy delirium of your household? How long are you planning to play house with the village dunce?"

"Stop!" Reed rose and slapped his hand hard against his desk. "No more!" Enraged, he pointed a finger at him. "No more sarcastic references, no more British, ironic slang. I don't want to hear it, Fred. Just keep your mouth shut! She's off limits from now on." Reed felt his fists clenching.

Fred backed up and bowed. "My sincere

apologies for the offense. I had not realized you were in love with her."

"I'm not . . ." Reed shook his head and sat down. "Just don't be disparaging toward her and especially don't be scornful of her."

"As you wish." Fred pulled on the lapel of his jacket. "We've been through a lot together. I know how much the land means to you, and if this is what you want . . ." He walked back to his desk. "If you need a best man, I will be the tightest-lipped chap in the church. If the reverend says amen, I will not even murmur my closure to the prayer."

Reed felt his breathing returning to normal. "Yes, I do want you and Janice to attend."

"Three days." Fred blew out a low whistle. "Things are quite different here in the American wilderness. Do you suppose your fellow rustics will reason why these nuptials ring hasty?"

"I don't care." Reed found the documents for his next case. "When the months go by, and they see she is not pregnant, the gossips will fade off."

"Then this is to be a marriage of convenience? An annulment could be in the future?" Fred asked.

"I don't know." Reed tried to read what was in front of him and sat back running fingers through his hair. "You've seen her. I tried to ignore her, which was impossible. I regret to say it but I have the worst urge to protect her and help her. And her child-like voice and her innocent thoughts they-they—*pull* me into a stillness that I could get lost in. But then when I can't rationalize her thinking, it's almost like panic rises in me. I have no idea how her illogical mind will play out, or what she'll say in front of others. And I hate that feeling." He clenched his jaw. "I'm sorry I snapped at you. This tension is worse than the four-hour tests at Oxford." He murmured returning to his paperwork.

"I do owe you," Fred said eagerly. "While you're gone on a holiday—" He stopped.

Reed's expression said it all.

"Poor Chappy, no honeymoon?"

CHAPTER 27

REED STOOD AND paced outside the brick and white paneled church. He'd never noticed the side wall of the church covered in ivy, just like the little cottage. The sun was warm on his back but under his good black suit and pressed white shirt was cold and sweaty skin. Gazing at the steeple and cross against the blue sky, Reed realized it had been years since he'd been in a church. Did he find it alarming he was about to marry a woman who believed she could talk to God and hear His leading? Often through bugs? Should he be feeling the same nausea as he did when they went to retrieve Robbie from the Union hospital? The cross at the top of the steeple held his attention.

God, I found the wherewithal to forgive. So I must have some faith in You. Have I rushed ahead like a disobedient child? Do you listen to those as far off as me? You owe me nothing, but if You could bless something in this day, I would welcome it.

Reed felt a hand on his shoulder and turned to see Fred and Janice standing next to him.

"Janice was just saying, prayer works." Fred

squeezed him. "Bernie dropped off the ring. I think we are ready? Shall we go in?"

Reed nodded and sucked in the day's fresh air. *This was only a wedding, not a firing squad,* he reminded himself.

Blinking, he noted the illuminating crimsoned reds and golds from the stained glass lining the tall sides of the church. In the front, Patience stood among the streaks of light talking to his mother in her rose and yellow dress. Her hair, shimmering in the light, was coiled in perfect thick knots at the base of her neck. She held a small bouquet of fresh flowers in her hand. He was thankful and pleased she looked like the stunning young woman he'd danced with the night of the dance. His father stood a few feet away from the front wooden pew, his hand protectively on the back of Robbie's wheeled chair. Reed lifted a painful smile. His swaying brother donned a starched white shirt and a small gray bow tie. Suddenly shocked by the emotion rising in his throat, he recognized the soft voice of the reverend's wife singing with a sweet melody at the piano.

> *I need Thee every hour, most gracious*
> *Lord;*
> *No tender voice like Thine can peace*
> *afford*
> *I need Thee, oh, I need Thee;*

Every hour I need Thee;
Oh, bless me now, my Savior,
I come to Thee.

Reed walked down the far right aisle and stood at the front, just a few feet from the piano. Fred stood a few feet behind him. Janice, the only attendee, sitting on the right side of the pews. The reverend stood and walked Patience to meet him in the middle of the center aisle. Reed tried unsuccessfully to swallow the emotions. The soft lyrics pricked something deep in him. He purposed not to look at his father or mother sitting on the other side. Lord, he didn't need to break down at his own wedding.

I need Thee every hour, stay Thou nearby;
Temptations lose their pow'r when Thou
*   art nigh.*
I need Thee every hour, in joy or pain;
Come quickly and abide, or life is vain.

He tried to steady the rapid rise and fall of his chest. What had the reverend just said? Patience reached her hands out to him. He took them, embarrassed for the quaking he felt running through his hands to hers.

"Let us pray," the reverend said as the song came to end. Reed sniffed and closed his eyes. Letting loose of Patience's hands, he grabbed his lapel hankie and swiped his damp face.

"Amen," the few voices said after the reverend finished.

"Dearly beloved, we are gathered today . . ."

Patience lifted a sweet smile at him. He must look ridiculous, this absurd display of emotion. He tried to focus on what the reverend was saying. Was he getting married? Right now? Forever and . . . ever?

". . . to join this man and this woman in holy matrimony."

He glanced behind Patience where his mother sat listening to the reverend. She'd been through so much yet looked steady and strong. Where would they all be without her love and prayers? His throat constricted again.

"This union, instituted by God, is not to be entered into lightly, but reverently . . ."

Reed snapped back at the words spoken, bowing his head. *Grandpa, I keep faltering somewhere between guilt and accomplishment.* When he looked up, he caught Patience's worried expression. Would his nerves never cease their blessed jittering?

"Do you, Patience Stephens, take Reed Michael Chapman as your wedded husband? To have and to hold, for richer and poorer, in sickness and in health. Forsaking all others. Till death do you part?"

Reed met her eyes. She should back out now

and have her own life. Just like the moment, they stood in the front H at Lennhurst, why did she put her life in his sweaty hands? This was a . . .

"I do."

"Do you, Reed Michael Chapman, take Patience Stephens as your wedded wife? To have and to hold, for richer and poorer, in sickness and in health. Forsaking all others. Till death do you part?"

"I do," came out clearly. Something shifting in his chest. Her smile warmed everything from his ice-cold toes to his fingertips.

"Is there a ring to be given?" The reverend asked.

Fred stepped forward and placed the ring in his hand. Reed prepared to put it on her finger and wondered why he'd never seen this ornate ring in his family's things. Patience stared with a curious gaze as he repeated after the reverend and slid it onto her finger.

"And Patience, do you have a token of your love and fidelity?"

Robert stepped away from Robbie and handed Patience a ring from his vest pocket. Of course, it was his grandfather's. He would never forget the rough metal soldered together. The warmth of her hand holding his was tangible as she slipped it on.

"With this ring," her voice floated, "I, Patience, take you, Reed . . ."

Good Lord, she was beautiful. Maybe tonight they could get to know each other a bit quicker than what he first thought.

"And with it, I bestow all my worldly goods to thee." She lifted a wary smile. His newly ringed finger and hand slipped from hers.

"Well done," the reverend said. "By the power vested in me as a minister of the gospel of Jesus Christ, I now pronounce you man and wife. You may kiss your bride." The reverend smiled at them.

Reed's eyes floated around the front of the church. That was it? Had he paid attention to any of the words spoken? Kiss, he needed to kiss Patience. He smiled remembering his last attempt. The reverend's wife sang and played the hymn again.

> *I need Thee every hour; teach me Thy*
> *   will;*
> *And Thy rich promises in me fulfill.*
> *I need Thee every hour, most Holy One;*
> *Oh, make me Thine indeed, Thou blessed*
> *   Son . . .*

Reed met her deep innocent eyes. "Hold still this time." He smiled drawing his finger over her cheek and rested his thumb under her chin. Bending his head forward, he closed his eyes . . ."

"Wait."

He opened his eyes only a breath away from her. "What?"

"Should everyone be watching?" she whispered. "It feels too personal."

"Patience, trust me." He breathed out. "It's a very small thing."

"Oh, okay." She lifted a nervous smile.

He placed a light kiss on her still lips. "See."

"Now I understand." She beamed. "Now do I kiss you?"

"If—If you want to." Reed dared not look at the expression on the reverend's face. Patience's pure countenance bore into his chest like the words of the soft hymn playing over them. He felt like everything she'd ever hoped for on her list, in this moment, had instantly found their place, joining with his life desires. Soft fingers touched the back of his neck, and she rose up on her toes. He caught the sweetest flash of a smile before he closed his eyes. Maybe it was her soft lips pressing on his. Maybe it was the way she pulled him close, the flickering hues of lights over closed eyes, the sweet church melody. His hands wrapped around her waist as one gentle slow kiss grew in desire to two and three a bit longer and four deeper.

The reverend snickered and tapped his shoulder until they broke apart. "Cake and punch are offered in the fellowship hall. If everyone could make their way. How about you two take a break from the kissing and lead the way?"

Reed felt his face flush. Stepping back he made the mistake of glancing at Fred rolling his eyes and waggling his head back and forth. Patience was right. The wind of vulnerable emotions swirling inside of him those last seconds, they probably shouldn't have been kissing in front of everyone.

CHAPTER 28

PATIENCE SMILED AND took the plate of cake from the reverend's wife. "I saw you at the dance last week," the square-faced woman said. "But you never hardly got a minute off the dance floor. Anyway, I'm Mrs. Pearce, and now there are, suddenly, two Mrs. Chapmans!" The lines around her eyes creased together with her broad smile. "We'd love to have you to Sunday service, and though it's hard for Arita to get away, we have ladies quilting, and Bible study on Wednesday mornings. I would love to introduce you to all the other women. Arita said you were from out of town. No family in the area?"

"Well, I feel as if my family are here with me." Patience watched Arita turn and join the conversation.

"The Pearces and the Chapmans go quite a ways back, don't we?" Arita changed the subject, rubbing Mrs. Pearce's back. "All our children running through those summer picnics we used to have. Patience, may I see the ring? It is rather intricate, and striking, could those be rubies?"

Patience held her hand up for the ladies to admire her ring. Reed walked up and smiled at her. Her stomach did a strange flip, Reed's wife, their sweet kisses still warming her awakened heart.

"I've never seen it in your things," Reed said to Arita.

"Oh, it's not mine. I assumed you had bought it." She shrugged.

"No." He stilled, watching Patience. "May I steal her away for a moment?" Patience took his extended hand as he led her to where Fred and Janice spoke with his father.

"There they are! Mr. and Mrs. Chappy. I want to congratulate you both and kiss the bride on the cheek. Would that be all right, Reed? Blimey, without all the discussion." He winked at Reed and placed a quick kiss on her cheek. Janice reached in to hug her.

"Say, Reed said there is no honeymoon trip." Janice chipped in. "So we want to have you two over to dinner this week. Say Wednesday? Reed and Fred could make the arrangements, but then it would never happen, so maybe I'll drive out to see you on my day off."

A friend, she looked and sounded so much like a friend. "I would welcome that. May I call you Janice?"

"Fred, you gave me the ring before the cere-mony. I thought you said Bernie gave it to you," Reed said.

Patience smiled and listened to Janice but

wanted to follow what the men were saying.

"It was on my desk yesterday with some other strange looking jewelry pieces. I have the box back at the office. It was the day Bernie picked up your things to move to your land, so I just assumed he'd left it."

Reed glanced at her then averted his eyes. "Thanks for standing up with me today, Fred."

"Good thing." Janice turned to him, covering a snicker. "From where I sat, I wasn't sure if you were going to faint or cry. Goodness, Reed."

Fred straightened, "Oh Beloved, if you only knew what you brides do to the hardened souls of man."

They all looked at Fred, wondering if he was serious. "More like what you do to us poor women." She rubbed her little-rounded belly. Fred placed his hand on her hers and kissed her on the cheek. "I love it when you talk cheeky."

"See what I have to deal with?" Janice squirmed, as Fred kissed her neck. "Oh, don't look so embarrassed Patience, I've been a victim of his uncontrollable passion for me, going on a year now. I hope I suffer all my days."

Patience tried to smile, but she had to look down. Arita had asked her about what she knew of marital duties. Of course, from what she assumed from books, really nothing. What would Reed want? Arita made it sound as if every young couple had their own way to love each other. To be honest and open with Reed with her questions. Didn't he say they would take their time to get to know each other? That meant the marital duties, didn't it?

"Go by and get the box. It's sitting on my desk." Fred pulled up still hugging Janice. "Now we must skedaddle, I have a sudden urge to victimize my own wife." They turned, still clutching each other. "That was the most positively endearing thing I've ever heard you say." Fred's voice trailed off as they said their goodbyes to the Chapmans and the Pierces.

Patience knew her cheeks still flushed as she gave Reed a small smile.

"We can go whenever you are ready," he said quickly and looked away. "Do you want another cup of punch?"

"No, thank you." She straightened her back. "I haven't had a chance to visit with Rob. "I'll do that and then be ready for you." *Ready, ready for you? Ugh, that's not what I meant to say.* She chewed her bottom lip as she walked over to Rob.

"I am now your sister." She grabbed his cold hands and began to warm them. "What do you think of that?" She watched his face contort as if he wanted to speak. "Reed looked very handsome today. And you, also handsome." She touched his trimmed beard before his head rocked back and forth. "You know him better than I do, Rob." She whispered close to his ear, and he stilled. "I'm not sure what was happening to him during the ceremony. Possibly regretful? As if he'd changed his mind?" Reed approached from the corner of her eye.

"More secrets between the two of you?" Reed notched his chin down, assessing them.

"No." She straightened. "Just some brotherly advice."

Reed squeezed Robbie's shoulders. The earlier reluctance showed in his face. "Robbie should have married before me," he murmured.

Arita stepped over and brought Patience a covered cake platter. Robert began to turn Rob around in his chair. "Congratulations, Reed, and Patience," he said over his shoulder. Patience wondered if something was wrong.

"There is half a cake in there. And Sarah said she'd left supper for you at the cottage." She hugged Reed. "Do not come over tomorrow, and we already told the Pearces we wouldn't be attending church." She leaned over Patience and the cake platter, kissing her on the cheek. "You two need time together." She patted Patience's cheek gently.

Patience felt a stab of uncertainty. Similar to leaving Lennhurst. Excited, yet nervous about the unknown. What were the Chapmans thinking? She watched as they walked out the side door. Did they approve of this marriage? Did they want her in the family? How often did they all look at her with confused expressions? Reed picked up her cape from a chair and laid it on her shoulders. He offered his elbow, and she curled her arm around his, clutching the cake plate with her other hand.

"Do you mind if we stop by my office?" he asked. "I'm curious about your ring. My father said it wasn't from him." He captured her hand in his larger one. As they walked out he angled her finger, and they studied the ring setting sparkling in the sun.

"I think it was my mother's."

Reed stopped and turned to her. "What?"

"I'm not sure why I said that. I was so young, but she wore many rings."

Reed took the cake plate as they walked down the two blocks to his office. Hancock was relativity quiet, only passing two boys on the sidewalk. Reed unlocked the door and went to Fred's desk. The square box was old with a plain brown lid.

"Do you recognize this?"

"No." She shook her head. "My mother had grand jewelry boxes with velvet and painted lids. Reed lifted the lid, and they both looked inside to a long pearl necklace, two large-stoned broaches. One purple and gold. The other with smaller red stones and silver plating, almost matching Patience's ring. "They look like rubies to me." He picked up a large hair comb with wings covered in flecks of garnet and amethyst.

"Butterfly wings." Patience touched the comb. "I remember my mother styled it in my hair one day. What a delight to see it again." Her eyes began to mist.

Reed tugged his finger between his neck and stiff collar, clearing his throat, he dropped it back in the box. "How would these get here Patience?" He shook his head. "I don't understand this." He held the box up to her and tossed it on Fred's desk. "I thought everything burned to the ground. How can these be from your family?" He paused. "Did you have this box in your things at Lennhurst?"

"No." She shook her head, watching his green eyes, once glossy at the wedding, now flashing distrust.

"Dr. Powell then? Or this benefactor you called him. Who would that be? And why would he have this box?"

"I don't know, Reed."

"Patience." He closed his eyes and ran his fingers through his hair. "We are married now. You don't have to hide from me. I vowed to keep you and provide and . . . and whatever else I said."

"I could tell you were distracted," she whispered. "And what would I hide?"

"We haven't been married a day, and you're

already trying to chastise me. Point taken. I am easily sidetracked. Especially when I don't understand what is happening."

"You didn't understand that you asked me to marry you today. What vows are?" Her eyes widened.

"No . . . I . . ." A strange chill ran through him and he turned away stalking over to his desk. "It turns my thinking inside and out when I don't know where that box came from and whose ring is on your finger. What should I be prepared for now that we are married?" He leaned on his desk and straightened abruptly. "Will our cottage burn down next or are these innocent gestures? I don't know who built the crosses or repaired the dock on my land."

"Your land?" She waited, hoping he would realize how dishonoring to her family that sounded.

"Yes," he said with wide eyes. "It's all Chapman land now."

CHAPTER 29

HIS PARENTS LOANED their family carriage to bring his new bride home. Home to his land, his rightful inheritance. Finally. He pulled King George to a stop. The only glaring problem was his young bride hadn't said one word to him since they left his office. If she clutched the box of jewelry and the platter of cake any harder, she would probably crush all of it. Why couldn't she clearly understand his position? He was trying to protect her. Just because all the unknowns hadn't been harmful, it didn't mean someone wasn't coming forward with ill plans or trying to do her wrong. Good Lord, someone burnt her childhood home to the ground, killing her entire family. He turned to help her and she ignored his outstretched hand, walking into the cottage. This wasn't quite what he was picturing for his first evening alone with her.

"WHAT IS A honeymoon?" She finally spoke after an hour moving through the cottage avoiding him.

Reed looked up from some paperwork, unable to concentrate. "It's a holiday of sorts. Usually, sometime after the wedding the couple might go to a city and stay in a hotel or something nice." The silence returned, and he went back to his reading.

"Does the family plan the trip? Was it part of the dowry the husband is supposed to receive?"

"Not necessarily." He knew where this was leading, and hoped she would drop it. "It's something we can plan for later." He noticed the sun was setting, drawing long shadows into the front room. "Are you cold? I could build up the fire."

"No. I don't like it as large as you do."

He wanted to remind her the last time he was in this cottage he was soaked to the bone by freezing lake water. Some recollected feelings came back from that strange day. Now he was married, if he wanted to have her, he could. He glanced over to where his things still sat untouched in his trunk. Asking her about where to unpack seemed a presumptuous question. He poked around the smoldering logs and caught her watching him. "Come and sit by me, Patience." He pointed to the other green chair as he took the opposite one. She came and sat, back straight and stiff, hands clasped in her lap, looking into the smoking fire.

"I know I've said something that . . . well, that caused you to be upset with me." He pulled off his shoes and kicked them aside. She rose quickly and picked them up and set them next to the front door. "And I said we still needed time to get to know one another." She finally glanced at him as she sat down. "So I'll start and tell you something about me, and then you can help me understand you." He saw a small nod of agreement.

"I know you have a great sentimental attachment to this place. You have risked everything to be here, that's one of the things I admire about you. You're not just a stubborn, stiff-backed, porcelain doll like I first thought." She sent him a sneering sideways glance. "Let me finish; you are kind and peace-loving and just loving, I would say." She stared at the ground. "But from this day forward you will have to grow up. Lennhurst kept you safe and alive, but it didn't help you with the harsh realities of this world."

"I can't make myself age any faster," she shot at him.

He scratched his head. "I mean to say. You're an adult now. Adulthood is about survival. We can only survive on this land if we use it wisely. The animals that live in the forest all around us, they use the land to survive. There is nothing wrong with a garden or a rare summer swim, but the land is about being used. Used for survival. Do you understand?"

"Yes, I told you I thought about having cabins or something around the lake, where people or creatures could come to rest and pray, meet with God."

Reed leaned back and gripped the arms of the

green chairs. "Chapman land is thick with trees." He steadied his tone. "Trees become lumber. Lumber is needed all over the east for building, for survival."

"You want to cut down the trees?" Her nose and mouth crinkled.

"Patience, do you understand, America is trying to rebuild after the war?" By the look on her face, he needed to go another direction. "Men like Robbie are coming home to barns and homes and entire towns burnt to the ground. There is a demand the Chapman mill may not even be able to keep up with. They need the lumber to rebuild their lives."

"I'm—I'm . . ." she floundered in thought for a moment, "I'm sorry." She stood and paced between the chairs and fireplace. "I know what it's like to have everything burnt down and taken from you. But how many trees did we pass from Brown Township to Hancock? A thousand or more? I don't see what growing up has to do with cutting down trees." She sent him a sideways glare as she passed his chair. "Is this why we didn't have a honeymoon? Because we should get to *know* each other?" Her voice held an unfamiliar sarcasm. "Get to know that *you* are going to . . . to destroy all that God has restored to me?"

"Hey! That's not fair." He rose and grabbed her waist and made her face him. "I will make *sure* the things you want to see happen will happen."

"I can't imagine how you will have time for my interests between your law office and cutting down trees." She rolled her eyes, pushed his hands off her and headed for the hall.

"Patience, wait." He moved swiftly, grabbing her upper arm as she tried to tug away.

"And this looks familiar," she growled, trying to pull away from him.

Something almost humorous hit Reed in thinking she could really escape him. He quickly picked her up in his arms as she twisted and pushed against his hold. "Those bruises were an accident." He tried to grab her escaped arm. "Patience. I . . . I . . . ." he searched for words, the right words to say this time. "I wanted to tell you how beautiful you looked today." He flinched as she elbowed him in the chest. "But now," he choked, tried to hold his composure, "that you won't calm down, your hair is falling out all over."

"Good then, just like my heart." She pushed her foot off the hallway wall and propelled them backward. Reed's shoulder caught Sarah's open door and toppled onto his back, her weight adding to the impact. He winced from the fall and let go of her as her thick skirts and legs covered him. A slender hand came from a mass of brown hair and pinched his neck.

"Oww!" He grabbed the offending limb.

"How's that for grown up!" she tried to rise off him, but he held her fast. "That's how sisters deal with bullies!" He scooted back quickly before her knee found his groin.

"I take back what I said about peace loving." He stood and grabbed her before she could get away. Pulling her backside against him, he trapped her offending arms in front of her. "Good night—that hurt." He grunted. "Seems a bit unconventional," he lifted her off her feet and walked into her room, "for a delicate fairy like yourself." He held back a laugh watching her legs and skirt swing wildly out in front trying to find the floor. Without warning, her boot heel came down swiftly, slamming into his shin.

"Ahhh!" He tried to lift the injured limb and steady her flailing torso. Losing his balance, they both fell onto the bed as it crashed off its frame to the floor. The thin wood headboard lunged forward as Reed swung on top of her taking the impact to his back. They both froze, and Reed debated if it was safe to release her pinned arms. After a moment of little movement, except the rise and fall of her body under his, he released her wrist and brushed the long hair off her face. "It's what you call, breaking in the bed." He chuckled.

A corner of a smile lifted, and she tried unsuccessfully to hold it back.

"Do you remember?" He gripped the headboard with his free hand and pushed it off his back.

"A long, long time ago, when we were standing in front of the reverend, and you kissed me?" Her eyes narrowed, and she tried to squirm out from under him, causing all variations of carnal distraction. "I would rather kiss you than fight with you any day. You're tougher than you look," he said, pulling more tousled hair off her face.

"Very well." Her breathy words and a tame hand reached up, surprising him. Running tender fingers through the hair behind his ear, he thought he saw surrender in the warmth of her eyes. Ready for her touch yesterday, he closed his eyes only a feather away from the most perfect, soft lips.

"Wait." Her hand pushed against his chest. Why had he ever let that hand go untethered?

"I need to get off my back."

"Of course, forgive me." He jumped back and pulled her to standing. She smiled, tucking her loose flowing hair behind her ear, and moved around him. Still holding her hand, he was about to pull her to him when suddenly she pushed him back onto the floored mattress and ran from the room. He popped up and grabbed the door frame, just in time to see the opposite door slam shut. The sound of something heavy pulled across the floor. It was the dresser he remembered from his time on that bedroom floor. He stood tapping his foot and had to chuckle.

Who knew, his fairy was part dragon.

CHAPTER 30

REED HEARD THE sound of a rooster crowing. He'd never heard that sound in town. He rolled to his side, and his hand flopped onto something hard. The floor was only inches below the mattress, and the headboard laid crooked against the other wall. The cottage, Patience's room, his wedding night, who would believe it? He rolled over to his back wondering if he could fall back to sleep. The rooster went off again. That ridiculous bird was getting moved away from the cottage today. He scanned her room. The simple brown dresser and ceramic basin, a brush and mirror, her two other dresses hung from hooks on the wall. Tidy. Had he come in and tried to move her orderly world? Was his *getting to know* each other speech, obvious with manipulation? Maybe the chicken coop could wait. He rose up and pulled his pants on. But some things could not.

After looking through every drawer and space in her room, the only secret thing was maybe her old crinkled dream list, and she'd already told him about it. It seemed everything she told him matched as true. Who could be helping her? He picked up her mirror and smoothed his hair back into place. His shoulders dropped seeing the purple-red bruise on his neck. Rolling his eyes, he tried to pull his collar closed over it.

Opening the door, there was no smell of coffee or breakfast. Scanning the small cottage, it was cold and silent. He looked at the other door. Was she in there? He tapped on her door. "Patience?"

He heard her faint yes and hesitated to find the right words. Chewing on his bottom lip, he squeezed her door frame and rehearsed a few apologies but they all sounded insincere, even to him.

"I'm going to return the buggy to my folks and work with my dad today. I won't be back till later."

"Very well." Her voice muffled through the closed door.

Wasn't that what she said before she pushed him back on the bed? He waited at the door, trying to think of something personal to say. Why was he so easily riled last night? How could he waver between laughter and anger, desire and wanting to govern her into submission? He looked back toward the messy bedding and broken bed. *Marriage. Harumph!*

SARAH KNOCKED ON the front door of the Chapman home. Arita opened it and invited her in.

"Good day, Mrs. Chapman. I thought I saw

Reed and Mr. Chapman ride off together. I wondered if Patience was here. I'd love to hear about the wedding."

"Have a seat, Sarah." Arita nodded to the table. "Can I get you coffee or tea?"

"Coffee with cream and sugar if it's not too much trouble."

"I'm not sure, but just Reed showed up this morning. Robert and I were going to do our Bible time, but before I knew it they were talking about the Polish property, pulling up barbed wire, then they were loading horses and away they went."

"I suppose the new bride might want to have some time to herself." Sarah's words held no conviction.

"Humph." Arita sat and sipped her coffee. "I hope nothing is wrong."

Both women studied their cups, thinking. Robbie's groan echoed from the parlor.

"What if I send Bernie over during Robbie's rest time? If Reed hasn't returned by then, you and I can take the wagon and check on her."

"Yes, I just took some turnovers out. I'll prepare a basket for them. Good idea. Tell Bernie around three," Arita said.

THAT AFTERNOON, PATIENCE pulled a fresh loaf of bread out of the oven. After so many fallen bread attempts, she could find little cheer for this successful loaf. Sarah was an excellent teacher, and Reed had offered for her to come for the days he was at work. But that offer couldn't lift her melancholy. She felt the tears reappearing without due cause. What was the matter with her? The only person she wanted for companionship was Reed Chapman, her husband. How could she be married and feel even more alone in body and soul?

Something reminded her of a verse in the Bible, and she sat and pulled her Bible close. Something about how a woman desires her—it was in Genesis. Where had she read about the husband? She flipped the pages back and forth. Genesis three, down the page. ". . . because you have done this thou art cursed above all the animals . . . and I will put enmity between thee and the woman . . ." Patience sighed, *God talking to the serpent,* reading on she found, "And thy desire shall be to thy husband, and he shall rule over thee." She rubbed her temple, looking out to the simple cottage and back to the Bible. "And I will greatly multiply thy sorrow in conception and bringing forth children. Cursed is the ground for thy sake." She slammed the Bible closed and dropped her forehead on it.

"Please Lord, forgive my folly and rebellion. I don't want to be cursed nor even the land." *Was there already a curse on this land? Is that what happened to my family?*

Hearing a noise, she looked up from her tearful jumbled prayers. Sarah and Arita stepped down from their wagon. She hurried to the door, knowing something was amiss. "Sarah. Arita? Is it Rob? Or something happened to Reed?"

"No, no, dear." Arita patted her on the back and walked in. "We just wanted to check on you." Arita stilled, looked her over and set a basket down. "I can tell you've been crying."

Sarah walked over to the warm bread and smiled. "The bread turned out good."

Patience whimpered with a crooked frown. "I'm a terrible, mean wife."

"Oh no," the older women said in unison. "It all takes time." Arita dropped her coat over a chair. "Two different people, from two different lives. It's going to take some adjustment."

"Are these Reed's things?" His mother walked over to the disarray of clothes in his trunk. "He should have unpacked this." She shook her head. "Why don't we do it together?" She pulled up the stack of his shirts and walked to the hallway and stopped at the bedroom door. Sarah walked up behind the frozen Arita.

"Oh Lordy, it didn't look like this when I left," Sarah announced. "No, someone had a hurricane in here." Wide-eyed, both women turned and looked everywhere but at Patience. Arita set the shirts back in the messy trunk. Patience felt herself crumbling inside. "When I kicked him

233

in the shin, we fell, and the frame just snapped under—"

"No. No need dear." Arita raised her hand, cutting her off. "What happens in the bedroom is between a husband and wife."

"That's a good thing coming from your mother-in-law." Sarah winked with a coy smile, "But I'm just an old widow, so why did you kick him?"

Patience heaved a sigh. If she told the story, they would either laugh or banish her from the Chapman family. The sound of arriving horses caused all three women to turn toward the front window to see Reed and his father ride up.

"Oh no." Patience cried and looked for somewhere to hide.

"Just breathe and smile." Sarah put her arm out and caught her from bolting by.

Reed and Robert tore into the house like it was on fire. "What happened?" Reed looked around with flushed cheeks, while all the women went mute. "Bernie said there was something the women had to help with." They all five stared at each other, the pressure killing Patience.

"I'm cursed!" Patience cried out. "I am!" She moved away from Sarah's steady arm. "I read it. I did." She scuffled left to right, eyes filling with tears. "It says so in the Bible." She gripped the chairs as she walked around the table, then into the small living area, circling and mumbling, watching the door.

"No love, you're not." Arita passed Reed reaching out to comfort her. "Reed Chapman, what is on your neck?"

Reed bundled his collar tighter. Patience thought she heard Sarah snicker or was it Robert? Did he know? Did Reed tell him everything?

"Have you seen the bedroom?" Sarah gestured at Robert, and he looked in the bedroom wide-eyed. "Oh, my . . . oooh my."

"Ahhh," Patience cried out. "I'm cursed, and the land is cursed!" She had to find a way through these people. Just as she broke through and came around Sarah, Reed's hands were on her arms.

"Patience, come with me, just for a minute. Please?"

Too vexed to resist, he shuffled her down the hallway and out the back door. Her hands covered her face.

"You're okay now." He pulled her close, lightly rubbing her neck and shoulders. "Goodness, you're shaking like a leaf."

She didn't understand why he was being kind, but her breathing and pounding heart slowed. Why did she agree to marry him? One minute she couldn't take her eyes off him for all different reasons, the next she fought to get away from him. It was too complicated for someone deemed immature, needing to *grow up*.

"Did you need to see my mother and Sarah?" he asked.

She shook her head against his chest. Maybe if she just never spoke they could stay like this.

"They just came to see you?" He tried again.

She nodded. "I thought you told them what I did. I was so embarrassed."

He squeezed her tight and let out a long breath. "I just assumed the worst, that you were ready to leave me. I rode King George like a lunatic to get here. Forget that word; I didn't mean—sorry. Today's all my fault. I should've stayed home. We needed to talk and straighten things out before I left. And—" He groaned. "I should have fixed the bed before we had company."

She wiped her cuff across her face, releasing a snort, laugh and cry all at once. They looked down and watched as the cat coiled around their ankles.

"You are not cursed, Patience," he whispered, running his hand down her long single braid. "Do you want to know why I was so distracted during our ceremony?"

Pulling back, she looked into his commanding, green eyes.

"It was the hymn. The one, the reverend's wife, played. 'I need Thee, oh I need Thee, every hour I need Thee.' You are not a curse. It's quite the opposite, you, your child-like faith, it reaches me in here." He rubbed his hand over his chest. "I've never allowed myself to hope in or need God.

I've lived all my years convincing myself I don't need anything, and suddenly, it frightens me, because for some reason that's all changed now."

CHAPTER 31

REED SET THE lantern on Patience's dresser and looked at the disastrous room. His family's timing was bad to say the least. He sighed spying the headboard. Living in town had its benefits. Thankfully they all made their polite excuses and hurried home. What was the piece of paper his mother had slipped into his hand? He reached into his pocket and pulled it out.

You can't draw water from an empty well. You need to court your wife!

Reed looked back to his closed door. They'd eaten supper in tired silence and Patience excused herself to read and go to bed. How would one court a young woman like her? Maybe he should have thought of these things before they rushed to the altar? Pulling off his boots, he kicked them to the corner.

How was he to know every single man in the county wanted time with her? How long till a proposal would've been in the works with one of those dandies? The way Joel had whispered something in her ear at the spring dance, still made his skin crawl. His mother was right, as usual. It might be worth the effort to help his wife gain long lasting affection for him.

PATIENCE AWOKE THE next morning and gripped her belly. As soon as she could engage her train of thought, she knew what was wrong. How could she take care of this with Reed living in this cottage? She flipped off the covers and heaved a sigh. She'd spotted through her nightgown and onto the sheets. Walking to the door, she leaned her ear against it, she could hear him in the kitchen. If he left for work soon, she would have the privacy she needed to take care of the wicked ladies' days. Another cramp made her grimace. Should she tell him? Maybe he could understand her erratic behavior or just like some of the ladies at Lennhurst, she needed to be sent away. His expression from the last time they spoke of women's monthly needs did not bode well for gaining his understanding.

"Reed." She called through the closed door. She could hear his steps from the kitchen only a few feet away.

"Yes, I'm here. I've made the coffee and oatmeal. Can you come to eat with me before I go?"

"No, no I can't." She rolled her head against the door. "I . . . I hoped you were leaving soon."

"Aren't you well? I can ride to get Sarah."

"No, please. I need the morning—the day to myself."

"Why won't you come out? I'm sure there is something I could say to make amends for today."

"No, please eat and then tell me when you're leaving."

She could tell he still stood by her door until she heard his steps fade. She turned and stripped the bed and dropped her things in a pile to wash. Wrapping her arms around her body, she winced against the cramps and freezing room. After what felt like hours, yet only minutes, she heard Reed at the door.

"All right. I'm leaving. Are you sure you don't need anything?"

"I'm sure." She listened as he finally closed the front door. Shivering, she opened her door and ran across to her room. Throwing on her robe and necessary things, she heard the back door open and jumped to close the door as a large black boot attached to a gray woolen suit blocked the closure.

"What are you doing Patience?" His chiseled chin shifted back and forth as he pulled the door wide. "You're going swimming, aren't you?"

"No. Just a bath and some wash." Her hair hung loosely around her downcast face.

"In the lake?" His eyes narrowed.

"No." She huffed, and her shoulders slumped. "It's my ladies' days. I wasn't keeping track with everything that has happened. So now you know why I behaved so badly and couldn't stop crying yesterday. And why today, I need to be alone. If you want to send me back to Lennhurst for all this, I wouldn't blame—"

"No." The word came out a bit sharp as he shook his head. "I don't want to send you," there was a long pause, "anywhere." A slow, small smile rose up on one side. "I shouldn't have barged in. I think I would do well to send myself away. I will see you this afternoon. Hopefully before dark."

She nodded, looking at his things strung all over the floor of her once pristine room. "Until then."

REED LET KING George have the lead until he pulled up abruptly approaching Hancock. George snorted and danced sideways under the restraint. "I know, yesterday was your favorite," Reed said, patting his long neck. He hadn't ridden out with his father on their land in more than fifteen years. George ran like the gods were after him, and Reed felt as invigorated as the day he stepped back on to American soil. It was so good to be home, back on his land. Oh, if he could just keep the peace with Patience Stephens.

He led George back to the small barn behind his office. Patience Chapman, he corrected himself. The woman who invited herself back to Hancock to live was now his wife. To think, just this morning, she'd opened the possibility for him to send her back to Lennhurst. And he had said *no*. The idea actually appalled him, as he walked in the back door and set his things on his desk. She was strange, but that asylum was chilling. Besides, he enjoyed someone much prettier than Fred keeping him enticed and aggravated.

Later in the afternoon, Reed closed a heavy law book, distracted by the note his mother had given him. Courting. What would have meaning and be something special to her? If there was a way to purchase a can of butterflies or ladybugs, but there wasn't. He drummed his fingers over the thick book. Joel had already built her boxes for her garden planting. It still seemed a bit early for seed planting. He glanced down at the law book. *Of course! She says, 'something I read in a book' all the time.* With a plan in mind, he headed for the door as Fred walked in.

"Chappy, I hope you've been here all morning, helping me with the Fisher investigation." Fred dropped his things on his desk.

"Yes, Fred, I have. I have four pages of testament and citations from as early as 1820." He handed the pages to him. "But I have to run to the library."

"More research I can only hope." Fred looked over Reed's work.

"Not for you." Reed smiled quickly, opening the door.

"Wait. I promised Janice I wouldn't forget." He handed Reed an invitation. "She's been busy at Dr. Nedows and won't have a chance to ride out for a social call. So, you are to be at our house Wednesday evening. And it's written right here, so all I have to do is read it and get you to come. Janice has everything. Chapmans don't need to bring anything."

Reed took the note. The Chapmans sounded odd to him.

"Annnd . . . blimey Reed, how did it go with your new wife?"

Reed stilled, rolling his lips together. He hated to give Fred any information to mock him with.

"Say no more. From the look on your face, an annulment is still on for the future." Fred nodded. "But legally the land is yours. You're certainly not considering quitting this fine establishment to go cut trees or anything?"

"No," Reed said abruptly. "Just get to work, so we can keep oil in the lamps and nappies for all those wet baby pants you are going to change."

"You don't say; I have to do nappies?" Fred blew out a huff and turned back to his desk.

REED CROSSED THE street and turned the corner onto South Avenue. A small, tinkling bell sounded over the library door as he entered. The place smelled like new paper, an obvious difference from his long nights at the stuffy Oxford library of books and antiquities. He noticed a shelf with a cookbook and many on how to keep house next to the Farmer's Almanac. A tall, thin woman with round glasses approached him. "May I help you find a book?"

"Humm." Reed scratched his chin. He didn't want to offend Patience. His mother and Sarah had taught her the basics. "I was thinking of something a new wife would find helpful."

"Oh well, yes." The woman smiled. "Any woman would enjoy this one. The author has included drawings with each recipe."

"All right. Thank you." He took the book and looked around.

"May I make one more suggestion?" The woman looked over her glasses at him. "For when her chores are all finished."

"Of course."

"We just got in a lovely fun tale." She reached around and grabbed a book off her desk. "It's called Alice in Wonderland." It appears to be a fantasy tale for children. But I've read articles that many of the references are based on Oxford and Christ's Church."

"Really, an English author?" His brow furrowed.

"Delightful story, I've read it myself." She smiled. "All kinds of animals come to life. Packs of playing cards dance, and there's even a caterpillar with pink hands."

Reed stilled. "I think we might save that for another time." He looked around until he found what he wanted. "I'll take the cookbook and Arabian Nights. That was a favorite for me." He checked out the books and thanked the librarian for her help. Coming back around his building, he loaded the books in his saddle bag. "Let's get home, George, maybe some reading is in order." He smiled as he saddled his horse and swung up. He didn't want any English authors, but he realized now, along with his new wife, he talked to animals.

CHAPTER 32

SOMETHING AKIN TO disappointment settled over Reed as he did his chores around the cottage Wednesday at dusk. Patience had been sincere and thankful for the books from the library. He'd read the first four chapters of Arabian Nights as they sat by the fire last night. It was the first resemblance of peace he'd known in weeks. She looked fine physically and he'd made a point to thank her for the simple dinner. Noticing earlier she'd packed a bag of cookies for someone then he remembered tonight they were at the mercy of Fred and Janice Beasley. After dropping fresh cut wood in the box next to the cook stove, he brushed the dirt off his sleeves.

From where he stood, a favorite past time distracted him. He could watch her in her room pinning her hair while holding a small mirror. Beautiful and graceful, her simple movements made his insides run warm. Truth be told, since Fred and Janice had married, he'd missed the companionship with his irritating friend. Cynthia Icely was an irksome substitute. But being married to Patience and sharing this little cottage, eating across from her and sometimes talking for hours had brought more comfort, more sentiment to him than he could have imagined. Or knew he needed. He'd never really pictured what it would mean to come home to a wife, to be settled down, but if this was it, it agreed with him. He swept to the door to grab her cape as she came out, knowing his face was flushed. He covered her shoulders then waited until she turned back to him to say, "You look wonderful."

The word desirable would have been closer to his thoughts.

She fastened the clasp at the neck and offered a small smile. He couldn't help but continue gazing at her, his wife. She'd twisted her long braid into a knot at her neck and looked timidly stunning in the flattering rose and yellow dress.

"So, you are ready?" He checked the fire, wishing they could just stay home. "Your first dinner party?"

"It's to be a party?" she said, wide-eyed.

"No, just the four of us." He grabbed his jacket and slid it on. "I wish I could guarantee Fred would stay verbally sober tonight."

"I don't understand." She squinted at him.

"I've never understood him either." He winked, lifted her hand and kissed the back. And there it was again. That strange sensation circling deep through his blood; a magnetic pull back to their childhood. Locking eyes with her he thought,

How could that pure trusting face make me question what I know has to be true. I've yet to see the actual burns on her back, but Lord above, it has to be her. Why else would this overwhelming—

"Reed?"

He came back to the moment. "Yes, we should be going."

SITTING AROUND THE small table of the Beasley home, Janice covered a giggle. "So then Reed says that Fred was loyal but untrustworthy. Smart but foolish. Moral but unprincipled. A vivacious weakling. What else Reed?"

"Jolly, with a load of rubbish." Reed imitated Fred's accent.

"And I knew right then." Janice pouted a silly smile at Fred. "That is the man for me!" Fred and Janice leaned over the table, lips pursed and kissed.

Reed looked to his quiet, reserved wife and flashed her a smile. She lifted a shy grin back.

Janice poured them all more coffee. "We've eaten and rattled on about ourselves the whole time. Please Patience, tell us what it was like to grow up in an insane asylum?"

Patience rolled her lips a few times, and her back stiffened. Was Janice's bluntness upsetting her?

"It was very difficult at first." Patience finally

249

looked at them. "I was on my stomach for weeks. My back was badly burned."

"Dear Lord, I've seen the peeling skin of burns from nursing in the war." Janice grimaced. "You poor child."

"And I spoke no English. So I cried a lot. I didn't understand what everyone was saying. I just wanted my family back. But then the fairies would come and comfort me."

Reed rubbed the crease between his eyes, cleared his throat and picked up his coffee.

"What do you mean, fairies?" Janice asked softly.

"When I could feel myself . . . um, drifting. I don't know the word. It was like falling asleep, but my eyes were open, and I could hear people talk or come in and out of the room. Kfall was the father fairy. He was strong with ebony legs and silver wings. He would come close to me and say, 'I will avenge.' Then there was the mother fairy. Her name was Delva. She would flutter close to me. Her wings were green like moss and blue, like the lake." She glanced at Reed. "The air from her wings would soothe the burning, and I could feel the comfort from her eyes. There were others who visited me." She eyed each of them. "I don't . . . think you want to hear about all that."

"It's fascinating, really," Janice said, leaning forward.

Reed held his breath hoping Fred wasn't going to find the humor.

"You were given laudanum for the pain, or maybe opium, I'm not sure," Janice added. "And your hallucinations came in the form of fairies visiting you. In your little child-like mind, they were the comfort you needed. Thank God for that, many people report demons and violent visions."

Patience moved her wedding ring back and forth on her finger. "Dr. Powell believed I needed to embrace them and what they mean to me."

Fred looked at Janice and back to Patience. "But you know now that fairies aren't real, right?"

"That's what Reed thinks," Patience murmured, looking at her cup. A long silence seemed to enhance the awkward moment.

"Tell us how you learned English?" Reed asked. So many things he didn't even know.

"Still laying on my stomach," she said somberly, "a teen girl named Anna, would lay on the floor with a slate and teach me the letters. Then she brought picture books with common objects, and I would practice the words. Sometimes she would bring items, like a fork or comb and hide them under a cloth. We would play games to see how many I could get right. Then little songs. Sometimes she would act out the little songs with little paper cutout characters."

"She sounds wonderful. She was a young nurse?" Janice asked.

"Anna? No," Patience shook her head. "She was a patient at Lennhurst. She'd killed her baby brother."

Fred rolled his wide eyes over to Reed, scratching under his chin.

"But it wasn't really her fault." Patience shrugged.

"So . . ." Janice searched for words. "As everyone there had different disabilities and mental limitations, they were allowed to roam free?"

"Not everyone. The building is like a large letter H. The front was for the less afflicted. The Friends of Pittsburg intended that every person would receive aid, sympathetic supervision, and religious oversight. I would say those residing in the back side of the building received *less* sympathy." She glanced at Reed. He nodded his agreement and smiled encouragement. "Anna and my friend Elias were from the back H. They were allowed to work and serve everyone. I never asked them, but I assumed they were without suitable funds and so Lennhurst allowed those that could to work."

"It makes sense." Fred nodded. "And those like you, who got there for other reasons were rehabilitated to join—join *us*—er—the rational ones."

"Oh yes," Janice elbowed Fred, "join us sane people? You know you had trouble finding your category." She laughed.

"I have some clients I'd like to send to the back H," Fred mumbled.

"And there are days I'd like to send you there," Reed said, mocking.

Patience turned to him. "Oh, Reed. Don't say that." The others reined in their snickers.

"I was born in Poland." Patience blinked. "Fred in England. This isn't our land of origin. When you come from so far away, it's hard to remove the sense of never belonging." The conversation stilled, and Fred ran a hand over his jaw. "So Fred is better at gaining belonging through what he does. He fights for people. He fights for their rights and gains justice. He stands up for them in the face of their accusers. Yes?" She looked at Fred, and he nodded back. "Fred is a champion in this foreign land, and he teases you Reed because he found he has weakness. He feels like he failed you when he was so sick, and so he tests you to see if you will still love him and assure him he belongs. And you do. You accept him and count him as a friend."

They all looked at each other and Reed thought something unusual misted in Fred's eyes.

Fred's hand trembled as he reached for his coffee. "Thank you for those words, Patience. Besides thinking you were just a plum pastry in the window, I couldn't see what my serious, determined Chappy saw in you. But now," he toasted her with his cup, "I understand."

CHAPTER 33

PATIENCE CAME OUT from her room the following Sunday morning, noticing a large brown paper package laying on the table. She glanced back at it as she started to make the coffee. Was it there last night when she went to bed? Reed opened the door to what was once Sarah's room. She was thankful to have her bed repaired and her own room back.

"Hello." She smiled at him. His hair was messy and shirt untucked. Rubbing his eyes, he stopped at the table and smiled at her.

"Is that your package?" She nodded to the table.

He shook his head and walked around her for a cup. "It's yours."

"Mine? I don't understand."

"The water is hot, would you like me to make your tea?" He quickly tapped the side of the kettle.

Patience looked down and saw his bare feet. It was still extraordinary to be living in a house with a man. "I'll do it. You know you have my curiosity."

"Then open it." He stood next to her.

Embarrassment is a strange emotion, she thought while unwrapping the paper. The heat rose up on her face as she touched a lovely blue and white flowered dress. "This is for me?" She lifted it in the air as it unfolded down near the floor. "It's beautiful." The white piping lined the bodice and sleeves. "I've never seen anything so fine." All the buttons looked like little pearls. "It must be store bought."

"Well, I didn't sew it." Reed seemed pleased with himself as he blew on his steaming coffee. "It's for you to wear to church today."

"I . . . I . . . don't know what to say. I am happy to stay with you and Rob."

"I know it's important to you. My parents will love having you. So now you have a new dress to wear."

She stilled, fingering the lovely fabric. "I have four dresses now. I can't imagine having that many."

"The two from Lennhurst are great for your work days, like when you want to garden. I'm going to get some eggs. I'll be right back." He set his cup down and went down the short hall and out the back door.

Shaking her head, she had to wonder. First the library books and reading to her at night. Then yesterday they had gone on a long ride on King George. Reed showed her the different sights and trails to their land. He knew so much, though trying to hold back, he was like a boy set free. The picnic he'd packed for lunch on the east side of the lake was special. He'd purchased two chocolate tarts from the bakery sometime before their outing. The thought of them made her mouth water. Now the opportunity to go to church in a new dress. Was this normal? A week ago they argued and fussed over the death of the trees, this week he was so generous. What would Dr. Powell say if she told him she was confused at which was to be real life with Reed Chapman?

She closed her eyes and tried to listen to her heart speak. The back door slammed, and Reed appeared with eggs held in his shirt. "Sorry I kicked it closed, I had my hands full." He carefully set them next to the basin and put the iron on the stove. "I'll cook these up while you get the wrinkles out."

Patience nodded. Delighted, but still confused, she flattened the dress on the table and admired it and the fine-looking giver.

THE REVEREND AND Mrs. Pearce stood outside the double doors after church. Patience watched them as she waited. The Pearces personally greeted each congregant with a touch, smile, or hug. Watching the little children laugh and run in from out front deeply warmed her soul. She could do this forever. A little girl smiled at her as she ran by. As Robert and Arita talked to people in line, she wished Reed could be standing by her. He said the hymn at their wedding had moved him. He would have enjoyed today. The songs were lifted to heaven as all the different families and voices sang their praise together. She inhaled a deep breath, standing in this lovely dress with all these people talking was more encompassing than she could even imagine. *"Thank you, Lord."* She whispered under her breath.

"Patience!" Mrs. Pearce turned and brought her forward for a hug. "How lovely to have you with us." Patience stiffened as Mrs. Pearce rubbed her hand up and down her back. "Robert and Arita are so delighted to have you in the family." Patience smiled, watching her in-laws laughing with the reverend just as a large plume of a feather attached to a broad-brimmed hat passed inches from them.

"Oh Miss Icely, you've had a chance to meet Mrs. Chapman?" Mrs. Pearce touched the bright pin-striped puffy sleeve.

Patience recognized the woman Reed had danced with at the spring dance.

"Not formally." The woman with pale skin batted bored eyes. "Forgive me, and I thought you were a friend of the family." Her eyes narrowed. "But if I had asked your last name, I would have noticed you must be a cousin or relation of Reed's."

Patience looked warily to Mrs. Pearce.

"Oh, how funny." Mrs. Pearce chuckled. "Last week she was just a friend, this week they have married and now she is a true family member."

Cynthia's eyes drooped. "How confusing. Who is she married to?"

Patience wondered why they held a conversation about her as if she wasn't standing in their midst. "I married Reed Chapman."

"No. No you didn't." Cynthia dropped her chin, sneering. "Is this some kind of inside joke?"

"Well ladies, why don't you talk down the steps?" Mrs. Pearce waved them on. "The line is backing up."

Patience looked to see the Chapmans already in another circle of people talking.

"You're married to Reed Chapman, that—that lives here in Hancock?" They stepped off the last step. "He's a lawyer and has a large horse named King George?"

"Yes," Patience said calmly.

"When did *that* happen?" Cynthia snapped.

Patience took a step back. Her lovely white skin was turning red. "Last Saturday."

"Really!" Her nose flared. "Not a week earlier he was escorting me to the spring dance. Putting on airs of courtship and favors only a man would want from a—a promised—ah—pre-declaration." She pursed her lips and flitted her eyebrows. "So I hope you know what you married. The man is as distracted as a grasshopper in a wheat field.

One woman one week, another woman the next. I only stepped out with him as a favor to my uncle. Really, it was always about getting King George in my uncle's thoroughbred line." She tapped along her perspiring eyebrow. "So sorry for you, you didn't even get a proper wedding." She looked past Patience. "I must go, my uncle is waiting." She turned so quickly Patience could feel the tempest of her presence move away.

Blinking back the impact of the woman's brash words, she watched as a young father lifted his boy in his arms and placed him carefully in the back of the wagon. His wife looked admiringly at him. Is that how it should be? Did she just assume Reed was a faithful, trustworthy person? What was the feeling this morning?

Was her heart trying to tell her to be careful? From their first meetings, he was helpful but rarely happy with her. She knew her ways and ideas could upset him. And then it turned so quickly, like this week had. What was she thinking the day he asked her to marry? She ran her hand down over the little pearl buttons. The beautiful fabric of the new dress, now light prickles making her back itch. Why hadn't they gotten to know each other better before marriage? Even when she was angry about the trees, he was almost laughing at her. Now Miss Icely's accusations mixed with her own. She brushed away the moisture from her eyes as the Chapmans approached.

"We didn't mean to leave you standing here." Robert smiled. "Arita has to catch all the news with everyone on Sundays. We should have warned you."

Arita turned and spoke with another woman.

"Robert," Patience said quietly, fighting the sharp pain her throat. "Can you tell me why you married Arita?"

"Ah, well." He rocked his head back and forth. "Look at her. She is warm and friendly, wants to help in any way she can. She's a great mother, but I guess I didn't know that, yet." He grinned. "So. I'd say because she loved me. I'd always admired her from afar. But when you know that wonderful person has true feelings for you, it's like a room filled with a warm light inside you."

"What are *true* feelings? What do they sound like or look like?"

"Oh goodness, Patience, you're asking me the tough ones." He shuffled his feet. "Are you sure you shouldn't ask Arita?"

Patience tried to blink away the rising tears. First Miss Icely's unpleasant words hurt beyond what she's known, and Robert didn't want to explain. How could she find serenity for her heart? Now she was the butterfly released without a safe leaf to land upon.

"Are we ready?" Arita turned. "I'm sorry I

gabbed so—Patience, something happened. I'm so sorry I lost track of time and—"

Patience shook her head. "No, no it's not you." She swallowed and wiped her face with her hand. "This is all just so new to me."

Arita glared at Robert, and he shrugged looking at the ground.

CHAPTER 34

PATIENCE SAT RIGID at Reed's parents' cloth-covered Sunday table. She'd helped set the rose point plates and silver. She held Robbie's hand at the meal prayer, but Reed could tell something was wrong. She wouldn't smile or look him in the eye. The agreeable sermon was discussed and the usual talk of the town, so what could have upset her? He'd bought her a new dress and arranged for her to attend church. Would she always be this hard to understand?

"So you *liked* church?" Reed asked Patience, trying to read her.

"Mmm, yes. Very much." She looked at her plate and stabbed a carrot.

"I don't know where I left my manners." Arita helped Robbie take a bite of mashed potatoes. "I should have introduced you to more people."

"She talked to—ah—" Robert snapped his fingers. "Mr. Edwin's niece. What is her name?"

Reed's head shot up. "Cynthia? Miss Icely?" He looked wide-eyed at Patience. She didn't respond. Her face flushed, and her eyes locked on her plate answered his question.

"Oh Lord, come quickly," he mumbled. "What did she say to you?"

She pushed some peas with her fork and barely shook her head. "Nothing," she whispered.

"Patience." He set his hand on her arm. She jerked from his touch and knocked her water all over her plate and starched tablecloth.

"Oh no!" She rose. "I'm so sorry." She picked up her plate and carried it to the basin. "Reed, I want to go. Can we go? Please." She dabbed the table with her napkin.

"Please, Patience. Get a new plate." Arita stood and helped her. "If I had a dime for every glass that spilled on this table, I could buy a new house. It's fine, dear, look it's all cleaned up."

Taking her cape, Patience was already heading toward the door. "Reed, you stay and finish." She reached for the handle. "I can ask Sarah for a ride."

She was out the door before he could get up from his seat. He took his last forkful of potatoes and gravy.

"Thank you." He mumbled with his mouth full. Grabbing his jacket, he hurried out the door.

"Patience, wait!" He went from jog to run to catch up with her. "Do you know you are strong and fast?" He tried to get her attention as he walked next to her. Grabbing her arm didn't seem like a good idea. "Let's go to the corral, and I'll get King George. I'll take you home."

She stopped suddenly, her face a mixture of pain and confusion. "Very well." She swung around him and marched toward the corral.

REED TETHERED KING George in the front of the cottage. She still hadn't said a word, and he was at a loss how to explain the nonsensical bitter Cynthia Icely. Her cat came around to greet her at the front door, but she walked past and shut the door. As he stepped onto the porch, he could see through the window she'd gone into her room and closed the door. He turned and sat on the low step of the porch. The cat came in purring and circled around his feet. He pulled his fingers through the soft fur and removed an old leaf from the cat's underside. Sighing, he dropped his chin on his arm resting on his knee. "I thought I was doing better. You got any ideas?" he said to the cat.

PATIENCE HAD CHANGED back into her gray plaid dress from Lennhurst and sat on her bed. *One woman one week and one woman the next,* rang back and forth in her head. She saw for herself he was with Cynthia at the dance. The two of them had an earlier dinner engagement the first night they sat at his parents' table. It was so confusing, was it her naiveté again or being misled by someone she longed to trust with her delicate affections? Both notions were crushing her heart. Why did Dr. Powell allow her to go with him? She dropped her head to the side. It wasn't Dr. Powell's fault. She wanted to come back to this land. She tried to find her own way. There was a soft knock at the door.

"Patience, would you come out and talk to me?"

"Lord, give me Your strength," she whispered and opened the door. They walked down the short hall and sat in the chairs in front of the fireplace. Reed rested his elbows on his knees and clutched his hands together, obviously tense.

"I wish you would tell me what she said. She's given me a few tongue lashings where I wondered if they left marks."

"What's a tongue lashing?"

"She's got a scorching mouth. Though she appears to be a Southern lady, when she's riled, all kinds of mean things fly from those lips."

"She did no such thing with me." Patience stood, her back starting to itch. "She commented on the haste of our wedding and your instability." She didn't want to talk about the root of her hurt; that he was capricious with women and they'd married too soon. She turned to look out the front window.

Reed sighed and rocked his head back and forth. "I wanted you to have a positive experience at church. I know that was something—"

"Did you or do you care for that woman?" She was surprised her voice did not waver.

"Now, no." He moved over to the window next to her, rubbing his temple.

"But at one time you cared for her?" She glanced up at him.

"Yes, but that's because I didn't really know how selfish and—and malicious she was."

"So you toyed with her affections before you got to know her?"

"I—don't like—" he gripped his forehead. "Really, Patience, I don't like—how that sounds. I didn't—what are you accusing me of?" His eyes narrowed.

"Toying with women, before you get to know them," she said, quickly.

"Women? Like I'm a rogue all over Hancock? Roaming to see who I can exploit?" Now his face turned red, and he clutched his hands behind his neck.

"I don't know," she declared. "I didn't know you long enough to know these things."

"You could have known me for a year, and you would see I don't 'toy' with women's affections. You can ask Fred." He stared at her. "I can tell by the look on your face. You don't believe me." He clenched his jaw until a vein began to bulge. "I have a wife who believes in fairies but doesn't believe me." He let out a low groan and turned away. "And maybe she shouldn't." He grumbled dropping into the chair running his hands down his face. Their differences were pulling her heart apart, again. "I don't know if you belong here," she murmured, "with me—" her tone sounding despondent. "I'm not sure if caring for one another is enough." She felt her body break out in cold sweat. "I never felt as happy as the day we said our vows in front of the reverend. But what do I do with this crushing of my heart? You have taken time to bring books and read and—" her tears quickened as she remembered his attempts at kindness. "And—and buy me lovely things—" she sucked in a sob.

Reed stood up and moved closer holding her quaking shoulders in his large, warm hands. "Don't you think I'm scared? You crank me up and down like the bucket from the well. I can't ever relax. Are we going to be lovers or—or are we just housemates, how long does one court his wife? And now I wonder if we can ever get past life's problems. Cynthia Icely is a problem." He gave her a small shake. "I don't know what she said, but she filled your head with doubt and regret." He brushed away a tear on her cheek. Heaven above, she loved it when he brushed her tears away. Something tender began to replace the ache in her body. She whispered, "How do you get rid of doubt and regret?"

"I don't know." He chuckled low, gently wrapping his arms around her. Her arms came up around him, and he kissed her temple. "Just don't kick me out yet. Please. Let me prove to you who I am."

She could feel his smooth muscled back through his shirt. It felt right to touch him. "When I first met you, all I could see was your cold presence. It's somehow part of your commanding manner." His embrace slackened. Patience ran her hands down his arms and leaned back watching his eyes narrow. "I think it has worked for you, the way you govern yourself. Your past, your time away from here has withheld your dreams, and so you rise up in an abundance of strength and control."

"Oh, I'd like to know where you get these insights." He whispered, pulling her closer, sliding his hands around her waist, slowly kissing near her ear, her cheek.

She began to forget what she was saying, and her limbs were strangely tingling. His lips were coming closer to hers. They both jumped and separated at the knock on the door. "I didn't hear anyone ride up." Reed went to the window and turned to her with piercing wide eyes.

"It's Dr. Powell. From Lennhurst."

CHAPTER 35

REED OPENED THE door and cleared his throat. "Dr. Powell, sir. How wonderful to see you, won't you please come in?" He took his coat and bag as Dr. Powell turned to Patience with out-stretched arms.

"Moj drogi." She ran into his embrace. "Jestes tutaj!"

Reed stood back like an uninvited guest. The embrace was touching, but what had she said to him? Did Dr. Powell speak Polish? He walked to the window. Just a small carriage sat out front. Was he here to take her back? He spun on his heel, his pulse drumming.

"I got lucky, I guess." Dr. Powell released Patience's hand, smiled and turned to Reed. There was only one place open for supper in Hancock, and the owner knew of you, Reed, and gave me directions. But I ended up at your parents' home, and they told me how to find the two of you here. I had some questions of course, but it was already getting dark, but this," he gestured wide, "this is the family land?" He looked back and forth from Reed to Patience.

"Yes, this is the Polish land." *It was also my*

family's land. Reed tried slowing his breathing, so he could think straight. "That Patience chose to live on. This was the caretaker's cottage."

Patience smiled. "It's perfect, really. I don't think I'd ever been inside as a child. But Reed found some people to help me make it livable. Now it feels like home." She beamed. "And I want to show you the lake. It's beautiful and, please, Dr. Powell, you must stay here with us." She looked at Reed quickly. "I will be starting my own garden area soon. I have many of the plants I enjoyed at Lennhurst ready to seed. Can you stay, we can go on a tour tomorrow."

"Yes, thank you. I would enjoy your hospitality." Dr. Powell nodded.

Reed flashed a smile and slipped away while they talked. Entering his room he grabbed all the clothing and papers strewn all over the floor and shoved them in the small wardrobe. Where would he sleep tonight? Does Dr. Powell know they are married? He walked back out to see their eyes on him.

"So Patience says you two were married. Just a week ago?" Dr. Powell looked skeptical.

Reed pressed his lips into a thin line and nodded. When would his conscience not hound him? "I know it seems somewhat too quick. But—"

"What happened to the woman you wrote me about?" Dr. Powell looked to Patience.

"Sarah." Patience spoke up. "She is still helping me a few afternoons while Reed is at work."

Of course, Patience had written him. Maybe this was just a friendly visit, to check on his favorite patient. Then why did he feel like his hand was caught in a steel trap?

"And Rob is your older brother?" he asked Reed.

"Yes, sir."

"Patience said he was a special man to the Union Army and to your family." He waited, looking Reed over. "I remember you talking about him when I first met you."

Reed nodded. Dr. Powell was assessing him. Almost as deeply as Reed assessed his bond with Patience. Dr. Powell was not God, and he was not the devil. As a lawyer, he was a trained negotiator for heaven's sake. He could handle this.

"I would love to meet him sometime." Dr. Powell nodded turning to Patience.

"Please come and sit." She extended her hand to the green chairs. "May I get you some coffee?"

Dr. Powell sat and waggled his head. "I think not, it was a long trip here, and I don't need it keeping me awake."

Reed watched them squeeze hands as Patience took the other green chair. "I'll go see to your horse." He grabbed his jacket off the peg and went out.

"I KNOW I could have just written you back." Dr. Powell smiled. "But after all my years at the asylum, I needed to have an excuse to do a home visit."

"Your timing could not have been better for me. I feel the leading of God and the confidence to walk ahead." She looked toward the door. "And then the next minute, I find myself upset and doubting. Not so much a loss of faith. I feel His presence every day."

"What do you doubt, Patience?"

"I think it is Reed. My wavering is usually centered on him. Do all new wives feel this way?"

Dr. Powell chuckled and rocked in his chair. "I've been a lot of things, but never a new wife."

"Certainly." She smiled.

"And, unfortunately, those at the asylum aren't in your position. Is it because it happened so fast? Do you think you love him?"

"Oh, Dr. Powell." She huffed. "What does love look like?"

"You might guess what I'm going to say." He gave her a fatherly look. "Love should be patient with one another. Mutual kindness, not trying always to be right. Also looking out for the welfare of the other person. When mistakes are made or hurts happen, can you forgive? Does he forgive you and not hold these things against you? Do you feel safe with him?"

She nodded.

"Does he—" They both looked up to hear Reed coming in the back door. "We will talk in the morning?"

She nodded.

"And if I have your permission, may I speak to him alone?"

"Yes." She answered as Reed walked into the kitchen and grabbed a chair from the table.

"Mr. Chapman, please. I have taken your place to rest at your hearth." Dr. Powell stood up slowly and gestured to the chair.

"No sir, I'll be fine."

Dr. Powell came close and patted him on the back. "I'm used to retiring early. Please take your place. You are so kind to offer an unexpected guest a place to sleep. Where will you put me that I won't be in your way?"

"That door on the right." Reed pointed to where he'd been sleeping. "The outhouse is just out the back door, and there is a nuisance of a rooster that won't allow any of us to sleep in."

"Perfect. Thank you both for taking me in. Patience, I look forward to talking tomorrow." He nodded as he headed down the short hallway.

Reed watched him and heard the door click closed. Taking a few steps into the parlor, he stood silent, feeling a myriad of conflicting emotions. Patience sat in the green chair, still and rigid.

"He wants to talk to you." She finally broke the silence.

"Good." Reed rubbed his creased brow. "I'm going to ask him about your benefactor. He must know who it is. And how that box of jewelry just showed up. Does he speak Polish?"

Patience finally looked into his eyes. "I—don't think so—why?"

"Because you said something to him when he walked in."

"I did?"

"I don't know what you said. But it wasn't English."

Patience watched the low embers of the crackling fire. "This was such a strange evening, and I don't remember saying anything." Her long lashes fluttered. Pulling her thick braid around to her chest she pulled out the tie. Drawing her fingers through her hair, it cascaded brown silk around her shoulders.

Reed watched his wife's slow, rhythmic movements, somehow strange desires awakened. He cleared his throat. "Where am I sleeping tonight?"

She pushed her hair to her back and looked around the small parlor. Her eyes revealed uncertainty as she stood and looked toward Dr. Powell's closed door.

"I suppose in my room." Patience twitched

her wedding ring back and forth on her finger.

He fought ten images coming at him all at once, the prominent one was imagining his hands and arms twisted throughout all her thick hair. He nodded, forcing a calm countenance.

CHAPTER 36

REED BANKED THE fire and dropped his boots by the chair. Patience picked them up and set them by the door and walked into her room. He wondered if he should offer to read while she prepared for bed. He smelled his shirt. Thankfully he was able to bathe today at his parents' while Robbie slept. A small flicker of light made a line on the wood floor of the short hallway. She'd left the blessed door open, which was too distracting. Walking to her door, he gripped the sides of the door frame. "Can I come in?"

She nodded twice, barely looking at him. She was sitting erect on the little chair, and that reminded him again of the first time he'd seen her. Little did he know then, she was no porcelain doll. He carefully closed the door. "Can I ask you a question?" He pulled his tucked shirt out.

"Mmm, hum." She tapped her fingers together on her lap.

"When you sit. I know it is proper for a woman not to slouch. But I wondered if that was because of your back or something you were taught."

He waited wondering if he'd offended her. One of her shoulders slumped awkwardly lower and lower. He questioned what that was about until her smile began to rise.

"Is that better, Mr. Chapman?" Her eyes sparkled with mischief.

Good Lord, she should not tease him. It made him want to grab her and forget her doctor wasn't in the next room. "Are you going to sit there and watch me undress?" He retaliated, pulling his shirt off.

"No." Standing quickly, she turned toward the window.

Reed dropped everything but his drawers. He sat on the edge of the bed. "You may turn around."

She glanced over her shoulder. "Are you not going to turn around for me?"

"Nope." His voice dipped. "I'm your husband, and I know the law. Somewhere it says I get to see everything."

"Oh no, you—" She reached for the lamp and blew it out just as he rose to catch her arm. "Please let me go." She broke away as the smoke swirled in the dark shadows. "Someone has left their things all over my floor." She stepped around him and pulled his things off the floor, setting them on her chair.

As soon as she turned, he grabbed her waist and pulled her against him. Feeling her warm hands on his skin was making what he had to say unreasonably difficult. "This might be the hardest thing I've ever done." He tried not to look at her soft lips. "And hear me when I say this Patience Chapman; I don't want anyone but you. Please believe that. But when you and I are going to—" he floundered for the right words, "to *be* together. There won't be any doubts in your head and there won't be anyone in the next room. This poor bed has already felt the two of us, and I don't want Dr. Powell wondering what you are doing to me."

She gasped and pushed away from his low chuckle. Watching him like a hawk, she backed up into the right corner of the room.

Her long hair covered her loveliness, but Reed enjoyed watching every teasing moment of every little hook and button she undid. He started to change his mind. What was that he'd just said about their being alone without company? He turned quickly toward the closed door and rested his forehead on the thin wood. Watching her undress was going to make him lose his common sense. Was it just a few hours ago she was ready to label him the town scoundrel, and he'd wondered if they had enough goodwill to stay married? Not to mention Patience voicing that doubt aloud. Right now he was feeling a lot more than goodwill towards his wife.

PATIENCE GRABBED HER nightgown from the drawer. She released one arm of her dress and quickly threaded her nightgown on that arm.

The thin white fabric came over her head, and she pulled her dress down as her nightgown fell over her body. Hanging her dress on the peg, she felt the room go from hot to cold as shivers ran over her skin. How would she ever find sleep? Just watching Reed lean into the door was exhilarating. Even in the dark, he had a strong back, narrow waist, and rounded muscular arms. Touching his skin moments ago was more dizzying than she could imagine. She backed into the corner again.

"Can I turn around?" he said softly.

"Yes," she whispered.

He started to say something and clamped his mouth. It was going to be a long night of staring at each other from the corners of the room.

"I do want to do the right things by you, Patience. I'm not perfect, but I'm not a rogue either."

Oh, if he only knew the torrid things conflicting her right now. The sincerity of his tone, intense, green eyes, and being alone with him all of it was melting her like wax.

"You look cold," he nodded toward the bed, "go to bed. I will wait till I think you're asleep."

It was only two steps from the corner to the end of her bed. She pulled up her gown to kneel on the bed and crawl forward. Pulling the bedding back quickly, she felt the cold sheets and pulled her gown down around her legs. Locking the pillow under her head, she faced the wall and prayed the darkness hid her unease and that Reed would suddenly become deaf so he couldn't hear her ragged breathing.

It seemed like an hour, but undoubtedly less, she heard her repaired bed creak under the weight of her husband's entrance. Would it hold both of them? How embarrassing to make any noise with Dr. Powell in the next room. The good doctor had often told her of his wife and nine children. Knowing Reed must be laying on his back, his shoulder lightly touched her back. What was she just thinking? *Oh, yes, Dr. Powell. Dr. Powell had nine children. Goodness, there must be a lot of love in his home. What had Janice said? She wanted to be a victim of her husband's passion all her days.* Warmth, suddenly radiated like a large warming pan, encompassing the entire bed. She pulled her pillow close and winced. Reed was lying on her hair. In all the nervousness, she forgot to braid it. Clutching her hair next to her neck, she tried to pull it free slowly. The bed rocked, and he came off his pillow.

"Am I on your hair?" he whispered.

"Yes, but I have it now." She twisted it, laying it along her neck. Please go back to sleep."

"I can't sleep." He murmured. "I keep thinking I'm going to come home from work tomorrow and you're going to be gone."

"Reed." Concern lined her tone. "This is my

home. Dr. Powell is just checking on me." She held her hair and laid on her back, their shoulders touching.

"What if he'd driven up after your talk with Cynthia? What if he'd driven up when you ran from my parents' home today?" He squeezed his brows together.

"But he didn't. God orchestrates our moments." She tugged the covers up. "I believe you when you say she is angry. This morning when Mrs. Pearce said we had gotten married, Miss Icely said 'no you didn't.' "

Reed turned his face to her. "It's my fault." He let go a gusty sigh. "I said clearly to Cynthia, we never had a future together. I reluctantly escorted her to the dance because I had forgotten to attend supper at her home. But she doesn't listen." He shook his head. "You were the only one I cared to dance with. If you wondered why I wanted to marry quickly, I was school-boy jealous how the other gentlemen fawned over you." He raised his hands, rubbing his face then reached past to grab the headboard.

Patience felt her stomach flip, his thick defined arms were so close. She swallowed hard and turned back to face her wall.

"I was afraid that you, being so fine, would make an attachment with someone else." He sighed.

Patience chewed her lip and drew the letters of

his name over the rough wood of the cottage wall she faced. His words were endearing. Maybe Dr. Powell could help her understand why his voice sounded regretful.

"Dr. Powell told me, to remember my favorite memories as I went to bed and thank God for His blessings." She turned back to look at him. His bare arms rested on top of the covers.

"Tell me your favorite memory." She whispered, unintentionally running her finger across his shoulder.

"Mmm." His eyes flashed to her touch, and she quickly hid her fingers back under the covers. "It would have to be working alongside my grandfather. In many ways, Rob was much like my dad. I'm trying to think why I admired my grandfather so." He reached under the quilt and found her hand. His fingers intertwined into hers. "I was just a boy, everything about him was grand. His vision for the mill, horses, and his time made me feel valuable." He turned to his side. All of his body just a feather away, at least their hands rested between them on the bed instead of on her. The peace lingered a few minutes. "That's really what you do for people." He sighed.

She stared at the ceiling. Was it his words or the wall and his masculine body trapping her that made her senses on alert? "I'm not sure what you mean," she said, breathless.

"You tell people things about themselves. Like

you know what they need to hear." He let go of her hand and brushed her hair up on her pillow. "Like the way you talk to Robbie or even Fred. I think you almost made Fred cry."

She glanced askance at him. "I—I didn't mean to."

"I wish my grandfather were alive." He yawned. "But then I couldn't be thankful for sleeping here next to you." Rolling to his stomach, he pushed his pillow up against the headboard. "Heavens above, you smell good." The little room lingered in stillness. "I need to focus on sleep. I should say goodnight."

Patience took in a deep breath, thankful he hadn't asked her a favorite memory. How could she try to explain this euphoric feeling of lying next to him? Without explaining how deep loneliness can paralyze a soul?

Feeling her own body relax, she listened to his breathing grow deeper. If his grandfather were alive, why could they not have met?

CHAPTER 37

DR. POWELL FOLLOWED Patience on the trail out to the ruins of the large house the next morning. "Ah, the sunshine and visit are good for my body and soul," he said. "As is seeing you rehabilitated." He flashed a sad grin. "Though I believe in restoration for every soul. You are one of the rare few I see go on to a productive life." The looming large brick fireplace came into view. "This is it?"

"Yes." She stopped and stared at the desolate ruins. They both seemed to need the reflective silence.

"Say, do you remember Elias Browne?" Dr. Powell spoke first.

"Yes." Her voice and face lit up.

"He is married and living in Denver City. Colorado territory. We got a letter from his wife, looking for Anna."

Patience's mouth hung open. Her two dearest friends from Lennhurst. "How wonderful." She felt a strange pang of delight mixed with remorse. "I always wondered about him." She murmured. "Living in Colorado, so far from the east. And what of Anna?"

"I will drop their addresses in the mail to you when I return. I don't know if I ever told you, but Anna was the one who picked your name. She said you were the most patient girl she'd ever met."

Following Dr. Powell as he walked around the area commenting on her few memories, Patience silently wondered if what Anna had said was true. She'd changed completely from the shy isolated girl who loved her time in the gardens. "How can I be more patient with my husband? I . . ." she sighed. "I don't know if it is proper to ask, but we are very different," she said touching a long piece of grass.

"Ahh, yes. A new marriage. I prayed for you last night." Dr. Powell stopped and looked at her. "I feel a bit remiss. Of all the things we talked about. We never talked about marriage." He breathed in deeply. "Men and women are different. That *is* what God intended. You won't ever see things in just the same light, except for the truth of God's Word, and the foundation you set for your marriage and family. Those important things you should agree on."

Patience shook her head. "And the times you don't agree." She looked away, remembering the riotous night they broke the bed.

"You must talk and share your feelings. There are reasons behind all our fears and worries." They walked on the trail toward the lake.

"Reed has plans for this land. It upsets me when he talks about cutting down the trees. Yet, I understand his reasoning. I just don't want to see the trees cut."

"All right." Dr. Powell followed the trail to the lake and stopped. "Beautiful. The mountains, trees, water, I can see why you wanted to return." After a few minutes of gazing at the soft blue water, he spoke. "What do the trees mean to you?"

Patience stewed for a moment. Scratching her head, "I don't know, besides homes for all the flying creatures. But it was the way he called it Chapman land. I guess I don't like that. Chapman trees, Chapman land. I feel left out. I feel like my parents' lives don't matter to him. At least not as much as the trees do."

"So, what is that feeling?"

Patience had missed these special times with his fatherly tone. "I guess feeling alone. Feeling left out." She murmured.

"Can I ask you to think of the overall days of your life? Where do those feeling usually connect?" he asked.

"With the death of my family." She inhaled slowly and exhaled quickly. "You think I need to look at those feelings of grief, over what Reed is wanting with the land?"

"Possibly," Dr. Powell said as they walked out onto the dock. "Can we pray now and listen for God's voice."

Patience breathed in the mossy fresh air coming off the water. Closing her eyes, she felt the increased stillness of God's presence hovering over her body and mind. "Wings. I see wings. They are very large and thick and they have an iridescent glow about them." Listening, she pulled her palms up from her sides, holding them open. "They're not mine." She chuckled, eyes still softly closed. "They are not my lovely fairies Kfall's or Delva's wings. Oh no, not close. They are the wings of an angel assigned to my care. The life of God pulses through these beautiful feathers. Oh! I hear a voice from heaven saying, 'I have always been with you. I have always covered you with My wings. Trust me, beloved child. I see you and will never leave you.'" She waited, the feeling of weightlessness surrounded her being.

"Amen." Dr. Powell reverently whispered. "Trees may be cut down and others grow back. But the wings of God's love and protection will never change."

Patience opened her eyes, smiling at Dr. Powell.

REED LOOKED UP from his desk when he heard someone at his office door.

"Sir." He stood quickly as Dr. Powell entered. "Is everything all right?" Coming around his desk, he wished his voice didn't sound so suspicious.

"Everything is fine." The older man nodded. The fine lines around his eyes creasing. "If you are here alone, may we talk for a while?"

"Yes, I apologize for leaving so early. Patience was asleep and—"

"No, no problem. We had a delightful morning walking and talking. The lake and surrounding areas do speak to tranquility and rest."

Reed pulled out the chair next to his desk for the doctor.

"I worried living back near her old home that it might cause some backlash for Patience." He looked long at Reed. "But she seems to be adjusting. And she has a husband."

Reed sat behind his desk, wringing his hands unseen. "Are you planning on staying tonight?"

"No. I've said my goodbyes to Patience and will return to Brown Township this evening."

If the silence was to make a point to Reed, it was working. He swallowed hard. "I hesitate to ask, but feel I must." Reed ran his fingers quickly from chin to neck. "Patience says she has a benefactor." He waited.

"Yes. She does," Dr. Powell said.

"Who could that be? Is it you?"

"It isn't me." He met Reed eye to eye.

"I don't understand. Maybe Patience has told you. Some strange things are happening around the property. Someone changed out all the rotten wood around the dock. Five crosses suddenly appeared by the house ruins. Things only some-one who knows the family would know. She has made friends with a few people from the mill, but they all deny it has been them. Then the box of fine jewelry shows up here at the office the day of our wedding."

"You sound worried."

"Of course I am. She is the only survivor of a terrible tragedy. What if someone wants her dead?" Reed stood, the chair scraping loud against the wood floors. "I was the one who knew she shouldn't be on that land. I never felt right about it." He stepped away and turned back.

Dr. Powell stared at him steadily. "You could sell it and take her to live somewhere else?" he said calmly.

"She's more stubborn than me," Reed huffed. "She wants to plant gardens and make a sani-tarium of some kind."

"But you are her husband. What would you do to keep your family safe?"

Reed chewed on his words. The land was everything. His family depended on it. He glanced at the doctor who waited for his answer. "My parents sent me to Oxford to keep me safe, and I've regretted it a hundred times."

Dr. Powell nodded. "The Stepanov family fled Poland to find safety. That seems to be what families do, but we cannot all pick the outcomes.

You are here, and they are not. Do you begrudge Mr. Stepanov for what he did?"

"No." Reed remembered that Stepanov was Patience's real last name. "He did what he thought was right." Reed clutched the back of his chair.

"And yet your family did what they thought was right."

Reed shook his head. How did this go from her benefactor to his problems? More silence hung in the air as he fought rising anger.

"I talked with Patience earlier about the things we believe." Dr. Powell rose and put the chair back. "There is no shame in protecting your own. I have nine children, and I would do anything in my power to keep them all safe. I would hope they have seen my attempts as a gift, a sacrifice for the things closest to our heart. Jesus went to the cross for the joy set before Him. His sacrifice would change all mankind. Now you are the husband. What will you choose to believe?"

Reed followed him to the door. He had no answer, and Dr. Powell didn't seem to need one.

"I will be praying for you, Mr. Chapman." Dr. Powell opened the door. "Your life and beliefs are more valid than your circumstances tell you they are." He nodded and walked out. Reed watched him pull his carriage to the side and climb in. What had Patience told the eccentric doctor? His beliefs are more valid than his circumstances?

Which circumstances would that be? That the land was now back as Chapman land? Or his disbelief of what he had done to gain it? Reed watched as Dr. Powell from Lennhurst Asylum drove his carriage down Main Street, Hancock, Pennsylvania. It seemed like watching something from a strange mismatched dream.

Chapter 38

DARK GRAY CLOUDS were rolling in late in the afternoon as Reed swung up on King George. "Great," he murmured, kicking George and leading him out of town. He'd already had to bring an hour or more of work home tonight due to Dr. Powell's visit.

It really wasn't the visit, it was the inability to focus after he left. Why couldn't the man just tell him what he knew about her benefactor? If no one was out to hurt her, then just spell it out. He was her husband, he had a right to know everything concerning her. Reed pulled his jacket tighter.

It was a little too late for Dr. Powell to pick apart his thoughts on family and sacrifice. His grandmother made her choice. His parents already put him on the boat. Robbie had already made the sacrifice. He'd done what was expected, built a lawyer business his family could be proud of. Had Dr. Powell figured out the night before the drive from his parents to the cottage was border to border with the Polish land? Likely so. A raindrop hit his face. *Take Patience and leave the area,* had been Dr. Powell's suggestion. The wise old doc was testing him. He was trying to see what he was made of. Four or five more drops hit his jacket and face and he gripped his satchel and let King George run. "Grit and tenacity, old man," he grumbled as he rode onto his land. Rain started to fall.

At least Patience had not left with Dr. Powell. He sighed, undeniably, there was something he needed from her. More than what he wanted last night, some attachment had woven in under his skin. The desire, like this moment, to see her at the end of the day. The way she moved around the small kitchen making their simple meals. Her smile and the way she pulled on her wedding ring when she was nervous. The utter calm and belonging he felt waking up to her this morning. To have her all to himself. He looked closer approaching the cottage. His father's horse was tied up to a tree. "Now what?" He sighed.

Reed dropped his satchel on the kitchen table and looked at Patience as she held two mugs of hot coffee.

"Looks like a bit of rain," Robert said as he walked from the green chairs to take the mug from her hand. Reed felt his chest relax. Nothing looked terribly wrong.

"Here you take this one," Patience offered as he dropped his coat on the chair.

"Thank you." He lifted a small smile.

She took his coat and hung it on the peg. The

way she watched him from under those long lashes, truly stunning eyes, made Reed's stomach flip. "Is everything all right at home?" he asked before taking a sip.

"Everything is fine." Robert set his coffee on the table. "I wanted to ask you a favor, but I think you and Patience should talk it over." He pulled some papers from his pocket. "I got two letters just this week." He handed them to Reed. "Both seem like good bids for our lumber. I've tried to determine which one is to our benefit. One is just for the trees, and one is for the milled wood. Both have the potential for us to supply the companies on a long-term basis."

Patience turned back to the stove and added some potatoes to a bubbling pot.

Robert kept talking. "I'd like you to think about going with me for a few days. Checking out the operations, looking over the numbers. But I feel it's a lot to ask, with a new wife and the load at the lawyer office."

"I'll go." Reed could feel the negotiations and opportunity pulsing in his blood.

"Patience," Robert spoke to her back. "I've already asked Arita, and she would love to have you for a few days."

"Please tell her thank you, but I'll be here, working on the garden." Her tone was different, unsettling to Reed's attuned ears.

Reed set the papers down and walked around

the table to the warm stove. "It could be raining for days. Would you think about it?" He let his hand rest on her back.

"I would be willing to *talk* it over."

Her words and tone nicked his conscience. Once again he'd jumped to a decision, forgetting her sensitivity to the trees. He pulled his hand away.

Turning back to the table, he held up the papers. "Half a day's ride to get to Ellenburg. Then onto Pittsburg. Depending on what other bids they might be taking, we should be able to see it through in two days. I'll need to talk to Fred." Patience's metal spoon dropped in the tin basin. "Then we would have to discuss how the mill would keep up with the demand." Reed turned to see her straight back wearing a large bow from her apron. "I have some ideas about that. We could talk about that on the road."

"All right. Let me know tomorrow. I'll let you two get to supper." Robert came over to Patience and wavered from patting her shoulder or back. He quickly bent and kissed her on the cheek. "Thanks for the coffee, Missy."

Patience turned and smiled at Robert. Reed recognized that soft mist in her eyes. She was upset or touched by his father's endearment or vexed with another female infraction. He blew out a breath walking his father to the door. This may not be easy.

HER CHIPPED BEEF gravy over potatoes was good, he'd told her twice. The cottage looked nice. He'd said that too, even *after* she dropped his boots in the room Dr. Powell had slept in.

"What of your visit with Dr. Powell?" He looked up at her as he reached for another oatmeal cookie. "These are good." Crumbs fell all over the table, and he swept them onto the floor.

"It was lovely." She leaned to look at the crumbs on the floor.

"Lovely because?" His hand reached out and caught hers, gently kneading her palm.

"Because . . . I . . . he helps me hear from the Lord. Helps me remember that God has not left me."

Reed wasn't expecting that. Sitting back, he slowly released her hand. Looking around at the evening shadows, he wanted to find the right words. "If I travel with my father, do you perceive me leaving you?"

She dropped her head to the side. "Of course. It is what you are doing."

"I mean . . . well, not in the count of days. But in your heart?"

She watched the rain dribble off the front porch. Her silence sliced through him.

"Then I'll just say it." He sat up. "I hate leaving you. I know we've only lived together a few weeks, but I don't like going through an hour at work without seeing you." His honest confession felt good.

Patience drew her fingers slowly over the rough wood table. "Dr. Powell said my fears are not about you cutting down my—I mean the trees."

"He did?" Reed found his opinion of the nosey doctor rising. "What did he say?"

"That my fear is from losing my family. That my anger should not be towards you and your decisions."

Reed wondered how soon Dr. Powell could come back. At this moment the man was a genius. "But there is something wrong." He reached for her hand and pulled her to standing. "I'm thinking I answered my father too quickly. I want to apologize for that." He pulled her close wrapping his arms around her stiffened back. "I'm so used to doing everything for myself that I agreed before we could talk about it." Pulling a strand of hair back, he kissed her temple. "If you don't want me to go, I won't." Good night, he would say anything, she smelled like talc and lavender. His body was spinning to have her touch.

"Loneliness is trying to creep back in my heart. But I trust you. You should go." She pulled back looking deep into his eyes. Her fingers ran slowly across his neck and into the back of his hair. The grace in her touch was overwhelming. "I do love you." He whispered the declaration just as his lips found their reward. Melding her pliable frame into his, she kissed him back. Like a woman who desired to be with her husband, each kiss grew more indulgent. Nothing in his life to this point had ever felt so good. Breaking away for one second, he wrapped his arms around her hips and picked her up, completely aware of what he wanted.

"Patience I . . ." His feet moved them to the hallway. "I've had some . . . some insightful experiences with you." He walked over the threshold of her room. "But there is one," a small smile raised from the corner of his mouth, "important experience we have not shared." He slowly set her down. His eyes drank in her beauty as he slowly pulled her braid from its tie. Separating her thick strands, his fingers played with the luxurious silk and caused longing to rise in his heart. She stilled and looked at the ground. He waited, praying, his hopes weren't about to be dashed.

"Can we keep the light off?" Looking up, she drew in a shaky breath, her body shuddering.

Nodding his head slowly, he closed the door blocking the only stream of light.

CHAPTER 39

PATIENCE FIGURED OUT her husband liked to sleep on his stomach. Wide bare back with strong arms and hands above his head was a new delight to study. With just the perfect gray morning light coming through the bedroom curtains, it was a new feeling to merely rest in bed and watch him. Should she arise before him and start breakfast? The way his short dark hair rested on the skin near his neck, it begged to be touched.

Breakfast could wait a few more minutes. After all the liberties of last night, surely, she could let her fingers touch his hairline while he slept.

"Patience." He whispered, rubbing his nose against the sheet. "You might be sorry for not letting me sleep." He pulled his arms down next to his sides. "I was having the best dream." He leaned up and pinched his eyes. "Did the rooster go somewhere?"

"He crowed hours ago." Her fingers twisted in little circles around his ear. He suddenly looked at her. "Oh no." He groaned.

She couldn't hold back a snicker. He was late for work, and for some reason it was amusing.

"And you laugh?" Turning, he bit his bottom lip and pulled her against him. "I'll skip breakfast." He began to kiss her neck and around her ear. His hands worked her nightgown up and over her head. She wiggled down deeper under the covers. "Where are you going?" He pulled her back next to him. She tried to relax in his arms, but somehow all this touching was different in the light.

"Are you cold?" he whispered, " 'cause you don't feel cold." His warm kisses trailed up to her lips. She couldn't focus, she loved kissing him. Their covers began to twist and fall away as they moved together.

Patience felt the cold air on her back. "Wait." She panted, grabbing at the covers and pulling them back over her. "I think I can only do this in the dark."

Reed had the strangest confusion on his face. "There is no rule that I know of." He pulled her hair back and started kissing her shoulder. "I think we are free to do this whenever we want. And if you don't want to, tell me quickly." His hand slid around her waist and up her back.

Patience flinched. He had to feel that awful knotted skin . . . she pulled away. "It's my back," she blurted, hating that she couldn't relax as before. "I don't want you to see my deformity. At night, it won't be . . . it isn't so appalling."

Reed rested his head on the pillow next to hers.

"Nothing is appalling about you. Except maybe the pinching and kicking." Smiling, he trailed his finger down her jaw. "I could feel your scars last night. They're part of you. Here, turn and lay on your stomach." He pulled on her arm as she resisted him. "Really. Obey your husband," he said lightly, turning her over. "I'm going to pull the sheet back." He wavered at her obvious tension as she struggled to turn back over.

"I'm going to look, Patience. Not just a little bit, but long. He held her arm tight and moved her hair away. "I wish this never happened to you," he said, compassionately, slowly pulling his fingers over her scars.

"I know, they're hideous." She shivered.

"No, they're not at all." Releasing her arm, he gently kissed her rippled skin. "They are part of you," he said, adding another caress of her skin and tender kisses on her shoulder blade. "I'm looking at everything, in the full light." He kissed the center of her back. "This would be the *last* thing that would keep me from loving you."

Patience breathed in a long breath. Her body began to relax, and her toes tingled. Cool, soothing water trickled through her veins. Losing what composure she thought she should have, she turned to Reed and pressed against him. "If this is what love is, then I know I have it for you." She searched his face finding the same truth in his eyes. Kissing him lightly at first seemed to bring him alive until there was no defining who wanted whom more.

"LONG MORNING AT the courthouse?" Fred said as Reed walked in, dropping his satchel on his desk.

"No, just getting out of the house late this morning." Reed pulled a stack of papers out.

"Mmm." Fred grimaced and rubbed his neck. "Look here, Chappy, I swore, I would keep my mouth shut. If I didn't owe you my life, I would have never vowed such a thing."

Reed finally looked at him. "What are you talking about?"

"Don't throw a paddy, but I've been a husband longer than you, mate. And I know you would never *just* be late, unless . . . your cup of tea added *some sugar?*" Fred waggled his brows. "Or you found her flying around the trees. I say, I'm hoping the first."

Reed wondered the best way to keep him at bay. "Yes, I love my wife. No, she does not fly. We are getting along, and I'm thankful we married. Can I ask you about your workload for the next couple of days?"

Fred shook his head. "Ah, okay," he drew out the word. "What's afoot?"

"My father had a couple of large bids come in for lumber." Reed poured some coffee. "I'd like to go with him and check them out. One would require just the trees, and one would require expanding the whole mill. My father hasn't had a new saw blade in ten years. I want to look over the contracts with him. I have some money saved that we could work with."

"You're a good egg, old Chap. Of course, I could cover here. Just leave me a list of your appointments and . . ." Fred paused, an uncommon silence held in the air. "Patience knows everything, I assume." His eyes bored into Reed's. "That the Polish land was once your family's?"

Reed set his cup down and pulled a law book off the shelf. "No, I haven't explained all that, yet."

"Chappy, I've met her. She's a decent pawn on the chess board. You'd better watch your moves."

Reed pinched the back of his neck. "I will." He flipped open the pages and tried to concentrate on what he needed to find. Tell her, before he left or after? They might not even get either bid. They were in a new, incredible place. He swallowed hard, nothing in his being wanted to disrupt what was growing between them. Why did it matter now? They loved each other. He flipped more pages, eyes scanning for what he was looking for.

THE NEXT MORNING Reed grabbed her hand across the kitchen table. "Patience, I'm serious.

Please don't cry. I feel bad enough."

She took her apron and swiped her wet face. "Are you sure you have enough food."

"Yes, love." He paused wondering if he should be going. Hearing his father ride up, he pulled her to standing. "It will be just a few days. If you need anything, you promise to have Sarah take you to my parents?"

"Yes, I promise." She whispered, tucked in his arms.

Feeling the warmth of her embrace, he was amazed at how bound he felt to her. "And no swimming while I'm gone."

"That I cannot promise," she said.

He pulled back, searching her damp eyes. A little twinkle appeared as she lightly pinched his side. They separated when he stepped back to see his father enter.

"Are you ready, Reed?" His father nodded at Patience. "Thank you for sparing him this week. This could set the future for your children and grandchildren."

Patience nodded, her half smile said she was unconvinced. Reed gathered his things and came close. He paused matching her same discontent expression. "I love you," he whispered and kissed her lips softly.

As Reed expected, she walked out and held King George's thick jaw talking to him like she did most days.

"The rain has let up, so maybe you can work on the garden after all." Reed swung up on the saddle and tipped his hat. Patience backed up as he turned the horse. He tried to look over his shoulder and smile, but King George was already prancing to take the lead.

CHAPTER 40

THE DAMP SOIL leading to the lake was an unexpected blessing as Sarah and Joel worked with Patience. With three shovels going, they could quickly clear the debris and map out the best route for the garden path. "Do you think it is too big?" She tossed an old, scrub bush to the side. Joel stopped and leaned on the shovel. "I think you should extend it over that knoll." He pointed with his good arm. "That way a bench would have the best view of the lake." Patience chewed on her bottom lip, studying the terrain.

"I think you're right. That large tree would provide hours of shade."

"Then you could curve it back to the right, into the trees. No need to plant anything up there, just leave it a nature trail."

"I love it, Joel." She beamed. "I think our gardener at Lennhurst had your kind of vision."

"Maybe I can work there." He smiled.

Patience continued to study the path they'd worked on all morning. "I'm sorry. What did you say? You want to be a gardener?"

"For you, I would." He plunged the shovel hard

into the soft earth and pushed with his foot till he could flip the ground over. "Mr. Chapman is talking about expanding, doing some hiring at the mill. I know I'm not much help, mill work is hard with only one decent arm."

Patience had rarely heard any melancholy in Joel. His high, rounded cheeks, usually displayed a pleasing countenance.

"Though I enjoy the work, I hope as more people come to enjoy it, I would need more help." She offered, "Would you like me to ask Reed?"

"I don't want to seem like I'm fishing for a new job. I'm grateful for the Chapmans allowing me and my ma to move in with Bernie. Funny, the mill house is bigger than the old cabin I grew up in." He raked a hand through his hair and pounded his foot against the shovel again. "But ever since I left the army, I just wanted to settle down and get my own place."

Patience watched him struggle under the weight of the rocks in the soil. "I'm so sorry I never asked you. Do you have someone special?"

"I did." He kicked some rocks off the path. "She was supposed to wait for me. We had an understanding. Well, I thought we did." He grunted picking up a large rock and chucked it away.

Patience remembered how Dr. Powell said it was essential to really listen to people. "What happened, Joel?" She picked up a smaller rock and tossed it from the new path.

"She never told me why she wouldn't wait. Well, when I asked her to marry me I was seventeen and she was sixteen. The Union was calling for men, and she wanted us to wait till after I served. I understood, she was a great help to her ma. She had six younger brothers and sisters."

"That was very generous of you, Joel. To see her family's needs over your own." They stepped along slowly tossing rocks and sticks from the path.

"Sometime during the first year in the army I got so sick I thought I was going to crumble away like a dry, ole leaf. So I didn't write, didn't know what to say. But then I got better and was sent back out to the field. I did write her from there but never received anything back. My hope was falling, but so many of the men held on to only two or three letters from home for all the years they were in the war. Then I caught a bullet to my shoulder. Didn't think I would live through that either." He chuckled.

Using the shovel again to loosen a small bush, Patience pulled while he lifted. It finally loosened, and she tossed it to the side. He dug the shovel in again. "Then three years passed. I had a useless arm, and my pa died. I'm not sure what hurt the most, finding out that she'd married her second cousin, having a crippled arm, or not seeing my pa one last time."

Patience looked over her shoulder to where Sarah piled rocks in a crate. The loss of her husband struck her heart. "I'm so sorry Joel. For you and Sarah. But for you, that is a lot for a soul to bear."

He paused, looking toward the tree line. "Those crosses, for all your kin?" He nodded at them. "That's a lot to lose." Patience followed suit and stared at the two larger and three smaller crosses. Since she'd married Reed, the strange pain in the pit of her stomach had lessened.

"And now, do you want to settle down? Or do you think she was your only love?"

He smiled shyly and lifted another rock off the path. He shook his head. "No, I don't think she was my only love." His face flushed red, and his eyes welled wet.

"Did I ask something too personal?" When would she learn better social etiquette?

He dropped his layered hands on top of the shovel handle. "No." The way his sodden eyes held hers, made her heart pound erratically.

"Why don't women wait?" His question set her at ease, remembering what his proposed had done to him.

"Maybe she didn't know if you wanted her. You said the letters were far between." She brushed the dirt off her hands.

"Why did you have to marry Mr. Chapman so quickly?"

Now Patience felt uncomfortable. "I—I guess it was quick. I'm not sure."

"Did you love him that fast?" Joel's voice sounded curious.

"Joel," She pulled up her shoulder, "you know where I come from. I told you." She struggled for the words. "I—wanted to live here and he offered me security so—"

Joel looked at the ground raking his fingers through his hair. "And you offered him his land back. And now the mill can grow."

Patience couldn't read his expression. "What do you mean?"

"Nothing." He stabbed the shovel into the dirt again. "I don't want to sound sore. The Chapmans have been good to my uncle and ma." He looked back down the path. "We're getting it to look more like your map." The side of his mouth lifted briefly. "Tomorrow we can lay out those seedlings we started and get things growin'."

Patience watched him as he walked away. He struggled to take the wheelbarrow from Sarah, and she couldn't help but stare after him. Did she make it sound as if she'd married Reed for security? They'd said they cared for each other. Though it took a few weeks, she was sure their love was real and growing.

Joel must be wondering something. It was

carefully unspoken in between everything else they talked about. She'd always counted him a friend. He never made any romantic gestures, only helping with all the improvements of the cottage and now the gardens.

Why don't women wait? Somehow she felt that directed toward her. The greater question was why Reed couldn't wait? For a man who sometimes displayed coldness and rigidness, at first barely tolerated her ways. He said he didn't want anyone else courting her, so he made haste? She stomped on the newly turned soil. The Chapmans were indeed a force. Something Joel also didn't say. Reed carried a fire in his gut. A driven man who knew what he wanted, and he proved he was used to getting it.

An hour before sunset, she waved goodbye to Sarah and Joel. They'd gotten so much done she felt pulled to walk back and look over the new paths. Dirty and sweaty from the long day, her tattered back itched for relief.

Walking out on the long dock, she watched the sun hover over the dense tall pines. Dots of sunlight glowed like snow over the blue water. Spring was lovely here. How often would she be completely alone to swim? She looked side to side. Only the squawk of a lonely hawk circling above the water could be seen or heard. Of course, she would stay close to the bank, she ruminated as she undid the row of buttons on her heavy gray dress. The land was so invigoratingly beautiful at sunset. With the cottage so tucked away in the dense woods, she missed seeing this sight. Maybe Reed would agree to build a house near the water.

She slipped out of her dress, petticoat, boots and stockings. With only a chemise, corset and drawers, the cool air met her skin in sweet respite. Looking down at her pile of things on the dock, a small smile inched upward. Walking backwards a few feet, she drew in deep breath, blew it out and took in another full breath and ran down the dock. Flying, if only for an instant, gave her the same elation as feeling her body crashing into the water.

Against her hot, sweaty skin the water was icy at first. She came up gasping. And then, just like that, she acclimated to its coolness and felt its refreshing presence.

No swimming, Reed had said. Her head went under again and popped up on the surface and she grabbed a quick breath. Laying back and pulling her belly to the top, her body floated with grace and ease. Playfully pulling her fingers under the water like small paddles, she came alongside the dock. The cold water chilled her to the bone, but she pulled her braid loose and enjoyed the freedom of swishing her long mane back and forth in the water.

Remarkably, she had found herself in all

ways a married woman but still felt like a child floating free. This diverse land, so unrestricted and opposite of what it was like to be a child at Lennhurst. Nearing the shore, she stood up and squeezed the water from her hair. This time her dress would be her warmth back to the cottage.

Walking up through the water, she tumbled forward when a sharp rock bit into her foot. "Ouch." She tried to find her balance and crept slowly from the water. Hopping on one foot, she turned and plopped onto the shore. Blood and lake water mixed over the bottom of her painful foot. Frowning, she looked at her pile on the dock. Thankfully nothing serious. No husband, no horse, she admitted it had been reckless. Anything worse could have put her in dire straits. Putting away childish things might be necessary, she could almost hear Reed's reprimand.

CHAPTER 41

THE NEXT MORNING Sarah sat at the cottage kitchen table sipping hot coffee. "You fared well enough on your own last night?"

"I did." Patience pulled her tea strainer from her cup. "I recalled those nights when you were back at the Chapmans'." She looked over to the crackling fireplace. "Except I didn't like being in my room alone, so I took the bedding and grabbed the cat and my Bible." She raised a small smile. "I slept on the floor in front of the fire with the cat and Bible." She shook her head taking another sip. "I know, silly."

"I remember firsthand, how a woman can get cold without a man in the bed." Sarah stood and took her cup to the basin. "Joel will be here later. He had a job at the mill to finish."

"Sarah." Patience rose and winced as she put too much pressure on her cut foot. She set her tea aside and turned to grab her boots. "Is Joel all right? He's always been so amiable, and—actually, he still is. He just doesn't seem the same."

"Ever since you married Mr. Reed." Sarah poured some hot water in the basin. "I've seen a

319

restlessness in him. I'm sure he had a feather in his cap for you, but he's lost his confidence since the war." She washed their few dishes.

Patience froze from lacing up her boots. She had a feeling. First, his betrothed didn't wait, then she didn't. "I hope in no way, that I led him on. I'm so backward in how these things work." She pulled her skirts back down and tried her weight on the sore foot.

"No, I don't think you did. But he did come alive around you. All the work he did on this cottage and even the grounds." Sarah dried her hands. "I'm sure he enjoyed some female company his own age." She lifted a small smile. "This morning, are we lining those new paths with the rocks?"

"Yes, ma'am." Patience reached out and grabbed her hand, patting it. "Thank you so much for your help."

BY AFTERNOON, THE sun was warm, and Joel set up some stumps and a plank in the shade for a planting table. Sarah had excused herself to go back to the millhouse while they studied the map for the best locations for each plant.

"Did you ever have a chance to read any Shakespeare?" Patience asked.

Joel shook his head smiling. "No."

"There is a play called *A Midsummer Night's Dream*. It has these fairies that live in the forest, Oberon the king of the fairies and Titania the queen. I always pictured their home. Much like this, woods and trees. I know it sounds different, but I want all the fairies and their friends to find this garden. To have a home."

Joel stepped back from her and went to the small plants in the boxes. "Does Reed know about this? This fairy garden?"

"Umm, yes and no. He knows about the garden. He knows I care for the thin-winged creatures. But his friends think I made these things up while I was a child. They gave me medication for my burns at Lennhurst."

Joel scratched his upper lip. "So this book by Shakespeare, it is just make believe. It's not a true story."

"True." She nodded. "It's actually a play." Joel looked around anywhere but at her. Like everyone else except Dr. Powell, she'd made him uncomfortable. "Very well." She straightened up. "Topiaries won't be ready for months. The boxwood we can start here. Fred and Janice gave us that ceramic urn, so I filled it with dirt and black-eyed Susan vine. Fred said it is a called a 'dolly bin.'" She pulled it off the shelf, and it slipped from her hands and landed on her foot. "Oh, oh, oh . . ." Joel quickly came next to her and lifted it from her foot.

"Are you all right?" he asked, as she turned to limp in a circle.

"It . . . oh, it just . . . oh! I had already cut my

foot last night." She bent grasping her ankle. "Now it's throbbing."

"Here," Joel brushed the dirt off another stump, "come and sit." He helped her sit and bent down in front of her. "I'm going to take off your boot." He pulled the strings from the hooks as she gritted her teeth against the pain.

"Blessed assurance, Patience. Your stocking is soaked in blood. I think you should let Dr. Nedows take a look. You might have broken a bone, or you might need some stitches."

"I don't know. Maybe I can just wrap it better." She winced, squeezing her hands together.

"No, you're going." He stood and brushed the dirt off his pants. "I won't have Reed angry about this, too. Put your arm around my neck."

As she did, he easily lifted her up with his good arm and walked her to the wagon. "Put your good foot on the floorboard." Sticking her good foot out, she hopped to the seat. Something pulsed from the bottom of her foot as Joel took his place. He slapped the reins, and the wagon jerked forward.

Patience felt a wave of nausea, certainly, her injury wasn't that serious. She hated medical procedures and, maybe worse, she would have to explain all this to Reed.

JOEL PULLED THE wagon to a stop next to the doctor's office. He jumped down and knocked on the door as Patience carefully scooted to the edge of the wagon seat. Isn't this where Janice had said she worked? Maybe she would be here. The door opened, an older gentleman with wrinkles and little round glasses hanging on the tip of his nose, stepped out. He looked up at Patience and wavered.

"Moje dziecko?" He whispered, eyes almost crinkled shut behind his glasses.

Patience clutched Joel's outstretched hand and froze. "Co? What did you say, sir?"

Joel helped her from the wagon and aided her into the office. "You speak Polish, sir?" Wide-eyed she stared at the older man as Joel helped her on a tall cot. The doctor stared at her, seemingly lost for words.

"Mowisz po poluku." Patience asked him again if he spoke Polish, amazed her native tongue came back so clearly. Joel stepped back from the exchange waiting for someone to speak.

"How is the shoulder, young man?" Dr. Nedows smiled to Joel.

"The oil you gave me brings the ache down at night." He eyed Patience, still looking lost.

"And your mother and uncle?"

Patience began to pull off her stocking. Maybe she hadn't heard him correctly. Now he speaks with no accent. Was her mind playing tricks?

"I guess this is what we need to take a look at." Dr. Nedows's cold hands gently lifted her heel.

She held her skirts together under her leg as he examined the bottom of her foot. "What caused this cut here?"

"Rocks." Her voice unsteady, trying not to stare at him. Did he know of her?

"Mistress gone barefoot outside?" He smiled briefly at Joel, who shrugged. "And the top, swollen and black and blue?"

"I dropped a heavy planter on it this afternoon." A shudder went up her back, and she felt like a confused child again, alone and uncomfortable. Swallowing hard, she wished Reed was here. "It's already feeling a bit better. I can't get my boot on but . . ."

She sucked in a sharp breath as Dr. Nedows held a cloth with something on it against her cut. Finding her breath, she gritted her teeth together and gripped the cot. "I don't like whatever liquid you placed on my wound. I don't like it at all." She felt the tears begin to form. She hated anything medicinal.

"I don't think you'll need stitches as long as it's kept clean. Stay off all rocks. Likely you have broken a small bone in your foot, so I will wrap that for you." Without looking at her, he took some white gauze off the shelf and carefully padded the bottom of her foot, wrapping a wider length around her ankle and back around her foot.

As soon as he stepped back, Patience scooted her legs and skirts to the corner of the cot. She reached for Joel, and he stepped forward to support her. She could swear Dr. Nedows said 'my child' in Polish. How dare he ignore her questions? The strong smells were giving her a headache. Did he know her family? She pressed her lips into a tight line as she hopped out of the office with Joel holding her arm steady. "You may send your bill to my husband, Reed Chapman. His office is a few blocks from here." She hopped out the door, never looking back at him.

"I know who your husband is." His voice sounded strangely dry and regretful.

PATIENCE RODE IN silence back to the cottage. Joel asked if she would like his mother to return to stay with her.

"No, thank you." Her words still sober and tense.

Joel set the brake and jumped down. "Here, just let me carry you." He reached for her with his good arm and Patience wrapped her arms around his neck. They stepped up on the porch, and she reached for the handle as the door opened by itself. Reed stood inside wide-eyed and stoic.

"How nice to see you two."

CHAPTER 42

JOEL SLOWLY LET Patience's legs drop and steadied her as she balanced on one foot. As soon as she felt his hands on her waist, he removed them as quickly. She hopped on one foot and sat in a chair at the table.

Reed closed the door and stood in the middle of the room looking like a bored schoolmaster. Patience knew he would wait, loving to see them squirm.

Joel cleared his throat. "Anything else, Patience?" Joel glanced at her and nodded at Reed. "I'll be by tomorrow to finish the planting." He blinked quickly, letting himself out.

A cold breeze lingered from the door or somewhere from Reed's person. "What happened?" He finally spoke.

"I . . ." Patience dropped her head to the side, rubbing her temple. "Went swimming."

"I certainly could not have heard that right?" He came closer to the table. "Were you swimming with Joel?"

"Of course not!" Patience shook her head, glaring at him.

Reed flinched back. "You bark at me?" He

walked around the table. "Yet, I was the one who came home to a home without a wife." He walked by her. "She was here when I left." His tone exasperated. "She seemed sad to see me go, so I pushed hard to get home before dark." Walking over to the fireplace, he leaned his forearm against the brick. "Then when I find no word or note, I rode to my parents. My mother hadn't seen you and had no idea where you could have gone, so I went to the mill house. Sarah says you were with Joel this afternoon." He pushed off the brick. "So I rode around the property, seeing where the path had been cut and the work is going on, but no Joel and no Patience."

"I'm sorry." Patience cut in. "I didn't know you would be here. I would have left you a note. I can see now—this has caused you a bit of worry."

"Seriously, Patience. A bit? No, not a bit. A lot! A lot of worry." He stalked back to the table. "And then you say—you hurt your foot swimming? The very thing I asked—"

"I float. I don't swim." She tucked her foot under the table. "I would never just start swimming out to the middle of the lake. I stay near the dock. I could stand in the water." Her voice trailed. "And when I did, I cut my foot on a rock."

"And somehow Joel was nearby to take you to Hancock or did he wrap that foot? Did he touch your foot, your ankle, humm?" He glared at her through narrowed slits.

"No, if you would just calm down so I could explain." She dropped her elbows on the table, her forehead on her palms. "There is nothing for you to be upset about."

"That's easy for you to say. You're not married to you."

Her chin shot up. To think only an hour ago she longed for his comfort. Rising from the chair, she stared at him from the depth of her pained brown eyes. "Good night." Grimacing, she walked on the heel of her injured foot.

"Wait." His voice calmed, he came up behind her. "Of all the things I looked forward to, this was the last thing I expected." His breath softly landed on her neck. "I don't want to fight with you." A gentle hand rested on the back of her arm, melting her resolve. "Seeing you with Joel riles me. Seeing you hurt riles me." His fingers lightly touched the hair behind her ear. "Not knowing where you were . . ."

"I apologized for that." Her tone blunt, her foot throbbing. She felt his touch drop and a wave of loneliness filled her being. Hobbling forward, she hated that her eyes were filling with stupid tears. First Dr. Nedows was ignoring her and now these cross words with Reed. She went into her room and closed the door.

REED AWOKE WITH the low flickering firelight and a stiff neck. He'd fallen asleep in the green chair. He stood with drooping eyes and added one more log to the fire. Walking the few steps to their bedroom door, he waited and sighed, she was long asleep and nursed a pained foot. He turned and went into his old room. Grabbing the blanket, he wrapped up and lowered onto the bed. In his ridiculous homecoming, he hadn't had a chance to tell her about the bid they had secured for the mill.

The next morning he realized he'd overslept and rose quickly. His trunk of belongings still remained in this extra room. Pulling out a change of clothes, he blew out a breath, realizing he had neglected to make their room look like he lived here.

Listening for Patience as he dressed, he wondered if she needed help today. With the work at the office and the details of the bid, there was little time for him to stay home and dawdle in a garden. But the idea of Joel helping her didn't sit well at all. Maybe she would agree to go to his mother's for the day. Joel wanted to work on her garden—fine. But she didn't need to be here. Stepping into the kitchen, a piece of paper glared at him. He'd seen her writing, from the quick glance at her Lennhurst list. Now looking over the note a rock dropped hard in his gut.

I need to speak with someone. I cannot walk so I have taken King George. I'm sorry for the inconvenience, but you will find him at your office. I will send for you when I am ready to come home.

Ready to come home? Reed's heart pounded. "What?" He sighed. Why hadn't he listened to her last night? Why did he always do all the talking? He knew the shortest trail to his parents' home. "Lord, please," he whispered taking off in a run. *Let this not have to do with Joel.* Speaking quickly with his mother and pretending everything was fine with his evasive questions, he grabbed one of his parents' horses. Even Joel seemed innocent and couldn't give any details to where she would have gone. *This is so strange.* He kicked the old mare into a run. Yet, everything to do with her was strange. The one thing he feared, tasted like sour milk in his mouth. Her unpredictability would push his nerves over a cliff. He had agreed to marry and now loved an unreasoned, childlike woman.

He pulled the mare up and let out a long breath to see King George behind his building with straws of hay hanging from his mouth.

"Loyal friend." He came around the large horse and looked into his eyes. "What is this about? Is she here?" He was doing it again, expecting an answer from King George. He turned and walked in the back door, feeling like a husband about to collapse under a mountain of guilt.

"Patience." He called looking up the stairs. Why had he ever taken her up to his apartment?

So much of his anguish was his own fault. He went up the stairs to see the empty apartment and then jogged back down.

"Looking for your wife *here,* Chappy?" Fred looked up from his pile of papers.

Reed went to his desk and blew out a long breath. In all his haste, he'd forgotten his work satchel. "I forgot my work. I need to take King George home."

"As . . . you should?" Fred gave him a perplexed grin.

"Have you seen Patience this morning?" Reed chewed on the inside of his cheek. "She said she had to see someone."

"And you think that someone is me?" Fred pulled on his thin nose. "Weren't you only gone a few days? And you are about to blame me for misplacing your wife?"

"No, just answer the question." Reed looked out their large front windows. "I pray to every angel in heaven that Cynthia Icely hasn't got ahold of her."

"Let's pray not." Fred shuffled his papers, looking down. "Maybe her fairy family came for a visit and they took her—"

Reed slammed his fist on his desk.

"All right, all right!" Fred stood and held his hands up. "Look here, old chap, a thousand blimey apologies. You go home and see if she's there and don't forget your work. I will walk

Main Street and look high and low. We meet back here in thirty minutes?"

Reed nodded, summoning all the calm he could find.

REINING KING GEORGE to a stop, Reed jumped off and ran into the cottage.

"Patience!" He called going into both little rooms and out the back door. Walking around the chicken coop, he stilled and tried to listen. "Patience!" He yelled again. Only the cat's low meow could be heard as the cat rubbed against the back door. Closing his eyes, he gripped his head.

It had been hours now, he looked around again and walked to where the new paths had been laid. All that work, done while he was gone. What in heaven and earth happened? Did she believe him irreparably angry? Lord knows he'd withheld his yearning to throw Joel across the room. And he'd succeeded based on only one thing, he really did trust her.

It was still unimaginable she'd taken King George somewhere by herself. He was a handful for him, and she was sporting a sore foot. Why did she leave the horse in town? She must still be in town. Who else would give her a ride home? He reentered the back door and moved into her room. Pulling out her drawer, her Bible and wrinkled list were gone. His heart thudded anew.

Did she take the stage back to Lennhurst? What did the note say? *She would send for him?*

Walking back to the table, another piece of paper laid on top of the first one. Surely there was only one note when he woke up this morning? He grabbed the paper and walked back out off the front porch and searched around, wishing she would just appear.

Squinting in the sunlight reflecting off the paper, he read,

Reed, I need more time to think. I am with family and safe.

Heaving a long sigh, he jogged out the door and down the path to the crosses. Family, of course. He tried to hold his expectation loose as he looked all around the area of the five wooden crosses. Backing up, he even looked high into the tall trees surrounding the area. Circling the ruins of the Polish house, and then scanning the dock and lake his countenance and spirit plummeted.

A woman, a child who believed in fairies and butterflies for companionship? Did he really think he could fall in love and mold her into his controlled world? After the marriage, the way she felt in his arms, and even the new bid for the trees, he had been exceptionally hopeful. *When will at least one thing in my life work for good?* He huffed. *What a sidetracked idiot, I am.* He turned on his heel and headed back for King George.

CHAPTER 43

ARITA CHAPMAN STOPPED at the large glass window as Reed looked up from his office desk. He offered no gesture or warm greeting, it had been two days since he'd found the short note from his wife and talking to his mother wasn't going to change anything. Patience had chosen to leave him.

Arita walked in with a small paper bag. "Just some leftovers, thought you might be hungry."

He nodded at his mother as she set the bag on his desk. "I'm finishing up the contract for the trees," he said, hoping she would see him busy and not try to talk. His parents had already heard everything. There wasn't any new news, he went back to adding the lengthy columns. She stood unmoving, waiting.

"Is Rob all right? I'm sorry, with everything, I haven't been much help." He glanced up quickly.

"Rob is fine. When are you going to Lenn-hurst?" she asked directly.

"I've told you, I'm not sure she is there. And when I get there, what would I say? She has made up her mind about me." He could feel his temper flaring, he didn't need to be accused of more than what he'd already tallied for himself. "Please don't ask me again what could have set her off, I'm as confused as anyone." He scribbled some figures on some scratch paper.

"She loved the land. You said she'd started the garden the day before. I talked to Joel and Sarah they can't—" Arita stopped short. Reed flashed her an angry, bloodshot stare. "And I don't like those daggers in your eyes, young man."

Reed pulled in a deep breath and sat back. He was going to get a tongue lashing, *fine,* but he wasn't ten and in trouble for forgetting to close the corral gate again. This was his adult life, his real, bone-crushing, never-winning life. He tapped his fingers together over his waist, wishing she would hurry up and leave.

"You have a terribly brilliant mind." Her expression spoke her unhappiness, and she shook her head. "But it runs like a single water pump when it wants something. Instead of seeing all you have, you only see what you want. Up and down, in and out until you draw out what you want."

"Really?" Reed sat forward. "I never wanted to go to Oxford, but I did it for the family. How incredibly single-focused and selfish of me," he scoffed.

"And you remind us of that in every conflict." She snipped back. "Patience was here in Hancock so you could get your grandfather's land back.

Sweet revenge for being sent abroad? For living instead of dying in the war," she rebuked. "Is that true or not?"

Reed planted his elbows on his desk and rubbed his face. "Yes, it's true. But I am paying the price for all my offensive ways. Does that make you happy?" Looking up, feeling the silence and seeing the set of her jaw, he wondered if she might reach across his desk and slap him.

Arita sighed softly and her tone was remorseful, "Did you really think you could play with her life, get the land back, and go on your merry way?"

"No, mother." Suddenly exhausted from two nights of little sleep, he closed his eyes. "I made the biggest mistake of all. I fell in love with my wife." He shook his head and rubbed his face. "Nothing has ever hurt as bad as this. I would sell that land." He murmured into his hands. "And yours, too, if I could have her back."

The air hung in heavy stillness until he heard his mother open his office door. "That's the first clear-headed thing I've heard you say." She walked out, pulling it shut behind her.

PATIENCE LISTENED FOR any movement from down stairs. Her guest room was quiet for reading, praying, and staring out the window, but the isolation was wearing thin. She moved carefully down the narrow stairs and peeked around the corner. The small kitchen was empty and a kettle of hot water rested on the little stove. Grabbing a cup from the counter, she heard a noise and turned quickly. Gasping with fright, she clutched her chest and recoiled with nowhere to go.

"Janice!" She turned the mug around in her hands next to her chest. "Dear Lord, you startled me."

"Patience." Janice stood with her knit wrap over her arm. "What are you doing here?"

"I . . . uh, I . . . am a guest here." She turned and set the cup down.

"Does Reed know you are here?" Janice asked. Patience felt her stomach drop. She'd been so safely hidden. There was no way she could win the allegiance of Reed's best friend's wife. They were like three strands of a rope; she was the outsider.

"No." Patience gripped her hands together. "I have prayed and listened and I still don't know what to do." The desperation in her own voice made her eyes fill with tears.

"You can tell me." Janice set her wrap over the back of a chair. Her small round belly evident through the layers of her skirts.

Patience rocked her wedding ring back and forth. "I came to see Dr. Nedows earlier. I don't think he meant to, but he spoke Polish to me." She swiped the back of her hand across her wet cheeks.

Janice's mouth hung open, then frowned.

"I . . . he . . . Dr. Nedows is my uncle." Patience whispered.

"What?" Janice blinked. "Your uncle?"

"I was just as shocked. He was the one who arranged for my parents to find asylum here in Hancock. He believed it would be a safe haven. My mother is—was his younger sister."

"Oh, my," Janice breathed. "And after the fire, he hid you away at Lennhurst?"

Patience nodded. "He believed I would be safe there. And when Reed brought up the need to sell the land, he wondered if it would be harmless for me to be found and release the land for sale. God's timing to let it go. He wanted to contact me but had to be sure no one was out to harm me. He's been watching everything. He paid for my years at Lennhurst, the repair of the dock, the crosses. The box of family heirlooms that held the ring. It was jewelry from our family." She pulled her hands loose and looked away.

"With everything Reed has done, Dr. Nedows thinks we should return to Poland. He stays in touch with other families that assure him the revolution, the uprising my father ran from, is over. My father wasn't a criminal." Patience looked her in the face, standing taller. "He led a revolt to abolish Polish serfdom. Entire villages of people were being dominated and worked without any pay." She pressed her hand against the rising and falling of her chest. Trying to stay calm was difficult. "Taking the lives of my family in a faraway country," her voice lowered, "was the clearest message of how corrupt our homeland had become."

Janice held her gaze, "So, can you talk to Reed about all this? He's been worried sick." She looked back to the quiet parlor. Thankfully Dr. Nedows was still out on a call. "What do you mean with 'with everything Reed has done'? What has he done? Was he cruel to you?"

Patience felt her eyes filling again. "Is it cruel to take advantage of someone for your own personal gain?" She rubbed her forehead and wiped her hand over her wet face.

"I suppose it is." Janice let out a long sigh, confusion and sadness shaping her expression. She reached for her wrap. "Fred will be wondering where I am." She slipped her wrap around her shoulders.

Patience reached out and touched her arm as new tears spilled down her cheeks. "These have been the hardest days I've ever had." Her voice broke. "I would rather have the dead skin pulled off my back than feel the crushing of this heart betrayed."

Janice dropped her hand over Patience's. "I will not say I know where you are." She forged a smile. "He would break in here, I believe. But will you meet with him? Can I tell him that? I can't listen to him and Fred speculate when I know where you are."

Patience pulled away. "I don't know how to face him."

"Do you remember those vows?" Janice asked. "They weren't that long ago. In good times and in bad. I think I heard you agree to that."

Patience let out a long breath and jumped at the sound of the front door. Janice leaned back to see. "It's just Dr. Nedows."

"Very well. Saturday I will meet him at noon. I can see the town square from my window. There is a bench. I will be there."

Janice squeezed Patience's trembling hands. "I will tell him." She nodded then hurried from the kitchen.

CHAPTER 44

REED TOSSED AND turned in the cold bed long before the rooster went off. He'd already decided in his heart and mind what the morning should look like. Today at noon he would meet with his wife. Janice had told him about seeing Patience. Reading between everything Janice wasn't trying to say, it didn't take much sense to figure out she was staying with Dr. Nedows. Janice had been the one to help him draw up the phony documents that started this foolish escapade. How ironic she was now the mediator.

Finishing his breakfast, he looked over the crinkled map of her fairy garden. He had sworn with any free minutes in his day, his next job would be to tear the barbed wire fence down for good. If he could finish the rest of her paths, he'd hopefully have time to build the small bridge that would go over the small creek. He wondered about some table and benches. If all went well maybe he could ask her what she preferred today.

Something tugged at his heart besides his usual chest pain. He was so inept at this, yet being around Patience had brought a simple child-like faith. He dropped his face in his hands.

God of Heaven, I believe You heard me as I forgave the offenses in my life. Now I am the one in need of an ocean of forgiveness. I have been a coward to keep things from my wife. I have been prideful and arrogant in light of what I want. Please forgive me, I never wanted to hurt her, yet I have. If You can take the callouses from my heart—I give its poor condition to you. He breathed in deeply then let it out slowly. *And please help me to stay calm today. No matter what.*

Just before noon, Reed entered his office and grabbed the journal and small wrapped gift. He stared at it a moment too long. Did it seem disingenuous also? A gift given as more bribery? He slapped the items against his hand. His nerves were kicking in, and he told himself he would stay calm. How could he guess her response? She was as unpredictable as the spring in Hancock. Swallowing the knot in his tight throat, he went out the office door and headed for the town square.

Reed's pace slowed to a painful eternity when he caught sight of her. She sat on the bench, stiffed-back, skin like porcelain and in the same dress she wore when he met her at Lennhurst. Her thick brown braid coiled in the same location at the nape of her neck. It was like being in the dark night of a repeating dream. Was this the same woman he'd caressed in his bed? Had he already dug his fingers through those shiny tresses? His heart pounded. Those were no dreams.

As he approached, she stood quickly, gripping her wedding ring. Thank God she was still wearing it. Every fiber wanted to reach out and touch her, but he stood broad-shouldered and solid.

"You look well." He spoke first.

Her chin quivered a bit, she looked fearful. "As do you."

"Do you want to sit here or walk?" He offered.

"Ahh . . ." She looked around. Only a woman pushing a baby buggy was nearby. "We could just sit here." They sat slowly.

"I brought you something." He reached out with the items.

"Thank you." She took them and held them on her lap.

Though it was a beautiful day, he felt a cold sweat wash over his body. Trying to keep his foot from tapping, he lifted a small smile, hoping.

"The reason I cannot return is—" she began, her tone as stiff as her rigid posture.

He bristled, she never did mince words.

"—that I feel you married me in haste to secure my land. And now by marriage, it is your land. Someone told me it was Chapman land before my parents settled there. I feel foolish, of course, your parents live adjacent to where we live. I never thought you would marry me, use me . . .

just to bring the land back together." She took a deep breath. "I thought you married me because you cared for me and wanted to keep me safe."

Reed's rebuttal pulsed on the tip of his tongue. *Stay calm* rang in his ears.

"So the time I needed away from you was very important." She stared ahead, brushing a small strand of hair back in place. The movement of her graceful fingers made his mouth go dry. "You have a grand influence over me." She swallowed hard. "A once isolated woman untrained in the ways of the world. You're a good . . . persuasive . . . a good lawyer."

The pointed sting of those words went straight down his throat, piercing his heart.

"You helped me leave Lennhurst. You invited me into your family." She looked down and gripped the items on her lap. "My Bible says to forgive and believe the best, but I can't, my heart is too hurt. My wings have been clipped back farther than imagination allows. I'm thinking of returning to Poland with my uncle. Doctor Nedows is my mother's older brother." She murmured, exhaling a broken sigh.

Reed stiffened like a fist to the gut; fighting remorse and anger in her plan to leave him for good. *Please, Lord,* he prayed. Waiting to settle himself, he took a deep breath. "Most of what you say is painfully true." He watched a group of small birds fly from the trees. "I have lusted after your land, like a spoiled child who can't have a toy." He shook his head. "Do you remember when I told you that you needed to grow up?"

With round eyes, and conflicted expression, she nodded.

"I have needed to grow up. My grandfather loved horses, land and the mill. Before he passed, he grabbed my arm and said, 'make me proud.' I still feel like that child with some mission to fulfill. I strive and scrape, but it never feels enough. I don't understand why everything in me has always been driven by necessity."

He touched her hand. "Until I married you. You make everything feel enough for me. Yes, I have lusted after the land, but I have known what it is to love you." He gripped her hand. "You invite me in, calming the clanging of my soul. A harmony I can't explain. My heart started beating for the first time when I saw you at Lennhurst. Really beating, really flying beyond myself. Something wild and wonderful, reigniting the time we met as children."

Patience looked up, looking confused.

"Please Lord," he whispered. "Patience, do you remember being five or six? Your hair was caught in the barbed wire fence. Past the old oak?" He waited. "Please say you remember this."

He couldn't read the emotion on her face. Was she unresponsive to show her strength? Or entertaining the past recollection, now shocked and crushed that it was him? She pulled her hand free from his.

Her jaw locked, but he could see the tremor in her chin. "Didn't I just say, you *can* have a grand influence over me?" She left the items on the bench and stood. "I suppose I am the only person who can do something about that." Stepping away from the bench, she rubbed her crossed arms and looked down the street.

Reed rose, all the grace and forbearance he prayed for, crumbled around his feet. "I'm just sorry. Sorry for everything. No." His shoulders shot up, and he grabbed the back of her arm. "I'm not sorry for falling in love with you." He waited until she met his eyes. "The path I cut was crooked, and you of all people deserve a fairytale."

She turned quickly from his grasp and swiped the tears from her face. "I have to go." She picked up her items from the bench. "Thank you for the gift."

He opened his mouth to beg for her not to leave him. At least give him another chance before she left the country. But he locked his jaw—he'd said too much. He was often too hasty. So what else was new?

PATIENCE HELD HER tears at bay as she walked in and passed Dr. Nedows reading in his chair. "I think I'll rest." She murmured, nodding at him.

Climbing the stairs, her feet weighed a hundred pounds. Reed's declarations were unbearably weighing her entire body down. Collapsing onto the bed, she laid on her side and wrapped her body around the pillow. The tears flowed freely as she eyed his gifts. Influence. Was he just trying to say all the right things? Wasn't the word love, unconditional? Or maybe convenient to get your way. Did he hope she would jump in his arms and pretend nothing was wrong? Certainly, her innocence had left her body the night she lay with him. *Oh, the deep piercing of a gullible heart.* She pulled the pillow in tighter. But what of the innocence of spirit and soul? How does one repair such broken trust? Can flesh and blood ever mend?

You can trust Me, came a quiet whisper as she closed and rested her tear soaked eyes. Trying to breathe in the Lord's comfort, she rolled onto her back. Her hand almost knocked the gifts off the bed. Blowing out a tired breath, she pulled the ribbon off the journal and little box. On the tan parchment front, she recognized Reed's handwriting. He'd written *Dream* across the front cover. Another folded paper fell out as she opened the journal. *New paper for all your new dreams.* He'd written inside the flap.

She leaned back onto the pillows and held it to her chest. Her childhood lists, fantasies and dreams seemed so far away. Could she see herself starting over in Poland? More despondence over-whelmed her being. She unfolded the paper that had fallen out. It was some kind of official paper from the courthouse, it had the county seal and her name on it. She rolled up to sitting. 'The above said land listed under Reed Chapman has been officially transferred in title and deed to a Mrs. Patience Chapman. The sole owner and proprietor from this day forward.' He had it recorded two days ago. It was hers again. She reread it again hoping it would evoke a response in her, but just more lonely tears fell. This was another grand gesture that somehow left her con-flicted and empty. Now the Chapmans could not fulfill the new bid for the mill. She tugged off the lid to the little square box. Laying along the red satin fabric, a delicate gold stick pin. On the end of the pin was a small gold and black jeweled ladybug.

CHAPTER 45

LATER AS THE week drug on, Patience stared out her upstairs window to the pearly gray skies. The last hour she'd finished the breakfast dishes for Dr. Nedows and folded a bit of his doctoring laundry. But now she was back in her room and could hear the voices of his patients come and go. Thankfully he was a gentle soul. He'd told her many times he didn't want to pressure her to take the trip to Poland. He was content with his life here, but if it was important to her, he would gladly take her.

Sitting on the bed, she picked up her Bible. She'd prayed for him as much as herself. He carried such guilt for bringing her family to America where their lives ended so violently. He'd expressed his deep regret he'd trusted Reed Chapman with her information. He mourned the poor slip in judgment, and he should have come for her himself and saved her the heartache. The night after Reed had given her the deed, she showed it to her uncle. It was a deed to land that was now in her name only. What she hadn't shared was that without trust in Reed as her husband, it held little appeal. She ran her hand over her dream journal. The empty pages matched the chambers of her heart. She slipped to her knees and bowed her head against the bed. *Dear Lord* . . .

"Patyana." A soft knock was at her door.

She smiled and stood. Her real name felt comforting from her uncle's voice. Opening the door, she met his crinkled eyes and low spectacles.

"Janice has arrived to watch the office. The Chapmans have asked for me to check on Robbie today. He's had a cold, and they are concerned with his lungs. I was going to go myself, but Janice said I should ask you if you wanted to go."

"He likes to be called Rob." She whispered without thinking, her neglect for this treasured life spurring her. "Yes, I would like to see him. Thank you for asking, I'll be down in a minute."

AS SOON AS her uncle's old carriage turned onto the Chapmans' lane, she felt something akin to her cold water swims over her skin. Was it the sight of the house, smell of the burning barrel from the mill or just seeing the animals grazing in the corral?

Her uncle clicked his tongue leading his horse around to the front. Even the cow looked up with a mouth of grass to watch them. Letting herself down on her healing foot, she spied the mill. Though far down the road, the sound of men's voices and movement tapped a longing in her. This place was always alive with people and family. Oh, how she missed it. Following her uncle to the door, she bit down on her lower lip. Unexpected emotions were flooding in fast as the door opened. She swallowed hard and walked in. Arita pulled back with wide eyes and grabbed her and squeezed her fully.

"Patience. I—oh, my goodness, I wasn't—I'm so glad to see you." Arita stared long at her. "Thank you for bringing her, Doctor." Her smile rising and falling. "We've missed you." Arita continued squeezing her arm and rubbing her back.

"I would love to be of any help." Patience surprised her words held steady. Arita was a generous and accepting woman. Thudding steps were heard coming up the porch, and Robert walked in smelling like fresh cut wood.

"Well, Patience!" He reached out for her hand and patted it. "What a wonderful surprise." He turned to Arita. "I came as soon as I saw the doc's carriage.

Dr. Nedows went to their basin and washed his hands. "So the drainage is green you say?" He looked to Arita.

"Yes, a bit thicker every day." They walked toward Rob's room.

Robert and Patience looked at each other. "I know you want to hear what the doctor says," she said, "But if I could have one minute?" She squeezed her hands together, hard. "You must know Reed signed the rights to our land over to me."

Robert looked down and nodded his head.

"But if it's not too late, I want to give you as many trees as you need to fulfill the contract you have. I want you to go ahead with what you need for the mill."

Robert blinked and looked out the front window. "I don't know what to say. I guess, thank you." He turned to her, rubbing his chin back and forth. "That is very generous of you."

Blast it, his gaze held hers for too long, that fatherly strength came towards her, but she didn't want to cry.

"Listen to me, Missy."

That did it. Those imprudent tears flowed over.

"Reed has made some unforgivable mistakes, and I take some responsibility for encouraging him." Robert's brows drew together causing a deep furrow. "And I'm not going to tell you what you should do. And I would have said this *before* you offered the trees." He nodded at her until she nodded back that she understood. "We love you." His direct words slicing her being. "Arita and I are moved by how much delight you have brought to the family. Since our girls have long married and gone, we didn't realize how cold and routine our lives had become. You were and are a much-needed breath of fresh air. Whatever happens between you and Reed, we are still your family." He reached out and pulled her into a warm hug. "We are keeping you, that is, if you want us." He patted her back and chuckled.

Speechless, Patience found her hankie in her reticule and blew her nose. She shook her head, willing the words to come out. "Thank you, Robert." Her voice cracked. "You and Arita have been true parents to me." They nodded to each other and walked into Rob's room.

"ANY KIND OF infection is dangerous for him." Dr. Nedows pulled his stethoscope around to the front of Rob's chest.

Patience could see Rob's breathing was labored, that special gleam in his eyes was gone. His rocking and jerking had fallen to small shudders and slow spasms. "We need to keep him upright through the night. I suppose you could strap him in the wheeled chair," Dr. Nedows pursed his lips, thinking, "but I would prefer a better angle, where his sinuses would drain like this." He held his hand out in a sloped position.

"I can do that."

Patience jumped. Reed stood in the bedroom doorway.

"I can get in the bed and keep his pillows on my chest. With my arms, I can keep him in place."

"Reed." His mother sighed. "You'll get no sleep. I'll come in and relieve you."

"No." Reed walked closer and stoked Rob's thick hair. "You care for him all day, and you keep the mill running all day." He glanced at his father. "I can take the nights."

"Keep the window open all night." Dr. Nedows spoke to Reed. "The cool air is good, though don't let him get a chill. His fever is low, so if we can keep ahead of that, he should pull through. His pulse is a bit shallow, and he's not getting as much oxygen as I'd like. If at any time it sounds like he can't get air, pound on his back, pull him up straighter."

Reed nodded. "Yes, sir."

Patience stared dumbfounded at Reed. How did the man encompass every room he was in? Was she the only one that felt it? Her eyes floated to Rob's blue Union uniform hanging from the wardrobe. Masculinity was such a strange thing. The protection of a silent uncle, the warm embrace of a father-in-law, a sacrificial, broken brother, a strong, driven man—*husband*. She looked at Reed, then looked away quickly, his eyes intense on hers.

"Would you step outside for a minute, Patience?" Reed asked, waiting for a response.

Without looking she knew every eye in the room was on her. "Yes." She moved from the small, crowded room and followed him out the front door.

"I was surprised to see you." He stepped down

the front step. "Though Janice did not say—but just knowing where she worked, I thought you might be at Dr. Nedows's, and then you told me the day at the town square."

Patience let out a long breath. "I'm very concerned about Rob." She had to change the subject before she wavered at his presence.

"Of course," he whispered, watching her.

Why was she still mesmerized by those green eyes that went on forever? This earnest home, these sincere people, it felt like someone yanked on the roots of her heart.

"Would you like to stay the day?" Reed asked. "Help my mother? I can take you back to Dr. Nedows's after work."

Patience rubbed her neck and walked to where King George was tied to the porch railing. "How are you, friend?" She fingered his velvet ears.

"It's no problem to stay, Patience." Reed stepped closer. "I can't imagine how, but I think my parents miss you more than me."

Patience froze, only her eyes glanced sideways at Reed who seemed oblivious to the endearment of his last words.

"Very well, I'll stay."

CHAPTER 46

PATIENCE LIFTED THE black and white photo of the four Chapman children. It was one of her favorite things about this home. Rob sat a few inches taller than Reed, his face more slender, he seemed to squint a tiny look of rebellion.

"Did Rob not want to sit for this photograph?" Patience watched Arita knead bread on the kitchen table.

"Oh, that he did not." She pounded the dough with her fist. "Some days I wished I'd born those boys first."

"Why?" Patience took the bread pan and lined it with grease.

"The girls were easy and compliant. I found out the hard way, oh those boys have a mind of their own. If they couldn't cut it, or throw it, or climb it, or shoot it, they were not happy. My girls would have sat another hour for that photograph, but it was pure torture for the boys. The girls made me assume I did motherin' so well. The boys tested everything I thought I'd done right." She chuckled, shaking her head.

Patience felt the old familiar pace she and Arita shared. Arita asked if she'd ever seen a photo of her family. Patience shook her head with great regret, did she look anything like her mother? Her internal melancholy was held at bay as the afternoon in this home gently offered her soul rest and comfort.

The daughter-in-law was grateful Arita never tried to knead and worry the woes of these last weeks like bread dough. She treated Patience like nothing had changed. Patience sighed and turned to wash her hands as Arita slid the bread into the oven. Patience glanced one more time at the photo. She remembered Reed at that age, tenderly kissing her hand, his—

"Be a dear and listen for Robbie." Arita brought her back to the present. "I want to get the clean sheets off the line. I'll be right back."

Before Patience could volunteer to do it, Arita was out the back door. Patience walked into Rob's room, his gate was up on his bed, but he leaned crookedly against a stack of pillows. His eyes were glossy with sickness, and she took a soft rag to wipe the drool from his chin. "Hello, beloved." She ran her fingers through his moppy hair just as Reed had. She tried to straighten his stiff body. His limbs felt cold, and she rubbed them with her hands. "Are you warm enough?" She pulled a blanket back up over his chest, his stillness and distant expression worrisome. Putting her hand on his chest, she could feel the labored breaths. "I don't want you to be in pain, dear warrior." His eyes drooped closed. "I know." Her heart hurt with the bittersweet moment. "You have felt worse pain than this."

She straightened up and watched his eyes flutter back open. "Your mother tells me stories about you as a boy. There is a sad looking fort up in a tree on the north side of the house. Did you build it?" She smiled. "Yes, that is when you didn't think you would become a carpenter." He shuddered back and forth, and she steadied him. "Let's try some water." She reached for it and held his chin up. Small drops flowed down his tongue as she caught the overflow on the rag under his chin. Turning to set the water down, Arita stood in the doorway.

"Maybe you should talk to your uncle." Arita smiled. "You're the most caring nurse." Arita let out a long sigh, dropping the folded sheets on the chair. "Reed offers to take the night shift with Robbie, like we don't know that he works all day, too."

Patience looked back, speaking to Rob. "If you don't mind, I'll stay in here, too." The words were out before she thought it through, and she glanced at Arita. "I want to be of help if it's okay with you or with Reed." Arita brushed Rob's cheek with the back of her fingers. "Whatever you two want to work out is fine with me."

• • •

FRIED PORK CHOPS, fresh buttered bread, and canned applesauce almost pleased Reed as much as sitting across from his wife at dinner. Earlier today she looked confused. Similar to last week, pale with puffy circles under her eyes. Maybe it was the soft glow of the lantern on the wall, but something in her lenient expressions brought a small sliver of hope. The day with his mother must've been good. He chewed another bite, wondering what she thought of the little ladybug pin. This woman could be so transparent and the next minute impossible to read. Maybe tonight they could talk more. He could only hope.

"Reed." His father set down his fork and wiped his face with the napkin. "I didn't have a chance to talk to you this afternoon, but Patience has agreed to go forward with the lumber bid and use of the trees on her land."

Reed hesitated, his expression guarded. "I—I don't think that is wise."

Patience looked up. "It's all right Reed. Your family has done so much for me. I want to do this for them."

"Then buy them a new blanket or something." His jaw locked, and he told himself to stay calm. "Not the land. No more back and forth, no more this and that. It's caused more problems than what it's worth."

The silence at the table screamed everyone's

362

discomfort. Reed rehearsed how he could have said that better. *Forget it;* he wasn't going to be able to say everything perfectly. Her hand quivered as she tried to eat, his one sliver of hope to connect with his wife was falling away.

"Mr. Edwin get back to you on the sale of—" Robert cut short when Reed's face shot him a fierce look.

Patience's wide eyes flashed between the men. "You're not talking about King George are you?"

Reed dropped his fork, leaned back in his chair and rolled his eyes to the ceiling.

"Sorry—I—" Robert looked away with an apologetic wave of his hand, "I'll go check on Robbie." His chair scooted back loudly against the wood floor.

Reed shook his head and raised his arms in the air with spread fingers and then clenched fists. Groaning, he held his fists against his forehead and stood up. "Patience." He released his face, revealing the red pressure points his fists made on his skin. "I believe as today, I am still your husband." He gripped the back of the chair. "I have vowed before God not to keep anything from you. So yes, I am selling King George."

She swallowed hard. "Why, why would you do that?" Her eyebrows tucked together in her confusion. Pleading, she looked to Arita.

"There were back taxes on the land. I would

have had to pay them when I purchased the land anyway, but I used the purchase money to expand the mill getting it ready for the orders we contracted. There's no other way to secure the land for you."

Arita began to clear the dishes.

"No, no there must be another way." Patience stood and went to the window. "Is King George here now?" She scanned the front yard.

"Yes, Mr. Edwin and I haven't settled on the price, but—I'm sorry, by tomorrow . . ."

Patience turned and swiftly approached the table. Grabbing his arms, she pleaded. "Please, Reed. Please don't do this. We'll find another way. My uncle will help us. He paid for my care at Lennhurst. This isn't your debt!" She shook him. "Please, please you love him. He was a gift from your grandfather, please." She appealed, gulping for air. "Go to the courthouse and put your name back on the deed. I never asked you to do that." The tears ran steadily down her stunned face.

"It doesn't work like that," he said quietly.

"Then take the trees you need." She tried to reach his downcast eyes. "The mill will make more money." She cupped his face, and he finally looked at her. "King George is part of you, and you are part of him, please Reed." She begged.

Robert appeared in the downstairs hall. "Arita, I wonder if Reed should go for the doctor,

Robbie's color is ashen, and I'm having trouble getting him to swallow."

Patience moved back with faltered steps. "My uncle needed to check on another patient tonight. He said he wouldn't be back until the morning." She raked her fingers down her face. "No, no, no." She began to pace around the living room. "Who will help Rob? No, you can't leave Rob. Oh no, oh no." She zigzagged between the furniture and across the open floor.

Reed watched his parents' gesture for him to do something.

"I don't think it's a good idea," he stayed motionless. "She's easily provoked by me." He glanced at his mother. "She'll want to fight me."

Patience rocked and paced, touching the top of the furniture and chairs. "Don't leave, don't leave." She repeated over and over. "Don't leave me here, George. Don't leave me here." Her voice echoed wall to wall while his parents looked at each other confused.

"MAMA, MAMA, OJCIEC, ojciec . . . Please come for me." She blocked the front door with her body then began to pace the room again. "Chartvea! Chartvea, beautiful butterfly, listen to me, stuchaj teraz, listen." Her breath caught, her eyes glossy with tears, she whispered low. "You can fly with me. Come. Come now. Let's fly away together."

Arita started to reach out for her as she paced by, but Reed shook his head no.

"Little Eella, trust me. My moga latac. We can fly. The fairies will guide us. Come now, come little bug, use your little wings." Her body swayed with the continual circling. "Please, *please* . . ." She yearned, reaching back and forth in the childless air. "Don't leave me, stay here. Just stay here." Just as chaotic as the stirring of the room, she stood still, staring at the rug. With pale face drenched in tears of despair, she looked up and found Reed. He took two careful steps toward her, but she fell onto a pile of fabric on the floor, her arms and legs under her. Her rocking and crying vacillated between deep sorrow and hiccups of murmuring more words in Polish. He knelt down next to her and carefully touched her back.

"It hurts, oh, oh, oh it's still burning." She whimpered.

He took his hand away and looked into the shocked faces of his parents. Feeling as if the wild wind in the room had left, he stayed next to her as his parents went to be with Robbie.

After what seemed like an hour, Reed gripped her arms and pulled her up. "Patience, come with me, I want you to rest." She stood, her usual stiff back slumped in fatigue as they took the stairs. He led her into his old room, knowing she'd slept there before. Pulling back the covers, he helped her sit, removed her boots and took the pins out of her thick bun. "Lay back." He tucked in her thick skirt and pulled the covers over her.

"Please." She found his hands and gripped them. "I—I want to be there. Promise you will come to get me . . . if . . . Rob . . . flies . . . I mean—"

"I know, I will." Unmoving, he gently stroked her hair until she drifted asleep.

CHAPTER 47

A SMALL SLICE of orange morning glow laid across the kitchen table. Patience gripped Reed's cold hand as she descended the stairs with him. The smell of dirty dishes and old coffee came from the area. He hadn't said anything, only the lantern light revealing his ragged and blotchy face told her what was happening.

Stepping into Rob's room, Arita fell into Patience's arms. "It wasn't even the fever." She choked out with tears streaking down her face. "He just couldn't breathe. He couldn't fight anymore . . . he's," she sobbed, "he's gone." Arita's body slacked, and Reed steadied his sobbing mother against his shoulders.

Patience moved around them and sat on Rob's bed, his wooden gate no longer needed. She laid her hands next to his thick beard that was hiding a sunken white face. "You have fought the fight. You have run the race. Now you can fly from your cocoon and be free." She looked up at the ceiling of the room. "Father in Heaven, would you give Rob a mansion with my family?"

Despondent Robert stood in the corner, Rob's uniform sleeve touched his grieving father's shoulder. Fatigue and pain etched deep in his face.

"Jesus was a man of sorrows acquainted with grief." She reached out her hand, and Robert took it. "Would you mind if I stayed with him, while you and Arita sleep a few hours?"

Robert nodded slowly and stepped to Arita, taking her elbow. Arita took one last, long look at her silent son and allowed Robert to lead her across the hall. Their door clicked closed.

A stream of yellow began to reflect off Rob's window sill, and Patience saw Arita's Bible sitting there. Standing, she took the book and flipped through the pages. Facing Rob, she read with firm conviction.

"He will swallow up death in victory;
and the Lord GOD will wipe away tears
from off all faces;
and the rebuke of his people shall he take
away from off all the earth:
for the LORD hath spoken it.
And it shall be said in that day,
Lo, this is our God;
we have waited for him, and he will save
us:
this is the LORD;
we have waited for him,
we will be glad and rejoice in his
salvation.

For in this mountain shall the hand of the LORD rest, Isaiah 25."

Reed stepped forward, taking the Bible from her hand. Patience's chin quivered, she knew she'd collapsed last night, but did Reed feel the peace and love coating this room? His hand carefully rested on her back.

"I know I waited in a long rebellious season, but God has saved me. I do believe those words you just read." His body wavered, his eyes were so weary. "But I don't know about you."

A shiver ran up her spine, feeling his brokenness.

"The first time I saw you at Lennhurst I was taken by your beauty. But when things don't make sense to me, I try to push them away. Only with you, I failed time and time again." Fresh tears rose up around his thick lashes. "I have to know." He swallowed hard and gripped her hands. "I've never been so low of mind and heart." He pinched his lips together and shook his head. "I've never been at the end of myself as I am this day. So please just tell me this. Can you ever forgive my callousness? Would you try to trust me again? Could you tolerate my over logical, easily distracted ways?" He waited in the heavy silence and released her hand and swiped his sleeve over his damp face. "I've been in a cage where I can't get out. Now I need you to set me free."

She closed her eyes and took in a long breath. "I would like to try."

STANDING WITH THE warmth of the afternoon sun on their backs, Patience listened. She'd never attended a funeral before. She heard Reverend Pearce say, "Let us pray."

"Father, grant us comfort today as we say good-bye to Lieutenant Robert Joseph Chapman, the third. A man with great respect for this country and for this family he leaves behind. May we remember his courage, his love, and his life well lived. Amen."

Patience felt Reed's warmth and strength leave her side as he helped the other men lower Rob's coffin into the ground. He came back to stand with her and his parents as their friends sang a closing hymn. Arita dabbed her face and stepped back as Robert's enclosing arm led her away from the family burial site. Patience noticed something moving around the other gravestone belonging to the Chapman grandfather. Could it be? Reed took her elbow to follow his parents, but she pulled on his suit jacket. "Look. Look there." She pointed with her hankie clutched in her palm. Finally pulling him close to her. "Do you see that?"

"A butterfly," he whispered, drawing her against him. His arms encircled her, and he rested his cheek on her temple. "Amazing."

• • •

AT DUSK, WHEN the last wagon rolled down the Chapman's road, Reed came inside as Patience finished drying the dishes. "Your mother has gone to bed. It has been a long day for her."

"For all of us." Reed had seen his father walking past the mill earlier. "I told my father I would be taking you home, or to Dr. Nedows's . . . or . . . where ever you want."

Patience looked down, folding her towel. "What do you want?"

Her soft question made his heart knock against his ribs. "I want to take you to your land. I'd like to show you something." The moment she was weighing his request seemed to last an hour.

"Very well," she finally said, lightly touching his sleeve.

RIDING QUIETLY ON King George, Reed wavered. "I'm sorry I upset you last night."

Patience waited and finally spoke. "And I am sorry, my childish behavior must have upset you and your parents, like caring for Rob wasn't enough. Dr. Powell should have come and taken me away." She sighed.

"No." He shook his head. "I couldn't have gone through losing Rob without you." He didn't want to remember all the things she had to endure since coming to Hancock. "I know I need to stop trying to control everything." He straightened, watching how the light was fading off the land. "I won't sell King George. I can think of something else." He felt her cheek settle on his back, and her arms squeezed his waist.

"Thank you," she exhaled. "And as of today, I should still have the say over the trees. I want you and your father to go forward with the contracts. It's all Chapman land. It's all for the good of the family." King George instinctively walked the trail onto their land.

"You are my family." He entwined his fingers with hers along his waist. "I don't want any of it without you. That would be a bitter life to—"

"Reed!" Patience looked ahead and wiggled behind him. "What is all this?" She tapped his arm, and he stopped, lowering herself to the ground. "Is this pebbled cobblestone?" She stepped onto the winding path lining the array of plants and flowers. "And this! A patio, tables, and chairs?" She spun and looked up. "What is this called?"

"A gazebo."

"With ivy? Is that a bridge over the little creek?" She walked quickly while looking at all the strange things hanging from the trees. "These are . . ."

He swung his leg over King George's head and jumped down. "They are really bird-houses. I bought them as a blueprint. You'll have to tell me if fairies like bigger or fancier."

"Reed." Perplexed, she stared at him. "What has come over you? This is even more than what *I* imagined."

"I don't do well with idle time, and funny thing," he looked around, "it helped me. It would calm me, and I actually enjoyed the work. I never understood the curative purpose for a garden until now."

She shook her head. "That makes my heart glad, but you didn't know if I would be coming back. Did you?"

"If you mean do I get those divine impressions about people like you do. No. But I could pray every morning and night." He lifted a coy smile, seeing her pleased like this, how interesting that from morning to night his world could come around. He hated to break the moment. "It's getting dark." Those velvet eyes he loved were assessing him.

"Reed, if I asked you something strange, would you consider it?"

"Depends." His eyes flashed. Strange could have a hundred different meanings for her.

"Could we grab the bedding from the cottage and sleep out on the dock tonight?"

He squinted.

"I want to see the heavens. I want to picture Rob in his new body, his new home."

Reed nodded. "Let's do that."

• • •

"GOD'S MASTERPIECE." PATIENCE sighed, watching the vibrancy of a billion stars against the black curtain of night. The lake water lapped peacefully against the dock, as rich evening air danced between land and water.

"I'm exhausted," Reed whispered holding her next to him under their blankets, "but I don't want to miss anything. I don't want to close my eyes. I'm afraid this is only a dream, and there is something else I need to say. I promised myself I wouldn't say it to you. I didn't want to be persuading or be *the lawyer.* Will you hear me out without taking it that way?"

"Yes. I can just listen." She nodded against his shoulder.

"I came to Lennhurst with a somewhat illegal plan. I made it sound as if the land had to be occupied, which it didn't. Never in a hundred years did I think a woman who grew up in that asylum would want to live on the very land that saw her family's demise. I guess I'd convinced myself that I was doing all of us a favor. I convinced myself that pushing in was the best way to get what I wanted. Meeting you has blatantly shown me the opposite. You live life with a sweet peace. Your heart really does fly. I can't have that and push at the same time." He let out a long sigh. "I'm truly sorry for all the things that I did that hurt you. I fell in love with you

376

on our wedding day." He suppressed a chuckle. "I was such a mess that day. I wanted to be your husband, I wanted to take care of you, but I knew you deserved an extraordinary life. Without a husband striving to get what he wanted."

Patience ran her hand over his stubbled jaw. "Since we are confessing, I might have used you a bit, too. That first night in your apartment? When you tried to take me to the boarding house the next morning?"

"Oh, I remember," he huffed.

"I knew that if I let you drop me off, I might not ever see you again." She turned a smile into his arm. "I can't really explain it either, and I have no knowledge of how men and women connect. I just wanted," she sighed contentedly, "you."

Reed kissed her forehead.

Patience took his hand and held it over her heart. "I know now you've been in here a long, long time. Of course, it *had* to be you." She whispered.

"When?" he asked.

"When we were children. I remember the boy who untangled my hair from the barbed wire. I remembered him because only a few months later, I woke up alone and terrified in Lennhurst. Besides my family, that brown haired boy with the commanding green eyes kept me alive. I would see you over and over, and often I wondered if it was just another dream. Did you kiss my hand?" She smiled up at him.

"I did." He laughed lightly. "It was so unlike me. Robbie was there that day too. We'd actually been trying to figure out how we could jump the fence for a swim."

"Oh, and I thought you were a boy on a white horse, rescuing young maidens. But really you were just trying to trespass."

"Yep." He watched the stars, his body warm with peace and comfort. "I wish I'd never misplaced that boy. He yawned. "If God can place each star in the sky, I suppose he can place the wonder and carefree spirit back into a soul. That's what you give to me." His husky voice trailed off.

"So, we can take a swim in the morning?" She lightly trailed a finger down his cheek.

"About that." He brushed back her hair. "Another thing with my idle time was deciding that if you came back, I would not keep you from swimming. I told myself, which would I prefer? Seeing my beautiful wife swim or flying from branch to branch around her new garden." He kissed her cheek.

"Swim all you want."

Epilogue

Patience breathed in the beautiful garden scents as she pulled out the bench and set her pen and dream journal down. The pottery urn the Beasleys had given them now overflowed with a butterfly banquet. Deep yellow lantana, purple verbena, creeping zinnias and French marigolds drew the winged beauties to flit and play. She turned in a circle, amazed at how the other plants and flowers had grown so much in the last few months. The sunny summer days and frequent rains blossomed her gardens into abundance and splendor. Each leaf and climbing ivy drew her to touch them again. "Hello lovely." She couldn't help wonder if heaven—just like at creation was mostly garden.

Sunday afternoons were her favorite time to open her journal and write a new list of gratitude to God. Maybe it was the joy of sitting with Robert, Arita and Reed each Sunday in church or seeing a very pregnant Janice standing next to Fred. Reverend Pearce made God's word so encouraging. The hymns sung by the families and children, moved the church with life.

She finally stopped looking around, turned to

sit at her bench, and rubbed her hand over the journal Reed had gotten for her. How amazing that this gift was put into her hand, the same day she contemplated going back to Poland. How close she'd come to making the worst decision possible.

Frightening how pain can try to lead you away, but the soft longing of her heart rose that night as she prayed. Without Dr. Powell or even Reed in her ear, she had to trust the Spirit of God for herself. Without really feeling clarity, the one thing she could trust in always, God would be with her wherever she chose to go. She felt the permission to be free to choose, to be free to trust Him with all her unknowns. So, for what others might have seen as just simple moments in Hancock—those moments had meant abundant love, belonging and healing for her.

One night she confided in her uncle about the possibility that the fairies that tended to her would be something her imagination contrived while she was on medicine for her burns. He gently agreed with Janice, they were deliriums. Easier than she thought, she had always trusted in God's leading, so she let go of her childhood friends.

With more clarity, she knew she would not return to Poland, she would trust God to help her, come what may. She tapped her pen over a new page, a new list of thankfuls. Her and her lists, she smiled, she drew the outline of a butterfly, so many blessings.

I dream today about the garden in heaven. She wrote. *What does Rob enjoy the most, Lord?* She listened and drew little flowers with the butterflies on her page. *You, Lord made us to walk and talk with you—to know the fruit of Your provision and sustenance. A garden of no worries, only a garden of trust.* She sketched vines and ivy along the outside of her text. *Thank you for the gardens in my life, for the garden at Lennhurst and this one around me. Thank you for the group of ladies that Dr. Powell will bring next week.*

She pulled out his letter and two more abundant blessings caught her eye. One was a letter with rough penmanship and many misspelled words. She pulled it close to her chest and closed her eyes. For some reason tears formed with the fullness of her heart. Elias Browne's letter meant the world to her.

How could God know this missing piece would finally find rest? Elias was a grown man now. He talked briefly about the war and his roundabout journey, his short hair and the woman he loved. But what had delighted her beyond words was his remembrance of their childhood. He called her a friend, and thanked her for taking the time to talk and laugh with him. How could she know the very things that she absorbed from him, were the things he said made his young life bearable?

She'd said the like to him when she wrote him back. She released a deep sigh, just like Rob, some will cross our garden path for only a season, but their touch never fades.

She pulled the second letter she had written to Anna from the pages of her journal. The first letter she had addressed to Mrs. Alfred Plugg, Centerville, Kentucky, as Dr. Powell had instructed. But it was returned with jagged script, saying: "No longer lives here." This one she would address as Anna Plugg and see if it would find a trail to the young woman who made many days at Lennhurst comfortable.

She never thought much about her words reaching people. But her new friends and family still often looked curiously at her when she told them something she saw in them. Didn't everyone see the good in others? Their God-given purpose? The gold lining of who they were on the inside? She tucked Elias's and her letter to Anna back into the folds of the paper. Reed walked her way, balancing a cup of tea.

"Don't let me interrupt." He smiled.

"MMM, TEA FROM some of my own dried leaves. Thank you, love, I was just writing and doodling a bit." She held the cup and took a sip. "You know I'm excited to have the guests from Lennhurst arrive next week. I was thinking since we don't have the lakeside cabins done, what about letting

Dr. Powell and the ladies stay in the cottage? He writes of their suffering from despondency, and maybe it would be more soothing than in town."

He straddled her bench. "And we would sleep . . . on the dock?"

"No." She smiled, remembering that wonderful night. "I thought your parents might take us in." She set her tea down and leaned back against him.

"I'm sure they would love it." He wrapped his arms around hers, pulling her close. "Yes, tell him the cottage is theirs. Did I tell you my sisters have both confirmed, they will bring their families here for Christmas?"

"Christmas?" Her voice rang excitement and concern. "Here? To the cottage?" She twisted to face him.

"No, my parents'." He nudged her. "Roberta and Steven have two boys, Charles and Anthony. My sister Rachel and Corbin have Rita, their own Robbie, and Rubin."

Patience rubbed her forehead. "I may have to write all that down. Frankly, I feel a little nervous about meeting your sisters. How will I fit in?" She squeezed his thigh. "My name starts with a P."

Reed lifted her long braid and kissed her neck. "They missed our wedding and Rob's funeral. It should be an interesting time together. Except for teasing me, they are fairly harmless."

Patience picked up her pen as Reed held her looking out over the garden.

I dream of Christmas, she wrote. *The refastening of the Chapmans clan. In their grief and in their celebrations. The laughter of the children, eating cookies and playing games.*

Reed returned to kissing her neck.

"You said you wouldn't interrupt." Her shoulder shuddered from the light brushes of his lips. "I can't think of what to write when you do that."

"I can leave." He sat up. "I know what it is to lose to distractions."

"Mmm . . . don't leave." She squeezed his warm hand. "I believe your presence is my favorite distraction." She turned, and he pulled her onto his lap. Running her fingers through his hair, she smiled, placing a string of soft kisses on his forehead, cheek, and lips. While his hands ran gently up her back, neither noticed the small ladybug landing on her pages of dreams.

THE GARDEN

By Kari Jobe,
inspired me—

I had all
But given up
Desperate for
A sign from love
Something good
Something kind
Bringing peace to every corner of my mind
Then I saw the garden
Hope had come to me
To sweep away the ashes
And wake me from my sleep

I realized
You never left
And for this moment
You planned ahead
That I would see
Your faithfulness in all of the green

I can see the ivy
Growing through the wall
'Cause You will stop at nothing
To heal my broken soul

I can see the ivy
Reaching through the wall
'Cause You will stop at nothing
To heal my broken soul
Ohh, You're healing broken souls
You're healing, You're healing broken souls

Faith is rising up like ivy
Cringing for the light
Hope is stirring deep inside me
Making all things right

Love is lifting me from sorrow
Catching every tear
Dispelling every lie and torment
Crushing all my fears

You crush all my fears
You crush all my fears
With your perfect love
With your perfect love

Now I see redemption
Growing in the trees
The death and resurrection
In every single seed

Songwriters: Kari Jobe
The Garden lyrics © Bethel Music Publishing,
Capitol Christian Music Group

A *MUST* Watch: The Garden Live, Kari Jobe
https://www.youtube.com
/watch?v=OiirKDvMjNY

I'll Fly Away

By Albert E. Brumley

Some bright morning when this life is over
I'll fly away
To that home on God's celestial shore
I'll fly away

I'll fly away, oh glory
I'll fly away in the morning
When I die, Hallelujah by and by
I'll fly away

When the shadows of this life have gone
I'll fly away
Like a bird from these prison walls I'll fly
I'll fly away

I'll fly away, oh glory
I'll fly away in the morning
When I die, Hallelujah by and by
I'll fly away

Oh, how glad and happy when we meet
I'll fly away
No more cold iron shackles on my feet
I'll fly away

I'll fly away, oh glory
I'll fly away in the morning
When I die, Hallelujah by and by
I'll fly away

I'll fly away, oh glory
I'll fly away in the morning
When I die, Hallelujah by and by
I'll fly away

Just a few more weary days and then
I'll fly away
To a land where joys will never end
I'll fly away

Watch for some Johnny Cash — I'll Fly Away:
https://www.youtube.com
/watch?v=uA4JyAONd_I

AUTHOR'S NOTE:

I do not have a green thumb to save my life, but I am a serial home decorator. I had made a stencil of the words *Restore, to bring to original intent.* And placed it on a big piece of wood. It actually turned out well. I like it because it represents one of my core beliefs. We had everything we'd ever want at the Garden of Eden. If our ancestors hadn't blown it, surely you or I would have. And in comes the restorer of all things, Jesus. So, what is He restoring to us? (Thank goodness not my skills to garden). My belief is He is restoring all that He had originally created us for. Not hard to picture from the accounts in Genesis 1 and 2. Peace, security, dominion, fellowship with a benevolent God, just to name a few. One of the ironies of walking with God is that any time (even with my good intentions) that I have swayed from the original intentions of God for Julia, He has had no problem pulling the rug. Like Holy Spirit did enough tapping, and my excuses were getting old so—rug pull—big ouch.

Two things have changed my life: High life pain & High Revelation of the Love of God. Usually in that order.

Reed was never intended to strive for significance. The Lord had already given that to him via his original God DNA.

How free, airy and restful is your garden?

I can hear James 4:1, "Why do you strive and fight and lust for what you do not have . . ." Because Julia doesn't trust God's Garden is enough for her to rest in. The temperature is surely nice, and the bugs all stay on the leaves, but just like Eve, maybe I should be helping God along with my plans. Ugg . . . the rug is jiggling under my feet.

Trusting the process of restoration
for *all of us* Garden searchers—
Julia

If you've read *Love Covers* and now *Love Flies*, I hope you're ready to meet Anna from Lennhurst Asylum in Love Protects. I had her storyline in my head for years and for some reason these two books flowed out before hers.

Please come to visit at
https://www.juliawrites.com/

Books are
produced in the
United States
using U.S.-based
materials

Books are printed
using a revolutionary
new process called
THINKtech™ that
lowers energy usage
by 70% and increases
overall quality

Books are
durable and
flexible
because of
Smyth-sewing

Paper is
sourced using
environmentally
responsible
foresting methods
and the
paper is acid-free

Center Point Large Print

600 Brooks Road / PO Box 1
Thorndike, ME 04986-0001 USA

(207) 568-3717

US & Canada:
1 800 929-9108
www.centerpointlargeprint.com